THE HOUSE OF
MARTHA

FRANK R. STOCKTON

1st WORLD
LIBRARY
Literary Society

The House of Martha

Frank R. Stockton

© 1st World Library, 2007
PO Box 2211
Fairfield, IA 52556
www.1stworldlibrary.com
First Edition

LCCN: 2007927758

Softcover ISBN: 978-1-4218-4538-8
Hardcover ISBN: 978-1-4218-4454-1
eBook ISBN: 978-1-4218-4622-4

Purchase *"The House of Martha"*
as a traditional bound book at:
www.1stWorldLibrary.com/purchase.asp?ISBN=978-1-4218-4538-8

1st World Library is a literary, educational organization
dedicated to:

- Creating a free internet library of downloadable ebooks

- Hosting writing competitions and offering book
publishing scholarships.

Interested in more 1st World Library books?
contact: literacy@1stworldlibrary.com
Check us out at: www.1stworldlibrary.com

1st World Library Literary Society

Giving Back to the World

"If you want to work on the core problem, it's early school literacy."

- James Barksdale, former CEO of Netscape

"No skill is more crucial to the future of a child, or to a democratic and prosperous society, than literacy."

- Los Angeles Times

"Literacy... means far more than learning how to read and write... The aim is to transmit... knowledge and promote social participation."

- UNESCO

"Literacy is not a luxury, it is a right and a responsibility. If our world is to meet the challenges of the twenty-first century we must harness the energy and creativity of all our citizens."

- President Bill Clinton

"Parents should be encouraged to read to their children, and teachers should be equipped with all available techniques for teaching literacy, so the varying needs and capacities of individual kids can be taken into account."

- Hugh Mackay

CONTENTS

I

MY GRANDMOTHER AND I

My grandmother sat in her own particular easy-chair by the open window of her back parlor. This was a pleasant place in which to sit in the afternoon, for the sun was then on the other side of the house, and she could look not only over the smooth grass of the side yard and the flower beds, which were under her especial care, but across the corner of the front lawn into the village street. Here, between two handsome maple-trees which stood upon the sidewalk, she could see something of what was going on in the outer world without presenting the appearance of one who is fond of watching her neighbors. It was not much that she saw, for the street was a quiet one; but a very little of that sort of thing satisfied her.

She was a woman who was easily satisfied. As a proof of this, I may say that she looked upon me as a man who always did what was right. Indeed, I am quite sure there were cases when she saved herself a good deal of perplexing cogitation by assuming that a thing was right because I did it. I was her only grandchild: my father and mother had died when I was very young, and I had always lived with her,—that is, her house had always been my home; and as I am sure there had never been any reason why I should not be a dutiful and affectionate grandson, it was not surprising that she looked upon me with a certain tender partiality, and that she considered me worthy of all the good that she or fortune could bestow upon me.

My grandmother was nearly seventy, but her physical powers had been excellently well preserved; and as to her mental vigor, I could see no change in it. Even when a little boy I had admired her powers of sympathetic consideration, by which she divined the needs and desires of her fellow-creatures; and now that I had become a grown man I found those powers as active and ready as they had ever been.

The village in which we lived contained a goodly number of families of high standing and comfortable fortune. It was a village of well-kept and well-shaded streets, of close-cut grass, with no litter on the sidewalks. Our house was one of the best in the place, and since I had come of age I had greatly improved it. I had a fair inheritance from my mother, and this my grandmother desired me to expend without reference to what I was receiving and would receive from her. To her son's son would come ultimately every-thing that she possessed.

Being thus able to carry out my ideas concerning the comfort and convenience of a bachelor, I had built a wing to my grandmother's house, which was occupied only by myself. It communicated by several doors with the main building, and these doors were nearly always open; but it was satisfactory to me to think that if I chose I might shut and lock them, and thus give my apartment the advantages of a separate house. The ground floor of my establishment consisted of a large and handsome library and study, with a good-sized anteroom opening from it, and above were my sleeping and dressing rooms. With the exception of the time devoted to reading, reflection, and repose, I lived with my grandmother.

Frank R. Stockton

Neither of us, however, confined ourself to this village life. The winters my grandmother generally spent with a married sister in a neighboring city, and I was accustomed to visit and journey whenever it pleased me. Recently I had spent a year in Europe, and on my return I joined my grandmother for a while, before going to our village home.

II

RELATING TO MY YEAR IN EUROPE

I do not suppose that any one ever enjoyed travel and residence in England and on the Continent more than I did; but I do not now intend to give any account of my experiences, nor of the effect they had upon me, save in one regard. I had traveled and lived for the most part alone, and one of the greatest pleasures connected with my life in Europe was the anticipation of telling my friends who had never crossed the ocean what I had seen, heard, and done.

But when I returned to America I met with a great disappointment: my glowing anticipations were not realized. I could find scarcely any one who cared to know what I had seen, heard, or done.

At this I was as much surprised as disappointed. I believed that I possessed fair powers of description and narration, and many of my traveling experiences were out of the common. In fact, I had endeavored to see things the ordinary traveler does not see, and to do things which he seldom does. I found, however, that my unusual experiences were of no advantage to me in making people desirous to hear accounts of my travels. I might as well have joined a party of personally conducted tourists.

My friends and acquaintances in town were all glad to see me, not that they might hear what had happened to me, but that they might tell me what had happened to them. This disposition sometimes threw me into a state of absolute amazement. I could not comprehend, for instance, why Mrs. Gormer, who had known me for years, and who I thought would take such an active interest in everything that concerned me, should dismiss my European tour with a few remarks in regard to my health in the countries I had passed through, and then begin an animated account of the troubles she had had since I had been away: how the house she had been living in had had two feet of water in the cellar for weeks at a time, and how nobody could find out whether it was caused by a spring in the ground or the bursting of an unknown water-pipe,—but no matter what it was, they couldn't stay there; and what a dreadful time they had in finding another house; and how the day appointed for Jennie's wedding coming directly in the middle of the moving, it had to be postponed, for she declared she would never be married anywhere but at home; and how several of Mr. Barclay's relations came down from New Hampshire on purpose to be at the wedding, and had to stay either at hotels or with friends, for it was more than a week before her house could be made ready for the wedding. She then remarked that of course I had heard of the shameful way in which John had been treated in regard to that position in the Treasury department at Washington; and as I had not heard she went on and told me about it, until it was time for me to go.

At my club, some of the men did not know that I had been away, but there were others who were very glad to hear that I had been in Europe, because it gave them an opportunity to tell me about that very exciting election of Brubaker, a man of whom I had never heard, who had been proposed by Shuster, with whom I was not acquainted, and seconded by Cushman, whom I did not know. I found no one desirous of hearing me talk about my travels, and those who were willing to do so were satisfied with a very few general points. Sometimes I could not but admire the facility and skill with which some of the people who stay at home were able to defend themselves against the attempted loquacity of the returned traveler.

Occasionally, in social gatherings, I met with some one, generally a lady, who did take an interest in hearing that I had been in such or such a place; but this was always some place in which she had been, and, after comparing experiences, she would go on to tell of things which she had seen and done, and often ended by making me feel very sorry for having neglected my opportunities.

"Yes," said one, "it must have been cold on the top of that lonely mountain, with nothing to warm you but those plump little wolves, and the constant fear that their mother might come back; but you ought to have been here during the blizzard." And then she went on with a full history of the great blizzard.

Everywhere I was met by that blizzard. Those people who had not moved, or who had not had a puzzling disease in the family, or who had not been instrumental in founding a free kindergarten, could always fall back on the blizzard. I heard how their fathers could not get home on the train, of the awful prices the people charged for clearing away the snow, of the way in which Jane and Adelaide had to get on without music lessons for nearly ten days, and of the scarcity of milk. No one who had seen and felt that irrepressible storm suffered from it as I did. It chilled the aspirations of my soul, it froze the unspoken words of my mouth, it overwhelmed and buried every rising hope of speech, and smothered and sometimes nearly obliterated my most interesting recollection. Many a time I have mentally sent that blizzard to regions where its icy blasts would have melted as in a hot simoom.

I truly believed that in our village I should find sensible people who would be glad to hear about interesting things which they never had seen. Many of them had not traveled, and a returned tourist was a comparative rarity in the place. I went down there on purpose to talk about Europe. It was too early for my grandmother's return to the country. I proposed to spend a week with my village friends, and, before their bright firesides, charm and delight them with accounts of those things which had so charmed and delighted me. The lives of city people are so filled with every sort of material that it is useless to try to crowd anything more into them. Here, however, were people with excellent intellects, whose craving for mental pabulum, especially in the winter, could be but partially satisfied.

But bless me! I never heard of such an over-stock of mental pabulum as I found there. It was poured upon me by every one with whom I tried to converse. I was frequently permitted to begin statements which I believed must win their way, if they were allowed a fair start; but very soon something I said was sure to suggest something which had occurred in the village, and before I could brace myself the torrent would burst upon me. Never did I hear, in the same space of time, so much about things which had happened as I then heard from my village neighbors. It was not that so much had occurred, but that so much was said about what had occurred. It was plain there was no hope for me here, and after three days I went back to town.

Now it was early summer, and my grandmother and I were again in our dear home in the village. As I have said, she was sitting by the open window, where she could look out upon the flowers, the grass, and a little of the life of her neighbors. I sat near her, and had been telling her of my three days in the Forest of Arden, and of the veritable Jaques whom I met there, when she remarked:—

"That must have been extremely interesting; and, speaking of the woods, I wish you would say to Thomas that so soon as he can find time I want him to bring up some of that rich wood-soil and put it around those geraniums."

This was the first time my grandmother had interjected any remark into my recitals. She had often asked me to tell her about my travels, and on every other occasion she had listened until she softly fell asleep. I now remembered having heard her say that it interfered with her night's rest to sleep in the daytime. Perhaps her present interruption was intended as a gentle rebuke, and no other kind of rebuke had ever come to me from my grandmother.

I went out to find Thomas, oppressed by a mild despair. If I were to tell my tales to a stone, I thought, it would turn on me with a sermon.

III

THE MODERN USE OF THE HUMAN EAR

During my lonely walks and rides through the country about our village, I began to cogitate and philosophize upon the present social value of the human ear. Why do people in society and in domestic circles have ears? I asked myself. They do not use them to listen to one another. And then I thought and pondered further, and suddenly the truth came to me: the ears of the present generation are not purveyors to the mind; they are merely agents of the tongue, who watch for breaks or weak places in the speech of others, in order that their principal may rush in and hold the field. They are jackals, who scent out a timid pause or an unsuspecting silence which the lion tongue straightway destroys. Very forcibly the conviction came to me that nowadays we listen only for an opportunity to speak.

I was grieved that true listening had become a lost art; for without it worthy speech is impossible. To good listening is due a great part of the noble thought, the golden instruction, and the brilliant wit which has elevated, enlightened, and brightened the soul of man. There are fine minds whose workings are never expressed in writing; and even among those who, in print, spread their ideas before the world there is a certain cream of thought which is given only to listeners, if, happily, there be such.

Modern conversation has degenerated into the Italian game of *moccoletto*, in which every one endeavors to blow out the candles of the others, and keep his own alight. In such rude play there is no illumination. "There should be a reform," I declared. "There should be schools of listening. Here men and women should be taught how, with sympathetic and delicate art, to draw from others the useful and sometimes precious speech which, without their skillful cooeeperation, might never know existence. To be willing to receive in order that good may be given should be one of the highest aims of life.

"Not only should we learn to listen in order to give opportunity for the profitable speech of others, but we should do so out of charity and good will to our fellow-men. How many weary sick-beds, how many cheerless lives, how many lonely, depressed, and silent men and women, might be gladdened, and for the time transformed, by one who would come, not to speak words of cheer and comfort, but to listen to tales of suffering and trial! Here would be one of the truest forms of charity; an almost unknown joy would be given to the world.

"There should be brotherhoods and sisterhoods of listeners; like good angels, they should go out among those unfortunates who have none to hear that which it would give them so much delight to say."

But alas! I knew of no such good angels. Must that which I had to tell remain forever untold for the want of one? This could not be; there must exist somewhere a man or a woman who would be willing to hear my accounts of travels and experiences which, in an exceptionable degree, were interesting and valuable.

I determined to advertise for a listener.

Frank R. Stockton

IV

I OBTAIN A LISTENER

The writing of my advertisement cost me a great deal of trouble. At first I thought of stating that I desired a respectable and intelligent person, who would devote a few hours each day to the services of a literary man; but on reflection I saw that this would bring me a vast number of answers from persons who were willing to act as secretaries, proof-readers, or anything of the sort, and I should have no means of finding out from their letters whether they were good listeners or not.

Therefore I determined to be very straightforward and definite, and to state plainly what it was I wanted. The following is the advertisement which I caused to be inserted in several of the city papers:—

"Wanted.—A respectable and intelligent person, willing to devote several hours a day to listening to the recitals of a traveler. Address, stating compensation expected, Oral."

I mentioned my purpose to no one, not even to my grandmother, for I should merely make myself the object of the ridicule of my friends, and my dear relative's soul would be filled with grief that she had not been considered competent to do for me so slight a service. If I succeeded in obtaining a listener, he could come to me in my library, where no one would know he was not a stenographer to whom I was dictating literary matter, or a teacher of languages who came to instruct me in Arabic.

I received a dozen or more answers to my advertisement, some of which were very amusing, and others very unsatisfactory. Not one of the writers understood what sort of services I desired, but all expressed their belief that they were fully competent to give them, whatever they might be.

After a good deal of correspondence and some interviewing, I selected at last a person who I believed would prove himself a satisfactory listener. He was an elderly man, of genteel appearance, and apparently of a quiet and accommodating disposition. He assured me that he had once been a merchant, engaged in the importation of gunny-bags, and, having failed in business, had since depended on the occasional assistance given him by a widowed daughter-in-law. This man I engaged, and arranged that he should lodge at the village inn, and come to me every evening.

I was truly delighted that so far I had succeeded in my plan. Now, instead of depending upon the whims, fancies, or occasional good-natured compliance of any one, I was master of the situation. My listener was paid to listen to me, and listen to me he must. If he did not do so intelligently, he should be dismissed. It would be difficult to express fully the delight given me by my new possession,—the ownership of attention.

Every evening my listener came; and during a great part of every day I thought of what I should say to him when he should come. I talked to him with a feeling of freedom and absolute independence which thrilled me like champagne. What mattered it whether my speech interested him or not?

He was paid to listen, without regard to interest; more than that, he was paid to show an interest, whether he felt it or not. Whether I bored him or delighted him, it made no difference; in fact, it would be a pleasure to me occasionally to feel that I did bore him. To have the full opportunity and the perfect right to bore a fellow-being is a privilege not lightly to be prized, and an added zest is given to the enjoyment of the borer by the knowledge that the bored one is bound to make it appear that he is not bored.

In an easy-chair opposite to me my listener sat and listened for two hours every evening. I interested myself by watching and attempting to analyze the expressions on his face, but what these appeared to indicate made no difference in my remarks. I do not think he liked repetitions, but if I chose to tell a thing several times, I did so. He had no right to tell me that he had heard that before. Immunity from this remark was to me a rare enjoyment.

I made it a point to talk as well as I could, for I like to hear myself talk well, but I paid no attention to the likings of my listener. Later I should probably do this, but at present it was a joy to trample upon the likings of others. My own likings in this respect had been so often trampled upon that I would not now deny myself the exercise of the right— bought and paid for—to take this sweet revenge.

On the evenings of nine week-days and one Sunday, when I confined myself entirely to a description of a short visit to Palestine, I talked and my listener listened. About the middle of the evening of the tenth week-day, when I was engaged in the expression of some fancies evoked by the recollection of a stroll through the Egyptian department of the Louvre, I looked at my listener, and beheld him asleep.

As I stopped speaking he awoke with a start, and attempted to excuse himself by stating that he had omitted to take coffee with his evening meal. I made no answer, but, opening my pocket-book, paid and discharged him.

Frank R. Stockton

V

CHESTER WALKIRK

It is not my custom to be discouraged by a first failure. I looked over the letters which had been sent to me in answer to my advertisement, and wrote to another of the applicants, who very promptly came to see me.

The appearance of this man somewhat discouraged me. My first thought concerning him was that a man who seemed to be so thoroughly alive was not likely to prove a good listener. But after I had had a talk with him I determined to give him a trial. Of one thing I was satisfied: he would keep awake. He was a man of cheerful aspect; alert in motion, glance, and speech. His age was about forty; he was of medium size, a little inclined to be stout, and his face, upon which he wore no hair, was somewhat ruddy. In dress he was neat and proper, and he had an air of friendly deference, which seemed to me to suit the position I wished him to fill.

He spoke of himself and his qualifications with tact, if not with modesty, and rated very highly his ability to serve me as a listener; but he did so in a manner intended to convince me that he was not boasting, but stating facts which it was necessary I should know. His experience had been varied: he had acted as a tutor, a traveling companion, a confidential clerk, a collector of information for technical writers, and in other capacities requiring facility of adaptation to exigencies. At present he was engaged in making a catalogue for a collector of prints, whose treasures, in the course of years, had increased to such an extent that it was impossible for him to remember what his long rows of portfolios contained. The collector was not willing that work among his engravings should be done by artificial light, and, as the evenings of my visitor were therefore disengaged, he said he should be glad to occupy them in a manner which would not only be profitable to him, but, he was quite sure, would be very interesting.

The man's name was Chester Walkirk, and I engaged him to come to me every evening, as my first listener had done.

I began my discourses with Walkirk with much less confidence and pleasurable anticipation than I had felt with regard to the quiet, unassuming elderly person who had been my first listener, and whom I had supposed to be a very model of receptivity. The new man I feared would demand more,—if not by word, at least by manner. He would be more like an audience; I should find myself striving to please him, and I could not feel careless whether he liked what I said or not.

But by the middle of the first evening all my fears and doubts in regard to Walkirk had disappeared. He proved to be an exceptionally good listener. As I spoke, he heard me with attention and evident interest; and this he showed by occasional remarks, which he took care should never be interruptions. These interpolations were managed with much tact; sometimes they were in the form of questions, which reminded me of something I had intended to say, but had omitted, which led me to speak further upon the subject, perhaps on some other phase of it. Now and then, by the expression on his countenance, or by a word or two, he showed interest, gratification, astonishment, or some other appropriate sentiment.

When I stopped speaking, he would sit quietly and muse upon what I had been saying; or, if he thought me not too deeply absorbed in reflection, would ask a question, or say something relative to the subject in hand, which would give me the opportunity of making some remarks which it gratified me to know that he wanted to hear.

I could not help feeling that I talked better to Walkirk than I had ever done to any one else; and I did not hesitate to admit to myself that this gratifying result was due in great part to his ability as a listener. I do not say that he drew me out, but he gave me opportunities to show myself in the broadest and best lights. This truly might be said to be good listening; it produced good speech.

Day after day I became better and better satisfied with Chester Walkirk, and it is seldom that I have enjoyed myself more than in talking to him. I am sure that it gave me more actual pleasure to tell him what I had seen and what I had done than I had felt in seeing and doing those things. This may appear odd, but it is a fact. I readily revived in myself the emotions that accompanied my experiences, and to these recalled emotions was added the sympathetic interest of another.

In other ways Walkirk won my favor. He was good-natured and intelligent, and showed that he was anxious to please me not only as a listener, but as a companion, or, I might better say, as an associate inmate of my study. What he did not know in this respect he set himself diligently to learn.

VI

MY UNDER-STUDY

In talking about my travels to Chester Walkirk, I continued for a time to treat the subject in the same desultory manner in which I had related my experiences to my first listener; but the superior intelligence, and I may say the superior attention, of Walkirk acted upon me as a restraint as well as an incentive. I made my descriptions as graphic and my statements as accurate as I could, and, stimulated by his occasional questions and remarks, I began to discourse systematically and with a well-considered plan. I went from country to country in the order in which I had traveled through them, and placed my reflections on social, political, or artistic points where they naturally belonged.

It was plain to see that Walkirk's interest and pleasure increased when my rambling narrations resolved themselves into a series of evening lectures upon Great Britain, the Continent, and the north coast of Africa, and his pleasure was a decided gratification to me. If his engagements and mine had permitted, I should have been glad to talk to him at other times, as well as in the evening.

After a month or more of this agreeable occupation, the fact began to impress itself upon me that I was devoting too much time to the pleasure of being listened to. My

Frank R. Stockton

grandmother gently complained that the time I gave to her after dinner appeared to be growing less and less, and there was a good deal of correspondence and other business I was in the habit of attending to in the evening which now was neglected, or done in the daytime, when I should have been doing other things.

I was not a man of leisure. My grandmother owned a farm about a mile from our village, and over the management of this I exercised a supervision. I was erecting some houses on land of my own on the outskirts of the village, and for this reason, as well as others, it frequently was necessary for me to go to the city on business errands. Besides all this, social duties had a claim on me, summer and winter.

I had gradually formed the habit of talking with Walkirk on other subjects than my travels, and one evening I mentioned to him some of the embarrassments and annoyances to which I had been subjected during the day, on account of the varied character of my affairs. Walkirk sat for a minute or two, his chin in his hand, gazing steadfastly upon the carpet; then he spoke:—

"Mr. Vanderley, what you say suggests something which I have been thinking of saying to you. I have now finished the catalogue of prints, on which I was engaged when I entered your service as a listener; and my days, therefore, being at my disposal, it would give me great pleasure to put them at yours."

"In what capacity?" I asked.

"In that of an under-study," said he.

I assured him that I did not know what he meant.

"I don't wonder at that," said he, with a smile, "but I will explain. In theatrical circles each principal performer is furnished with what is termed in the profession an under-study. This is an actor, male or female, as the case may be, who studies the part of the performer, and is capable of going through with it, with more or less ability, in case the regular actor, from sickness or any other cause, is prevented from appearing in his part. In this way the manager provides against emergencies which might at any time stop his play and ruin his business. Now, I should like very much to be your under-study, and I think in this capacity I could be of great service to you."

I made no answer, but I am sure my countenance expressed surprise.

"I do not mean," he continued, "to propose that I shall act as your agent in the various forms of business which press upon you, but I suggest that you allow me to do for you exactly what the under-study does for the actor; that is, that you let me take your place when it is inconvenient or impossible for you to take it yourself."

"It strikes me," said I, "that, in the management of my affairs, it would be very seldom that you or any one else could take my place."

"Of course," said Walkirk, "under present circumstances that would be impossible; but suppose, for instance, you take me with you to those houses you are building, that you show me what has been done and what you intend to do, and that you let me make myself familiar with the whole plan and manner of the work. This would be easy for me, for I have superintended house-building; and although I am neither a plumber, a mason, a carpenter, a paper-hanger, or a painter, I know how such people should do their work. Therefore, if you should be unable to attend to the matter yourself,—and in such case only,—I could go and see how the work was progressing; and this I could do with regard to your farm, or any other of your business with the details of which you should care to have me make myself familiar,— always remembering that I should not act as your regular agent in any one of these affairs, but as one who, when it is desirable, temporarily takes your place. I think, Mr. Vanderley, that it would be of advantage to you to consider my proposition."

I did consider it, and the next evening I engaged Chester Walkirk as an under-study.

VII

MY BOOK

In order to be at hand when I might need him, Walkirk took up his residence at the village tavern, or, as some of us were pleased to call it, the inn. To make him available when occasion should require, I took him with me to the scene of my building operations and to my grandmother's farm, and he there showed the same intelligent interest that he gave to my evening recitals. I had no difficulty in finding occupation for my under-study, and, so far as I could judge, he attended to the business I placed in his hands as well as I could have done it myself; indeed, in some instances, he did it better, for he gave it more time and careful consideration.

In this business of supplying my place in emergencies, Walkirk showed so much ability in promoting my interests that I became greatly pleased with the arrangement I had made with him. It was somewhat surprising to me, and I think to Walkirk, that so many cases arose in which I found it desirable that he should take my place. I was going to look at a horse: some visitors arrived; I sent Walkirk. There was a meeting of a scientific society which I wished very much to attend, but I could not do that and go to a dinner party to which I had been invited on the same evening; Walkirk went to the meeting, took notes, and the next day gave me a full report in regard to some particular points in which I was

Frank R. Stockton

interested, and which were not mentioned in the short newspaper notice of the meeting.

In other cases, of which at first I could not have imagined the possibility, my under-study was of use to me. I was invited to address my fellow townsmen and townswomen on the occasion of the centennial anniversary of the settlement of our village, and as I had discovered that Walkirk was a good reader I took him with me, in order that he might deliver my written address in case my courage should give out. My courage did not give out, but I am very sure that I was greatly supported and emboldened by the knowledge that if, at the last moment, my embarrassment should not allow me to begin my address, or if in the course of its delivery I should feel unable, for any reason, to go on with it, there was some one present who would read it for me.

It had long been my habit to attend with my grandmother, bi-monthly, an early evening whist party at the house of an elderly neighbor. I had a bad headache on one of these appointed evenings, and Walkirk, who was a perfectly respectable and presentable man, went with my grandmother in my stead. I afterward heard that he played an excellent hand at whist, a remark which had never been made of me.

But I will not refer at present to any further instances of the usefulness of my under-study, except to say that, as I found his feet were of the same size and shape as my own, I sent him to be measured for a pair of heavy walking-shoes which I needed; and I once arranged for him to serve in my place on a coroner's jury, in the case of a drowned infant.

The evening listenings still went on, and as the scope of my remarks grew wider, and their purpose became better defined, it began to dawn upon me that it was selfish to devote these accounts of remarkable traveling experiences to the pleasure of only two men, myself and my listener; the public would be interested in these things. I ought to write a book.

This idea pleased me very much. As Walkirk was now able to take my place in so many ways, I could give a good deal of time each day to composition; and, moreover, there was no reason why such work should interfere with my pleasure in being listened to. I could write by day, and talk at night. It would be all the better for my book that I should first orally deliver the matter to Walkirk, and afterward write it. I broached this idea to Walkirk; but, while he did not say so in words, it was plain to me he did not regard it with favor. He reflected a little before speaking.

"The writing of a book," he said, "is a very serious thing; and although it is not my province to advise you, I will say that if I were in your place I should hesitate a good while before commencing a labor like that. I have no doubt, judging from what I have already heard of your travels, that you would make a most useful and enjoyable book, but the question in my mind is, whether the pleasure you would give your readers would repay you for the time and labor you would put upon this work."

This was the first time that Walkirk had offered me advice. I had no idea of taking it, but I did not resent it.

"I do not look at the matter in that way," I said. "An absorbing labor will be good for me. My undertaking may result in overworking you, for you will be obliged to act as my under-study even more frequently than you do now."

"Oh, I'm not afraid of work," said he; "I can stand any amount of it. But how about the evening discourses,—will they come to an end?"

Frank R. Stockton

"Not at all," said I; "I shall go on giving you an account of my travels, just as before. This will help me to judge better what to put in and what to leave out."

"I am very glad to hear that," he said, with animation; "I do not hesitate to own to you that I should very greatly regret to lose those most interesting accounts of your experiences."

This was very complimentary, but, as he was paid to listen, the remark did not possess the force it would have had, had he paid to hear me.

Enthusiastically I went to work upon my book, and I found that talking about my travels to Walkirk helped me to write about them for the public. But a week had not passed when I came to the conclusion that writing was in no way so pleasant as talking. I disliked labor with the pen; I disliked long sitting at my desk. The composition of the matter was enough for me; some one else should put it on paper. I must have a secretary. I went immediately to Walkirk, who was at the inn, working upon some of my accounts.

"Walkirk," said I, "I can get somebody else to do that sort of thing. I want you to act as my amanuensis."

To my surprise his face clouded. He seemed troubled, even pained.

"I am very, very sorry," he said, "to decline any work which you may desire me to do, but I really must decline this. I cannot write from dictation. I cannot be your amanuensis. Although it may seem like boasting, this is one of the few things I cannot do: my nervous temperament, my disposition, in fact my very nature, stand in the way, and make the thing impossible."

I could not understand Walkirk's objections to this sort of

work, for he was a ready writer, a good stenographer, and had shown himself perfectly willing and able to perform duties much more difficult and distasteful than I imagined this possibly could be. But there are many things I do not understand, and which I consider it a waste of time to try to understand; and this was one of them.

"Then I must get some one else," said I.

"If you decide to do that," said Walkirk, "I will attend to the matter for you, and you need trouble yourself no further about it. I will go to the city, or wherever it is necessary to go, and get you an amanuensis."

"Do so," said I, "but come and report to me before you make any engagement."

The next day Walkirk made his report. He had not been as successful as he had hoped to be. If I had been doing my work in the city, he could have found me stenographers, amanuenses, or type-writers by the hundred. By living and working in the country, I made his task much more difficult. He had found but few persons who were willing to come to me every day, no matter what the weather, and only one or two who would consent to come to our village to live.

But he had made a list of several applicants who might suit me, and who were willing to accept one or the other of the necessary conditions.

"They are all women!" I exclaimed, when I looked at it.

"Yes," said he; "it would be very difficult, perhaps impossible, to find a competent man who would answer your purpose. The good ones could not afford to give you part of their time, which is all you require, and you would not want any other. With women the case is different; and besides, I am sure, from my own experience, that a lady amanuensis would suit your purpose much better than a man: she would be more patient, more willing to accommodate herself to your moods, in every way more available."

I had not engaged Walkirk to be my under-study in matters of judgment, and I did not intend that he should act in that capacity; but there was force in his remarks, and I determined to give them due consideration. Although I had apartments of my own, I really lived in my grandmother's house; and of course it was incumbent upon me to consult her upon this subject. She looked at the matter in her usual kindly way, and soon came to be of the opinion that, if I could give a worthy and industrious young woman an opportunity to earn her livelihood, I ought to do it; taking care, of course, to engage no one who could not furnish the very best references.

I now put the matter again into Walkirk's hands, and told him to produce the persons he had selected. He managed the matter with great skill, and in the course of one morning four ladies called upon me, in such a way that they did not interfere with each other. Of these applicants none pleased me. One of them was a dark-haired, dark-eyed, rather spare person, whose youthful energies had been so improved by years that I was sure her briskness of action, her promptness of speech, and her evident anxiety to get to work and to keep at it would eventually drive me crazy.

Another was a skilled stenographer, who could write I forget how many hundred words a minute; and when I told her there were no minutes in which I could dictate as many words as that, even if I wanted to, and that there would be many minutes in which I should not dictate any words at all, she said she was afraid that if she fell into a dilly-dally, poky way of working it would impair her skill, and it might be difficult, when she left my employment, to regain her previous expertness. She was quite willing, however, to engage with me, and thought that if I would try to dictate as fast as possible I might, in time, be able to keep her nearly up to her normal standard.

A third one was willing to write longhand, and to work as slowly and as irregularly as I pleased. I gave her a short trial, but her writing was so illegible that I could not discover whether or not she made mistakes in spelling. I had, however, my suspicions on this point.

The fourth applicant I engaged to come for a week on trial. She exhibited no prominent disabilities, and I thought she might be made to answer my purpose; but as she possessed no prominent capabilities, and as she asked me to repeat almost every sentence which I dictated to her, I found it very tiresome to work with her, and I punished Walkirk by making him act as my under-study on the third and fourth days of her engagement. I requested him to dictate to her some detailed incidents of travel which I had told him, and which I was sure he remembered very well. He undertook the task with alacrity, but after two mornings' work he advised me to discharge her. Dictating to her, he said, was like talking into a tin spout with nobody at the other end. Somebody might come if you shouted long enough, but this was tiresome.

VIII

THE MALARIAL ADJUNCT

The fifth applicant on Walkirk's list had a morning to herself. So soon as she entered my study I hoped that she would suit me, and I had not talked with her ten minutes before I decided that she would. Her personality was exceedingly agreeable; she was neither too young nor too old. She expressed herself with a good-humored frankness which I liked, and appeared to be of a very practical turn of mind. She was a practiced stenographer, was accustomed to write from dictation and to read aloud, could correct proof, and had some admirable references. Her abilities appeared so excellent, and her demeanor was so agreeable to me, that I engaged her.

"I am very happy indeed, Mr. Vanderley," she said, with the pretty dimpled smile which had so frequently shown itself in the course of our conversation, "that you have given me this position. I am sure that I shall like it, and I shall try very hard to make my work satisfactory. I shall come up every morning in the nine o'clock train, as you desire; and I shall be obliged to bring my husband with me, but this will not in any way interfere with my work. He is suffering from a malarial disease, and is subject to periods of faintness, so that it would be impossible for me to leave him for the whole morning; but he can sit outside anywhere, under a tree, or perhaps somewhere in the house if it happens to rain. He is perfectly contented if he has a comfortable place to sit in. He is not able to attend to any business, and as I now have to be the bread-winner I am most deeply grateful for this work which you have given me. I am sure that the little trip in and out of town will do him good, and as I shall buy commutation tickets it will not be expensive. He came with me this morning, and if you will excuse me I will bring him in and introduce him." And without waiting for any remark from me she left the room, and shortly returned with the malarial subject. He was an extremely mild-mannered man, of light weight and sedate aspect. The few words in which he indicated his gratification with his wife's engagement suggested to me the need of sulphate of quinia.

This revelation of a malarial adjunct to the labors of myself and this very agreeable lady greatly surprised me, and, I must admit, threw me back from that condition of satisfaction in which I had found myself upon engaging her; and yet I could think of no reasonable objection to make. The lady had promised that he should not be in the way, and the most I could say, even to myself, was that the arrangement did not appear attractive to me. Of course, with no reason but a chaotic distaste, I would not recede from my agreement, and deprive this worthy lady of the opportunity of supporting herself and her husband; and the two departed, to return on the following day prepared to labor and to wait.

I inquired of Walkirk, I fear with some petulance, if he had known of the incumbrance attached to this candidate; and he replied that she had informed him that she was married, but he had no idea she intended to bring her husband with her. He was very sorry that this was necessary, but in his judgment the man would not live very long.

My grandmother was greatly pleased when I told her of the

arrangement I had made to assist a devoted wife to support an invalid husband. She considered it a most worthy and commendable action, and she was rejoiced that such an opportunity had been afforded me. She would do what she could to make the poor man comfortable while his wife was at work; and if he had any sense at all, and knew what was to his advantage, he would be very careful not to interfere with her duties.

The next morning the couple appeared, and the lady was ensconced in the anteroom to my study, which I had fitted up for the use of my secretary, where, through the open window in front of her, she could see her husband, seated in a rocking-chair, under a wide-spreading apple-tree. By his side was a table, on which lay the morning paper and some books which my grandmother had sent out to him. For a time she gave him also her society, but, as she subsequently informed me, she did not find him responsive, and soon concluded that he would be happier if left to his reflections and the literature with which she had provided him.

As an amanuensis I found my new assistant everything that could be desired. She wrote rapidly and correctly, never asked me to repeat, showed no nervousness at the delays in my dictation, and was ready to write the instant I was ready to speak. She was quick and intelligent in looking up synonyms, and appeared perfectly at home in the dictionary. But in spite of these admirable qualifications, I did not find myself, that morning, in a condition favorable to my best literary work. Whenever my secretary was not actually writing she was looking out of the window; sometimes she would smile and nod, and on three occasions, while I was considering, not what I should say next, but whether or not I could stand this sort of thing, she went gently to the window, and asked the invalid, in a clear whisper, intended to be entirely undisturbing, how he was getting on and if he wanted anything.

Two days after this the air was damp and rain threatened, and the malarial gentleman was supplied with comfortable quarters in the back parlor. I do not know whether or not he liked this better than sitting under a tree, but I am sure that the change did not please his wife. She could not look at him, and she could not ask him how he was getting on and if he wanted anything. I could see that she was worried and fidgety, although endeavoring to work as faithfully and steadily as usual. Twice during a break in the dictation she asked me to excuse her for just one minute, while she ran into the parlor to take a peep at him.

The next day it rained, and there seemed every probability that we should have continued wet weather, and that it would be days before the malarial one could sit under the apple-tree. Therefore I looked the situation fairly in the face. It was impossible for me to dictate to a nervous, anxious woman, whose obvious mental condition acted most annoyingly upon my nerves, and I suggested that she bring her husband into her room, and let him sit there while she worked. With this proposition my secretary was delighted.

"Oh, that will be charming!" she cried. "He will sit just as still as a mouse, and will not disturb either of us, and I shall be able to see how he feels without saying a word."

For four days the malarial gentleman, as quiet as a mouse, sat by my secretary's window, while she wrote at the table, and I walked up and down my study, or threw myself into one chair or another, endeavoring to forget that that man was sitting by the window; that he was trying his best not to do anything which might disturb me; that he did not read, or write, or occupy his mind in any way; that he heard every word I dictated to his wife without indicating that he was not deaf, or that he was capable of judging whether my words were good, bad, or unworthy of consideration. Not only did I endeavor not to think of him, but I tried not to see either him or his wife. The silent, motionless figure of the one, and the silent but animated and vivacious figure of the other, filled with an eager desire to do her work properly, with a bubbling and hearty love for her husband, and an evident joyousness in the fact that she could love, work, and watch, all at the same time, drove from my mind every thought of travel or foreign experiences. Without the malarial husband I should have asked for no better secretary; but he spoiled everything. He was like a raw oyster in a cup of tea.

I could not drive from my mind the vision of that man even when I knew he was asleep in his bed. There was no way of throwing him off. His wife had expressed to my grandmother the delight she felt in having him in the room with her while she worked, and my grandmother had spoken to me of her own sympathetic pleasure in this arrangement. I saw it would be impossible to exile him again to the apple-tree, even if the ground should ever be dry enough. There was no hope that he would be left at his home; there was no hope that he would get better, and go off to attend to his own business; there was no hope that he would die.

From dictating but little I fell to dictating almost nothing at all. To keep my secretary at work, I gave her some notes of travel of which to make a fair copy, while I occupied myself in wondering what I was going to do about that malarial husband.

At last I ceased to wonder, and I did something. I went to the city, and, after a day's hard work, I secured a position for my secretary in a large publishing establishment, where her husband could sit by a window in a secluded corner, and keep as quiet as a mouse. The good lady overwhelmed me with thanks for my kindness. She had begun to fear that, as the season grew colder, the daily trip would not suit her husband, and she gave me credit for having thought the same thing.

My grandmother and Walkirk were greatly concerned, as well as surprised, at what I had done. The former said that, if I attempted to write my book with my own hand, she feared the sedentary work would tell upon my health; and my under-study, while regretting very much that his efforts to provide me with an amanuensis had proved unsuccessful, showed very plainly, although he did not say so, that he hoped I had found that authorship was an annoying and unprofitable business, and that I would now devote myself to pursuits which were more congenial, and in which he could act for me when occasion required.

IX

WALKIRK'S IDEA

Walkirk very soon discovered that I had no intention whatever of giving up the writing of my book, and I quieted the fears of my grandmother, in regard to my health, by assuring her that the sedentary work connected with the production of my volume would not be done by me. Secretaries could be had, and I would get one.

This determination greatly disturbed Walkirk. He did not wish to see me perform a service for myself which it was his business to perform for me, and in which he had failed. I know that he gave the matter the most earnest consideration, and two days after my late secretary and her husband had left me he came into my study, his face shining with a new idea.

"Mr. Vanderley," said he, "to find you an amanuensis who will exactly suit you, and who will be willing to come here into the country to work, is, I think you will admit, a very difficult business; but I do not intend, if I can help it, to be beaten by it. I have thought of a plan which I believe will meet all contingencies, and I have come to propose it to you. You know that institution just outside the village,—the House of Martha?"

I replied that I knew of it.

"Well," he continued, "I did not think of it until a day or two ago, and I have since been inquiring into its organization and nature. That sisterhood of Martha is composed of women who propose not only to devote themselves to a life of goodness, but to imitate the industrious woman for whom they have named themselves. They work not only in their establishment, but wherever they can find suitable occupation, and all that they earn is devoted to the good of the institution. Some of them act as nurses for the sick,—for pay if people can afford it, for nothing if they cannot. Others have studied medicine, and practice in the same way. They also prepare medicines and dispense them, and do a lot of good things,—if possible, for money and the advantage of the House of Martha. But every woman who joins such an institution cannot expect immediately to find the sort of remunerative work she can best do, and I am informed that there are several women there who, at present, are unemployed. Now, it is my opinion that among these you could find half a dozen good secretaries."

I laughed aloud. "Those women," said I, "are just the same as nuns. It is ridiculous to suppose that one of them would be allowed to come here as my secretary, even if she wanted to."

"I am not so sure of that," persisted Walkirk; "I do not see why literary, or rather clerical, pursuits should not be as open to them as medicine or nursing."

"You may not see it," said I, "but I fancy that they do."

"It is impossible to be certain on that point," he replied, "until we have proposed the matter to them, and given them the opportunity to consider it."

"If you imagine," I said, "that I have the effrontery to go to that nunnery—for it is no more nor less than that—and ask the Lady Abbess to lend me one of her nuns to write at my dictation, you have very much mistaken me."

Walkirk smiled. "I hardly expected you to do that," said he, "although I must insist that it is not a nunnery, and there is no Lady Abbess. There is a Head Mother, and some sub-mothers, I believe. My idea was that Mrs. Vanderley should drive over there and make inquiries for you. A proposition from an elderly lady of such high position in the community would have a much better effect than if it came from a gentleman."

Walkirk's plan amused me very much, and I told him I would talk to my grandmother about it. When I did so, I was much surprised to find that she received the idea with favor.

"That Mr. Walkirk," she said, "is a man of a good deal of penetration and judgment, and if you could get one of those sisters to come here and write for you I should like it very much; and if the first one did not suit, you could try another without trouble or expense. The fact that you had a good many strings to your bow would give you ease of mind and prevent your getting discouraged. I don't want you to give up the idea of having a secretary."

Then, with some hesitation, my good grandmother confided to me that there was another reason why this idea of employing a sister pleased her. She had been a little afraid that some lady secretary, especially like that very pleasant and exemplary person with the invalid husband, might put the notion into my head that it would be a good thing for me to have a wife to do my writing. Now, of course she expected me to get married some day. That was all right, but there was no need of my being in any hurry about it;

and as to my wife doing my writing, that was not to be counted upon positively. Some wives might not be willing to do it, and others might not do it well; so, as far as that matter was concerned, nothing would be gained. But one of those sisters would never suggest matrimony. They were women apart from all that sort of thing. They had certain work to do in this world, and they did it for the good of the cause in which they were enlisted, without giving any thought to those outside matters which so often occupy the minds of women who have not, in a manner, separated themselves from the world. She would go that very afternoon to the House of Martha and make inquiries.

X

THE PLAN OF SECLUSION

My grandmother returned from the House of Martha disappointed and annoyed. Life had always flowed very smoothly for her, and I had rarely seen her in her present mental condition.

"I do not believe," she said, "that that institution will succeed. Those women are too narrow-minded. If they were in a regular stone-walled convent, it would be another thing, but they are only a sisterhood. They are not shut up there; it's their business and part of their religion to go out, and why they should not be willing to come here and do good, as well as anywhere else, I cannot see, for the life of me."

"Then they objected to the proposition?" I asked.

"Yes," she replied, "they did, and without any reason whatever. I saw their superior, whom they call Mother Anastasia, and from her I learned that there were several women in the establishment who were thoroughly competent to act as secretaries; but when I proposed that one of them should come and write for you, she said that would not do at all. I reasoned the matter with her: that literature was as high a profession as medicine, and as much good could be done with the practice of one as the other; and if the sisters went out to nurse and to cure, they might just as well go out to write for those who cannot write for themselves. To that she answered, it was not the writing she objected to,—that was all well enough,—but it was decidedly outside of the vocation of the order for one of the sisters to spend her mornings with a young gentleman. If he were sick and suffering, and had no one else to attend to him, it would be different. Upon this, I told her that you would be sick if you were obliged to do your own writing, and therefore I couldn't see the difference.

"But I must admit she was very good-natured and pleasant about it, and she told me that if you chose to come to their visitors' room and make yourself comfortable there, and dictate, one of the sisters would sit at the table behind the grating and would write for you. I replied that I did not believe you would like that, but that I would mention it to you."

I laughed. "So much for Walkirk's brilliant idea," I said. "I fancy myself going every morning to that nunnery to do my work in their cheerless visitors' room!"

"Cheerless? I should say so!" exclaimed my grandmother,—"bare floors, bare walls, and hard wooden chairs. It is not to be thought of."

That evening I informed Walkirk of the ill success of my grandmother's mission, but to my surprise he did not appear to be discouraged.

"I don't think we need have any trouble at all in managing that affair," said he. "Why shouldn't you have a grating put up in the doorway between your study and the secretary's room? Then the sister could go in there, the other door could be locked, and she would be as much shut off from the world as if she were behind a grating in the House of

Martha. I believe, if this plan were proposed to the sisters, it would be agreed to."

I scouted the idea as utterly absurd; but when, the next morning, I mentioned it to my grandmother, she caught at it eagerly, and no sooner had she finished her breakfast than she ordered her carriage and drove to the House of Martha.

She returned triumphant.

"We had a long discussion," she said, "but Mother Anastasia finally saw the matter in its proper light. She admitted that if a room could be arranged in this house, in which a sister could be actually secluded, there was no good reason why she should not work there as consistently with their rules as if she were in the House of Martha. Therefore, she agreed, if you concluded to carry out this plan, to send a sister every morning to write for you. So now, if you want a secretary from the House of Martha, you can have one."

To this I replied that I most positively wanted one; and Walkirk was immediately instructed to have a suitable grating made for the doorway between my study and the secretary's room.

Nearly a week was required for the execution of this work, and during this time I took a rest from literary composition and visited some friends, leaving all the arrangements for my new secretary in the hands of my grandmother and Walkirk. When I returned, the iron grating was in its place. It was a neat and artistic piece of work, but I did not like it. I object decidedly to anything which suggests restraint. The whole affair of the secretary was indeed very different from what I would have had it, but I had discovered that even in our advanced era of civilization one cannot always have everything he wants, albeit he be perfectly able and willing to pay for it.

XI

MY NUN

At nine o'clock on the morning of the appointed day my new secretary came, accompanied by one of those sisters called by Walkirk sub-mothers.

My grandmother received the two, and conducted them to the secretary's room. I was sitting in my study, but no attention was paid to me. The sub-mother advanced to the grating, and, having examined it, appeared satisfied to find that it was securely fastened in the doorway. The nun, as I called her, although Walkirk assured me the term was incorrect, stood with her back toward me, and when her companion had said a few words to her, in a low tone, she took her seat at the table. She wore a large gray bonnet, the sides and top of which extended far beyond her face, a light gray shawl, and a gray gown. She sat facing the window, with her left side turned toward me, and from no point of my study could I get a glimpse of her features.

The sub-mother looked out of the window, which opened upon little more than the once husband-sheltering apple-tree, and then, after a general glance around the room, she looked at me, and for the first time addressed me.

"I will come for the sister at twelve o'clock," she said, and with that she followed my grandmother out of the room, and locked the door behind her.

I stood and looked through the grating at my new secretary. I am not generally a diffident man, and have never been so with persons in my employment; but now, I must admit, I did not feel at my ease. The nun sat perfectly motionless; her hands were folded in her gray lap, and her gray bonnet was slightly bowed, so that I did not know whether she was gazing down at the table or out of the window.

She was evidently ready for work, but I was not. I did not know exactly how to begin with such a secretary. With the others I had been outspoken from the first; I had told them what I wanted and what I did not want, and they had been ready enough to listen and ready enough to answer. But to this silent, motionless gray figure I did not feel that I could be outspoken. No words suggested themselves as being appropriate to speak out. If I could see her face but for a moment, and discover whether she were old or young, cross-looking or gentle, I might know what to say to her. My impulse was to tell her there was a hook on which she could hang her bonnet and shawl, but as I did not know whether or not these sisters ever took off their bonnets and shawls, I did not feel at liberty to make this suggestion.

But it would not do to continue there, looking at her. She might be a very shy person, and if I appeared shy it would probably make her all the shyer; so I spoke.

"You will find paper," I said, "in the drawer of your table, and there are pens, of different sorts, in that tray." She opened the drawer, took out some paper, and selected a pen, all without turning her head toward me. Having broken the ice, I now felt impelled to deliver a short lecture on my requirements; but how could I say what I required without knowing what manner of person it was of whom I required it? I therefore postponed the lecture, and determined to begin work without further delay, as probably that would be the best way to put us both at our ease. But it had been more than two weeks since I had done any work, and I could not remember what it was that I had been dictating, or endeavoring to dictate, to the lady with the malarial husband. I therefore thought it well to begin at a fresh point, and to leave the gap to be filled up afterward. I felt quite sure, when last at work, I had been treating of the south of France, and had certainly not reached Marseilles. I therefore decided to take a header for Marseilles, and into Marseilles I plunged.

As soon as I began to speak the nun began to write, and having at last got her at work I felt anxious to keep her at it, and went steadily on through the lively seaport; touching upon one point after another as fast as I thought of them, and without regard to their proper sequence. But although I sometimes skipped from one end of the city to the other, and from history to street scenes, I dictated steadily, and the nun wrote steadily. She worked rapidly, and apparently heard and understood every word I said, for she asked no questions and did not hesitate. I am sure I never before dictated so continuously. I had been in the habit of stopping a good deal to think, not only about my work, but about other things, but now I did not wish to stop.

This amanuensis was very different from any other I had had. The others worked to make money for themselves, or to please me, or because they liked it. This one worked from principle. The money which I paid for her labor did not become her money. It was paid to the House of Martha. She sat there and wrote to promote the principles upon which the House of Martha was founded. In fact, so far as I was concerned, she was nothing more than a principle.

Now, to interfere with the working of a principle is not the right thing to do, and therefore I felt impelled to keep on dictating, which I did until the hall door of the secretary's room was unlocked and the sub-mother walked in. She came forward and said a few words to the nun, who stopped writing and wiped her pen. The other then turned to me, and in a low voice asked if the work of the sister was satisfactory. I advanced to the grating, and answered that I was perfectly satisfied, and was about to make some remarks, which I hoped would lead to a conversation, when the sub-mother—whose name I subsequently learned was Sister Sarah—made a little bow, and, saying if that were the case they would return at nine the next morning, left the room in company with the nun. The latter, when she arose from the table, turned her back to me, and went out without giving me the slightest opportunity of looking into her cavernous bonnet. This she did, I must admit, in the most natural way possible, which was probably the result of training, and gave one no idea of rudeness or incivility.

When they were gone I was piqued, almost angry with myself. I had intended stopping work a little before noon, in order to talk to that nun, even if she did not answer or look at me. She should discover that if she was a principle, I was, at least, an entity. I did not know exactly what I should say to her, but it would be something one human being would be likely to say to another human being who was working for him. If from the first I put myself on the proper level, she might in time get there. But although I had lost my present chance, she was coming again the next day.

I entered the secretary's room by the hall door, and looked at the manuscript which had been left on the table. It was written in an excellent hand, not too large, very legible, and correctly punctuated. Everything had been done properly, except that after the first three pages she had forgotten to number the leaves at the top; but as every sheet was placed in its proper order, this was an omission which could be easily rectified. I was very glad she had made it, for it would give me something to speak to her about.

At luncheon my grandmother asked me how I liked the new secretary, and added that if she did not suit me I could try another next day. I answered that so far she suited me, and that I had not the least wish at present to try another. I think my grandmother was about to say something regarding this sister, but I instantly begged her not to do so. I wished to judge her entirely on her merits, I said, and would rather not hear anything about her until I had come to a decision as to her abilities. I did not add that I felt such an interest in the anticipated discovery of the personality of this secretary that I did not wish that discovery interfered with.

In the evening Walkirk inquired about the sister-aman-uensis, but I merely answered that so far she had done very well, and dropped the subject. In my own mind I did not drop the subject until I fell asleep that night. I found myself from time to time wondering what sort of a woman was that nun. Was she an elderly, sharp-faced creature; was she a vapid, fat-faced creature, or a young and pleasing creature? And when I had asked myself these questions, I snubbed myself for taking the trouble to think about the matter, and then I began wondering again.

But upon one point I firmly made up my mind: the relationship between my secretary and myself should not continue to be that of an entity dictating to a principle.

XII

EZA

The next day, when the nun and Sister Sarah entered the secretary's room, I advanced to the grating and bade them good-morning. They both bowed, and the nun took her seat at the table. Sister Sarah then turned to me and asked if I had a gold pen, adding that the sister was accustomed to writing with one. I answered that I had all kinds of pens, and if the sister wanted a gold one it was only necessary to ask me for it. I brought several gold pens, and handed them through the grating to the sub-mother, who gave them to the secretary, and then took her leave, locking the door behind her. My nun took one of the pens, tried it, arranged the paper, and sat ready to write. I stood by the grating, hoping to converse a little, if it should be possible.

"Is there anything else you would like?" I said. "If there is, you know you must mention it."

She gently shook her head. The idea now occurred to me that perhaps my nun was dumb; but I almost instantly thought that this could not be, for dumb people were almost always deaf, and she could hear well enough. Then it struck me that she might be a Trappist nun, and bound by a vow of silence; but I reflected that she was not really a nun, and consequently could not be a Trappist.

Having been unsuccessful in my first attempt to make her speak, and having now stood silent for some moments, I felt it might be unwise to make another trial just then, for my object would be too plain. I therefore sat down and began dictating.

I did not work as easily as I had done on the preceding morning, for I intended, if possible, to make my nun look at me, or speak, before the hour of noon, and thinking of this intention prevented me from keeping my mind upon my work. From time to time I made remarks in regard to the temperature of the room, the quality of the paper, or something of the kind. To these she did not answer at all, or slightly nodded, or shook her head in a deprecatory manner, as if they were matters not worth considering.

Then I suddenly remembered the omission of the paging, and spoke of that. In answer she took up the manuscript she had written and paged every sheet. After this my progress was halting and uneven. Involuntarily my mind kept on devising plans for making that woman speak or turn her face toward me. If she would do the latter, I would be satisfied; and even if she proved to be an unveiled prophetess of Khorassan, there would be no further occasion for conjectures and wonderings, and I could go on with my work in peace. But it made me nervous to remain silent, and see that nun sitting there, pen in hand, but motionless as a post, and waiting for me to give her the signal to continue the exercise of the principle to which her existence was now devoted.

I went on with my dictation. I had left Marseilles, had touched slightly upon Nice, and was now traveling by carriage on the Cornice Road to Mentone. "It was on this road," I dictated, "that an odd incident occurred to me. We were nearly opposite the old robber village of"—and then I hesitated and stopped. I could not remember the name of the village. I walked up and down my study, rubbing my forehead, but the name would not recur to me. I was just thinking that I would have to go to the library and look up the name of the village, when from out of the depths of the nun's bonnet there came a voice, low but distinct, and, I thought, a little impatient, and it said, "Eza."

"Eza! of course!" I exclaimed,—"certainly it is Eza! How could I have forgotten it? I am very much obliged to you for reminding me of the name of that village. Perhaps you have been there?"

In answer to this question I received the least little bit of a nod, and the nun's pen began gently to paw the paper, as if it wanted to go on.

I was now really excited. She had spoken. Why should I not do something which should make her turn her face toward me,—something which would take her off her guard, as my forgetfulness had just done? But no idea came to my aid, and I felt obliged to begin to dictate the details of the odd incident, when suddenly the door opened, Sister Sarah walked in, and the morning's work was over.

I had not done much, but I had made that nun speak. She said "Eza." That was a beginning, and I felt confident that I should get on very well in time. I was a little sorry that my secretary had been on the Cornice Road. I fancied that she might have been one of those elderly single women who become Baedeker tourists, and, having tired of this sort of thing, had concluded to devote her life to the work of the House of Martha. But this was mere idle conjecture. She had spoken, and I should not indulge in pessimism.

I prepared a very good remark with which to greet the sub-mother on the next morning, and, although addressing Sister Sarah, I would be in reality speaking to my nun. I would say how well I was getting on. I had thought of saying *we* were getting on, but reflected afterward that this would never do; I was sure that the House of Martha would not allow, under any circumstances, that sister and myself to constitute a *we*. Then I would refer to the help my secretary had been to me, and endeavor to express the satisfaction which an author must always feel for a suggestion of this kind, or any other, from one qualified to make them. If there was any gratitude or vanity in my nun's heart, I felt I could stir it up, if Sister Sarah would listen to me long enough; and if gratitude, or even vanity, could be stirred, the rigidity of my nun would be impaired, and she might find herself off her guard.

But I had no opportunity of making my remark. At nine o'clock the door of the secretary's room opened, the nun entered, and the door was then closed and locked. Sister Sarah must have been in a hurry that morning. Just as well as not I might have made my remark directly to my nun, but I did not. She walked quickly to the table, arranged her paper, opened her inkstand, and sat down. I fancied that I saw a wavy wriggle of impatience in her shawl. Perhaps she wanted to know the rest of that odd incident near Eza. It may have been that it was impatient interest which had impaired her rigidity the day before.

I went on with the odd incident, and made a very good thing of it. Even when on well-worn routes of travel, I tried to confine myself to out-of-the-way experiences. Walkirk had been very much interested in this affair when I had told it to him, and there was no reason why this nun should not also be interested, especially as she had seen Eza.

I finished the narrative, and began another, a rather exciting one, connected with the breaking of a carriage wheel and an exile from Monte Carlo; but never once did curiosity or any other emotion impair the rigidity of that nun. She wrote almost as fast as I could dictate, and when I stopped I know she was filled with nervous desire to know what was coming next,—at least I fancied that her shawl indicated such nervousness; but hesitate as I might, or say what I might,—and I did say a good many things which almost demanded a remark or answer,—not one word came from her during the whole morning, nor did she ever turn the front of her bonnet toward me.

XIII

MY FRIEND VESPA

I was very much disgusted at the present state of affairs. Three days had elapsed, and I did not know what sort of a human being my secretary was. I might as well dictate into a speaking-tube. A phonograph would be better; for although it might seem ridiculous to sit in my room and talk aloud to no one, what was I doing now? That nun was the same as no one.

The next day was Sunday, and there would be no work, and no chance to solve the problem, which had become an actual annoyance to me; but I did not intend that this problem should continue to annoy me and interfere with my work. I am open and aboveboard myself, and if my secretary did not choose to be open and aboveboard, and behave like an ordinary human being, she should depart, and I would tell Walkirk to get me an ordinary human being, capable of writing from dictation, or depart himself. If he could not provide me with a suitable secretary, he was not the efficient man of business that he claimed to be. As to the absurdity of dictating to a mystery in a barrow bonnet, I would have no more of it.

I do not consider myself an ill-tempered person, and my grandmother asserts that I have a very good temper indeed;

but I must admit that on Monday morning I felt a little cross, and when Sister Sarah and the nun entered my antechamber I bade them a very cold good-morning, and allowed the former to go without attempting any conversation whatever. The nun having arrived, I would not send her away; but when the sub-mother came at noon, I intended to inform her that I did not any longer desire the services of the writing sister, and if she wished to know why I should tell her plainly. I would not say that I would as soon dictate to an inanimate tree-stump, but I would express that idea in as courteous terms as possible.

For fifteen minutes I let the nun sit and wait. If her principles forbade idleness, I was glad to have a crack at her principles. Then I began to dictate steadily and severely. I found that the dismissal from my mind of all conjectures regarding the personality of my secretary was of great service to me, and I was able to compose much faster than she could write.

It was about half past ten, I think, and the morning was warm and pleasant, when there gently sailed into the secretary's room, through the open window, a wasp. I saw him come in, and I do not think I ever beheld a more agreeable or benignant insect. His large eyes were filled with the light of a fatherly graciousness. His semi-detached body seemed to quiver with a helpful impulse, and his long hind legs hung down beneath him as though they were outstretched to assist, befriend, or succor. With wings waving blessings and a buzz of cheery greeting, he sailed around the room, now dipping here, now there, and then circling higher, tapping the ceiling with his genial back.

The moment the nun saw the wasp, a most decided thrill ran down the back of her shawl. Then it pervaded her bonnet, and finally the whole of her. As the beneficent insect sailed down near the table, she abruptly sprang to her feet and pushed back her chair. I advanced to the grating, but what could I do? Seeing me there, and doubtless with the desire immediately to assure me of his kindly intentions, my friend Vespa made a swoop directly at the front of the nun's bonnet.

With an undisguised ejaculation, and beating wildly at the insect with her hands, the nun bounded to one side and turned her face full upon me. I stood astounded. I forgot the wasp.

I totally lost sight of the fact that a young woman was in danger of being badly stung. I thought of nothing but that she was a young woman, and a most astonishingly pretty one besides.

The state of terror she was in opened wide her lovely blue eyes, half crimsoned her clear white skin, and threw her rosy lips and sparkling teeth into the most enchanting combinations.

"Make it go away!" she cried, throwing up one arm, and thereby pushing back her gray bonnet, and exhibiting some of the gloss of her light brown hair. "Can't you kill it?"

Most gladly would I have rushed in, and shed with my own hands the blood of my friend Vespa, for the sake of this most charming young woman, suddenly transformed from a barrow-bonneted principle. But I was powerless. I could not break through the grating; the other door of the secretary's room was locked.

"Don't strike at it," I said; "remain as motionless as you can, then perhaps it will fly away. Striking at a wasp only enrages it."

"I can't stay quiet," she cried; "nobody could!" and she

sprang behind the table, making at the same time another slap at the buzzing insect.

"You will surely be stung," I said, "if you act in that way. If you will slap at the wasp, don't use your hand; take something with which you can kill it."

"What can I take?" she exclaimed, now running round the table, and stopping close to the grating. "Give me something."

I hurriedly glanced around my study. I saw nothing that would answer for a weapon but a whisk broom, which I seized, and endeavored to thrust through the meshes of the grating.

"Oh!" she cried, as the wasp made a desperate dive close to her face, "give me that, quick!" and she stretched out her hand to me.

"I cannot," I replied; "I can't push it through. It won't go through. Take your bonnet."

At this, my nun seized her bonnet by a sort of floating hood which hung around the bottom of it and jerked it from her head, bringing with it certain flaps and ligatures and combs, which, being thus roughly removed, allowed a mass of wavy hair to fall about her shoulders.

Waving her bonnet in her hand, like a slung-shot, she sprang back and waited for the wasp. When the buzzing creature came near enough, she made a desperate crack at him, missing him; she struck again and again, now high, now low; she dashed from side to side of the room, and with one of her mad sweeps she scattered a dozen pages of manuscript upon the floor.

The view of this combat was enrapturing to me; the face of my nun, now lighted by a passionate determination to kill that wasp, was a delight to my eyes. If I could have assured myself that the wasp would not sting her, I would have helped him to prolong the battle indefinitely. But my nun was animated by very different emotions. She was bound to be avenged upon the wasp, and avenged she was. Almost springing into the air, she made a grand stroke at him, as he receded from her, hit him, and dashed him against the wall. He fell to the floor, momentarily disabled, but flapping and buzzing. Then down she stooped, and with three great whacks with her bonnet she finished the battle. The wasp lay motionless.

"Now," she said, throwing her bonnet upon the table, "I will close that window;" and she walked across the room, her blue eyes sparkling, her face glowing from her violent exercise, and her rich brown hair hanging in long waves upon her shoulders.

"Don't do that," I said; "it will make your room too warm. There is a netting screen in the corner there. If you put that under the sash, it will keep out all insects. I wish I could do it for you."

She took the frame and fitted it under the sash.

"I am sorry I did not know that before," she said, as she returned to her table; "this is a very bad piece of business."

I begged her to excuse me for not having informed her of the screen, but I did not say that I was sorry for what had occurred. I merely expressed my gratification that she had not been stung. Her chair had been pushed away from the table, its back against the wall, opposite to me. She seated herself upon it, gently panting. She looked from side to side at the sheets of manuscript scattered upon the floor.

"I will pick them up presently and go to work, but I must rest a minute." She did not now seem to consider that it was of the slightest consequence whether I saw her face or not.

"Never mind the papers," I said; "leave them there; they can be picked up any time."

"I wish that were the worst of it;" and as she spoke she raised her eyes toward me, and the least little bit of a smile came upon her lips, as if, though troubled, she could not help feeling the comical absurdity of the situation.

"It is simply dreadful," she continued. "I don't believe such a thing ever before happened to a sister."

"There is nothing dreadful about it," said I; "and do you mean to say that the sisters of the House of Martha, who go out to nurse, and do all sorts of good deeds, never speak to the people they are befriending, nor allow them to look upon their faces?"

"Of course," said she, "you have to talk to sick people; otherwise how could you know what they need? But this is a different case;" and she began to gather up her hair and twist it at the back of her head.

"I do not understand," I remarked; "why is it a different case?"

"It is as different as it can be," said she, picking up her comb from the floor and thrusting it through her hastily twisted knot of hair. "I should not have come here at all if your grandmother had not positively asserted that there would be nothing for me to do but to listen and to write. And Mother Anastasia and Sister Sarah both of them especially instructed me that I was not to speak to you nor to look at you, but simply to sit at the table and work for the good of the cause.

That was all I had to do; and I am sure I obeyed just as strictly as anybody could, except once, when you forgot the name of Eza, and I was so anxious to have you go on with the incident that I could not help mentioning it. And now, I am sure I don't know what I ought to do."

"Do?" I asked. "There is nothing to do except to begin writing where you left off. The wasp is dead."

"I wish it had never been born," she said. "I have no doubt that the whole affair should come to an end now, and that I ought to go home; but I can't do that until Sister Sarah comes to unlock the door, and so I suppose we had better go to work."

"We"! I would not have dared to use that word, but it fell from her lips in the easiest and most conventional manner possible. It was delightful to hear it. I never knew before what a pleasant sound the word had. She now set herself to work to gather up the papers from the floor, and, having arranged them in their proper order, she took up her bonnet.

"Do you have to wear that?" I asked.

"Certainly," she answered, clapping it on and pulling it well forward.

"I should think it would be very hot and uncomfortable," I remarked.

"It is," she admitted curtly; and, seating herself at the table, she took up her pen.

I now perceived that if I knew what was good for myself I would cease from speaking on ordinary topics, and go on with my dictation. This I did, giving out my sentences as

Frank R. Stockton

rapidly as possible, although I must admit I took no interest whatever in what I was saying, nor do I believe that my secretary was interested in the subject-matter of my work. She wrote rapidly, and, as well as I could judge, appeared excited and annoyed. I was excited also, but not in the least disturbed. My emotions were of a highly pleasing character. We worked steadily for some twenty minutes, when suddenly she stopped and laid down her pen.

"Of course it isn't right to speak," she said, turning in her chair and speaking to me face to face, as one human being to another, "but as I have said so much already, I don't suppose a little more will make matters worse, and I must ask somebody's help in making up my mind what I ought to do. I suspect I have made all sorts of mistakes in this writing, but I could not keep my thoughts on my work. I have been trying my best to decide how I ought to act, but I cannot make up my mind."

"I shall be delighted to help you, if I can," I ventured. "What's the point that you cannot decide?"

"It is just this," she replied, fixing her blue eyes upon me with earnest frankness: "am I to tell the sisters what has happened or not? If I tell them, I know exactly what will be the result: I shall come here no more, and I shall have to take Sister Hannah's place at the Measles Refuge. There's nothing in this world that I hate like measles. I've had them, but that doesn't make the slightest difference. Sister Hannah has asked to be relieved, and I know she wants this place dreadfully."

"She cannot come here!" I exclaimed. "I don't believe I ever had the measles, and I will not have them."

"She is a stenographer," said she, "and she will most certainly be ordered to take my place if I make known what

I have done to-day."

"Supposing you were sure that you were not obliged to go to the Measles Refuge," I asked, "should you still regret giving up this position?"

"Of course I should," she answered promptly. "I must work at something, or I cannot stay in the House of Martha; and there is no work which I like so well as this. It interests me extremely."

"Now hear me," said I, speaking perhaps a little too earnestly, "and I do not believe any one could give you better advice than I am going to give you. What has occurred this morning was strictly and absolutely an accident. A wasp came in at the window and tried to sting you; and there is no woman in the world, be she a sister or not, who could sit still and let a wasp sting her."

"No," she interrupted, "I don't believe Mother Anastasia could do it."

"And what followed," I continued, "was perfectly natural, and could not possibly be helped. You were obliged to defend yourself, and in so doing you were obliged to act just as any other woman would act. Nothing else would have been possible, and the talking and all that came in with the rest. You couldn't help it."

"That's the way the matter appeared to me," said she; "but the question would arise, if it were all right, why should I hesitate to tell the sisters?"

"Hesitate!" I exclaimed. "You should not even think of such a thing. No matter what the sisters really thought about it, I am sure they would not let you come here any more, and you would be sent to the measles institution, and thus actually be punished for the attempted wickedness of a wasp."

"But there is the other side of the matter," said she; "would it not be wicked in me not to tell them?"

"Not at all," I replied. "You do not repeat to the sisters all that I tell you to write?"

"Of course not," she interrupted.

"And you do not consider it your duty," I continued, "to relate every detail of the business in which you are employed?"

"No," she said. "They ask me some things, and some things I have mentioned to them, such as not having a gold pen."

"Very good," said I. "You should consider that defending yourself against wasps is just as much your business here as anything else. If you are stung, it is plain you can't write, and the interests of your employer and of the House of Martha must suffer."

"Yes," she assented, still with the steady gaze of her blue eyes.

"Now your duty is clear," I went on. "If the sisters ask you if a wasp flew into your room and tried to sting you, and you had to jump around and kill it, and speak, before you could go on with your work, why, of course you must tell them; but if they don't ask you, don't tell them. It may seem ridiculous to you," I continued hurriedly, "to suppose that they would ask such a question, but I put it in this way to show you the principle of the thing."

She withdrew her eyes from my face, and fixed them upon

the floor.

"The truth of the matter is," she said presently, "that I haven't done anything wrong; at least I didn't intend to. I might have crouched down in the corner, with my face to the wall, and have covered my head and hands with my shawl, but I should have been obliged to stay there until Sister Sarah came, and I should have been smothered to death; and besides, I didn't think of it; so what I did do was the only thing I could do, and I do not think I ought to be punished for it."

"Now it is settled," I said. "Your duty is to work here for the benefit of your sisterhood, and you should not allow a wasp or any insect to interfere with it."

She looked at me, and smiled a little abstractedly. Then she turned to the table.

"I will go on with my work," she said, "and I will not say anything to the sisters until I have given the matter most earnest and careful consideration. I can do that a great deal better at home than I can here."

It was very well that she stopped talking and applied herself to her work, for I do not believe it was ten minutes afterward when Sister Sarah unlocked the door, and came in to take her away.

XIV

I FAVOR PERMANENCY IN OFFICE

As soon as my secretary had gone I went into her room and looked for my friend Vespa. I found him on the floor, quite dead, but not demolished. Picking him up and carrying him to my study, I carefully gummed him to a card. Under his motionless form I wrote, "The good services of this friend I shall ever keep in grateful remembrance." Then I pinned the card to the wall between two bookcases.

During the rest of that day I found myself in a state of unreasonable exaltation. Several times I put to myself the questions: Why is it that you feel so cheerful and so gay? Why have you the inclination to whistle and to dance in your room? Why do you light a cigar, and let it go out through forgetfulness? Why do you answer your grand-mother at random, and feel an inclination to take a long walk by yourself, although you know there are people invited to an afternoon tea?

I was not able to give an adequate answer to these questions, nor did I very much care to. I knew that my high spirits were caused by the discoveries the good Vespa had enabled me to make, and the fact that this reason could not be proved adequate did not trouble me at all; but prudence and a regard for my own interests made it very plain to me that other people should not know I had been exalted, and how. If I desired my nun to continue as my secretary, I must not let any one know that I cared in the least to hear her voice, or to have the front of her bonnet turned towards me.

At dinner, that day, my grandmother remarked to me:—

"Are you still satisfied with the House of Martha's sister? Does she do your work as you wish to have it done?"

I leaned back in my chair, and answered with deliberation:—

"Yes, I think she will do very well, and that after more practice she will do better. As it is, she is industrious and attentive. I place great stress upon that point, for I do not like to repeat my sentences; but she has a quick ear, and catches every word."

"Then," asked my grandmother, "you do not wish to make a change at present?"

"Oh, no," I said; "it would be very annoying to begin again with a new amanuensis. I am getting accustomed to this person, and that is a very important matter with me. So I do not wish to make any change so long as this sister does her work properly."

"I must say," resumed my grandmother, after a little pause, in which she seemed to be considering the subject, "that I was not altogether in favor of that young woman taking the position of your secretary. She can have had but little experience, and I thought that an older and steadier person would answer your purpose much better; but this one was unemployed at the time, and wished very much to do literary work; and as the institution needed the money you would pay, which would probably amount to a considerable sum if your book should be a long one, and as you were in a great hurry, and might engage some one from the city if one of the Martha sisters were not immediately available, Mother Anastasia and I concluded that it would be well to send this young person until one of the older sisters, competent for the work, should be disengaged. I thought you would be very anxious to have this change made as soon as possible, so that you might feel that you had a permanent secretary."

"Oh, no," said I, trying very hard not to appear too much in earnest. "This person is very steady, and there is a certain advantage in her being young, without much experience as a secretary. I wish any one who writes for me to work in my way; and if such a person has been accustomed to work in other people's ways, annoyance and interruption must surely result, and that I wish very much to avoid. A secretary should be a mere writing-machine, and I do not believe an elderly person could be that. She would be sure to have notions how my work should or should not be done, and in some way or other would make those notions evident."

"I don't quite agree with you," said my grandmother, "but of course you know your own business better than I do; and I suppose, after all, it doesn't make much difference whether the sister is young or not. They all dress alike, and all look ugly alike. I don't suppose there would be anything attractive about the Venus de Milo, if she wore a coal-scuttle bonnet and a gray woolen shawl."

"No," I answered, "especially if she kept the opening of her coal-scuttle turned down over her paper, as if she were about to empty coals upon it."

"That's very proper," said my grandmother, speaking a little more briskly. "All she has to do is to keep her eyes on her work, and I suppose, from what you say, that the flaps of her bonnet do not interfere with her keeping her ears on you. But if at any time you desire to make a change, all you have to do is to let me know, and I can easily arrange the matter."

I promised that I would certainly let her know in case I had such a desire.

That evening Walkirk remarked to me that he thought nothing could be more satisfactory for me than to have on tap, so to speak, an institution like the House of Martha, from which I could draw a secretary whenever I wanted one, and keep her for as long or as short a time as pleased me; and to have this supply in the immediate neighborhood was an extraordinary advantage.

I agreed that the arrangement was a very good one; and I think he was about to ask some questions in regard to my nun, but I began my recital, and cut off any further conversation on the subject.

My monologue was rather disjointed that evening, for my mind was occupied with other things, or, more strictly speaking, another thing. I felt quite sure, however, that Walkirk did not notice my preoccupation, for he gave the same earnest and interested attention to my descriptions which he had always shown, and which made him such an agreeable and valuable listener. Indeed, his manner put me at my ease, because, on account of the wandering of my mind, his general expression indicated that, if I found it necessary to pause in order that I might arrange what I should say next, he was very glad of the opportunity thus given him to reflect upon what I had just said. He was an admirable listener.

XV

HOW WE WENT BACK TO GENOA

The next morning I awaited with considerable perturbation of mind the arrival of my nun. I felt assured that, after the occurrences of the previous day, there must certainly be some sort of a change in her. She could not go on exactly as she had gone on before. The nature of this anticipated change concerned me very much,—too much, I assured myself. Would she be more rigid and repellent than she had been before the advent of the wasp? But this would be impossible. On the other hand, would she be more like other people? Would she relax a little, and work like common secretaries? Or,—and I whistled as I thought of it,—having once done so, would she permanently cut loose from the absurdities enjoined upon her by the House of Martha people, and look at me and talk to me in the free, honest, ingenuous, frank, sincere, and thoroughly sensible manner in which she had spoken to me the day before?

After revolving these questions in my mind for some time, another one rudely thrust itself upon me: would she come at all? It was already seven minutes past nine; she had never been so late. Now that I came to think of it, this would be the most natural result of the wasp business. The thought shocked me. I ceased to walk up and down my study, and stopped whistling. I think my face must have flushed; I know my pulse beat faster. My eyes fell upon the body of him who I believed had been my friend. I felt like crushing his remains with my fist. He had been my enemy! He had shown me what I had to lose, and he had made me lose it.

Even in the midst of my agitation this thought made me smile. How much I was making of this affair of my secretary. What difference, after all—But I did not continue the latter question. It did make a difference, and it was of no use to reason about it. What was I to do about it? That was more to the point.

At this instant, my nun, followed by Sister Sarah, entered the adjoining room. The latter merely bowed to me, went out, and locked the door behind her. I was very glad she did not speak to me, for the sudden revulsion of feeling produced by the appearance of the two would have prevented my answering her coherently. I do not know whether my nun bowed or not. If she did, the motion was very slight. She took her seat and prepared for work. I did not say anything, for I did not know what to say. The proper thing to do, in order to relieve my embarrassment and hers,—that is, if she had any,—was to begin work at once; but for the life of me I could not remember whether my dictation of the day before concerned Sicily or Egypt. I did not like to ask her, for that would seem like a trick to make her speak.

But it would not do to keep her sitting there with an idle pen in her hand. I must say something, so I blurted out some remarks concerning the effect of the climate of the Mediterranean upon travelers from northern countries; and while doing this I tried my best to remember where, on the shores of this confounded sea, I had been the day before.

Philosophizing and generalizing were, however, not in my line: I was accustomed to deal with action and definite observation, and I soon dropped the climate of the Mediterranean, and went to work on some of the soul-harrowing improvements in the Eternal City, alluding with particular warmth to the banishment of the models from the Spanish Stairs. Now the work went on easily, but I was gloomy and depressed. My nun sat at the table, more like a stiff gray-enveloped principle than ever before. I did not feel at liberty even to make a remark about the temperature of the room. I feared that whatever I said might be construed into an attempt to presume upon the accidental intercourse of the day before.

For half an hour or more she went on with the work, but, during a pause in my dictation, she sat up straight in her chair and laid down her pen. Then, without turning her face to me, she began to speak. I stood open-mouthed, and, I need not say, delighted. Whatever her words might be, it rejoiced me to hear them; to know that she voluntarily recognized my existence, and desired to communicate with me.

"I have spoken to Mother Anastasia," she said, her voice directed towards the screen in the open window, "and I told her that it was impossible for me to work without sometimes saying a few words to ask for what I need, or to request you to repeat a word which I did not catch. Since I began to write I have lost no less than twenty-three words. I have left blanks for them, and made memoranda of the pages; but, as I said to her, if this sort of thing went on, you would forget what words you had intended to use, and when you came to read the manuscript you could not supply them, and that therefore I was not doing my work properly, and honestly earning the money which would be paid to the institution. I also told her that you sometimes forgot where you left off the day before, and that I ought to read you a few lines of what I had last written, in order that you might make the proper connection. I think this is very necessary, for to-day you have left an awful gap. Yesterday we were writing about that old Crusader's bank in Genoa, and now you are at work at Rome, when we haven't even started for that city."

Each use of this word "we" was to me like a strain of music from the heavens.

"Do you think I did right?" she added.

"Right!" I exclaimed. "Most assuredly you did. Nothing could be more helpful, and in fact more necessary, than to let me know just where I left off. What did the sisters say?"

"I spoke only to Mother Anastasia," she replied. "She considered the matter a little while, and then said that she could see there must be times when you would require some information from me in regard to the work, and that there could be no reasonable objection to my giving such information; but she reminded me that the laws of the House of Martha require that the sisters must give their sole attention to the labor upon which they are employed, and must not indulge, when so engaged, in any conversation, even among themselves, that is not absolutely necessary."

"Mother Anastasia is very sensible," said I, "and if I were to see her, I should be happy to express my appreciation of her good advice upon the subject. And, by the way, did she tell you that it was necessary to wear that hot bonnet while you are working?"

"She did not say anything about it," she answered; "it was not needful. We always wear our bonnets outside of the House of Martha."

I was about to make a further remark upon the subject, but restrained myself: it was incumbent on me to be very prudent. There was a pause, and then she spoke again.

"You are not likely to see Mother Anastasia," she said, "but please do not say anything on the subject to Sister Sarah; she is very rigorous, and would not approve of talking under any circumstances. In fact, she does not approve of my coming here at all."

"What earthly reason can she have for that?" I asked.

"She thinks it's nonsensical for you to have a secretary," she answered, "and that it would be much better for you to do your own work, and make a gift of the money to the institution, and then I could go and learn to be a nurse. I only mention these things to show you that it would be well not to talk to her of Mother Anastasia's good sense."

"You may rest assured," said I, "that I shall not say a word to her."

"And now," said she, "shall we put aside what I have written to-day, and go back to Genoa? The last thing you dictated yesterday was this: 'Into this very building once came the old Crusaders to borrow money for their journeys to the Holy Land.'"

We went to Genoa.

"How admirably," I exclaimed, when she had gone, "with what wonderful tact and skill she has managed the whole affair! Not one word about the occurrences of yesterday, not an allusion which could embarrass either herself or me. If only she had looked at me! But she had probably received instructions on that point which she did not mention, and it is easy to perceive that she is honest and conscientious."

But after all it was not necessary that I should see her face. I had seen it, and I could never forget it.

Whistling was not enough for me that day; I sang.

"What puts you into such remarkably good spirits?" asked my grandmother. "Have you reached an unusually interesting part of your work?"

"Indeed I have," I answered, and I gave her such a glowing account of the way the Red Cross Knights, the White Cross Knights, and the Black Cross Knights clanked through the streets of Genoa, before setting sail to battle for the Great Cross, that the cheeks of the old lady flushed and her eyes sparkled with enthusiastic emotion.

"I don't wonder it kindles your soul to write about such things," she said.

XVI

I RUN UPON A SANDBAR

Day by day, the interest of my nun in her work appeared to increase. Every morning, so soon as she sat down at her table, she read to me the concluding portion of what had been written the day before; and if a Sunday intervened, she gave me a page or more. Her interest was manifested in various ways. Several times she so far forgot the instructions she must have received as to turn her face towards me, when asking me to repeat something that she did not catch, and on such occasions I could not for some moments remember what I had said, or indeed what I was about to say.

Once she stopped writing, and, turning half round in her chair, looked fairly at me, and said that she thought I had made a mistake in saying that visitors were not allowed to go up the Tower of Pisa without a guide; for she, with two other ladies, had gone to the top without any one accompanying them. But she thought it was very wrong to allow people to do this, and that I should be doing a service to travelers if I were to say something on the subject.

Of course I replied that I would make the correction, and that I would say something about the carelessness to which she referred. Then there ensued a pause, during which she turned her face towards the window, imagining, I have no doubt, that I was busy endeavoring to compose something suitable to say upon the subject; but I was not thinking of anything of the sort. I was allowing my mind to revel in the delight which I had had in looking at her while she spoke. When her pen began to scratch impatiently upon the paper, I plunged into some sort of a homily on the laxity of vigilance in leaning towers. But, even while dictating this, I was wondering what she would look like if, instead of that gray shawl and gown, she were arrayed in one of the charming costumes which often make even ordinary young ladies so attractive.

As our daily work went on, my nun relaxed more frequently her proscribed rigidity, and became more and more like an ordinary person. When she looked at me or spoke, she always did so in such an unpremeditated manner, and with such an obvious good reason, that I could not determine whether her change of manner was due to accumulative forgetfulness, or to a conviction that it was absurd to continue to act a part which was not only unnatural under the circumstances, but which positively interfered with the work in hand. Some of her suggestions were of the greatest service, but I fear that the value of what she said was not as fully appreciated as was the pleasure of seeing and hearing her say it.

Thus joyously passed the hours of work, and in the hours when I was not working I looked forward with glad anticipation to the next forenoon; but after a time I began to be somewhat oppressed by the fear that my work would come to an end before long for want of material. I was already nearing the southern limit of my travels, and my return northward had not been productive of the sort of subject-matter I desired. In my recitals to Walkirk I had gone much more into detail regarding my experiences, and had talked about a great many things which it had been pleasant to talk about, but which I did not consider good

Frank R. Stockton

enough to put into my book. In dictating to my nun I had carefully sifted the mass to which Walkirk had listened, and had used only such matter as I thought would interest her and the general reader. My high regard for the intelligence of my secretary and her powers of appreciation had led me to discard too much, and therefore there was danger that my supply of subject-matter would give out before my nun grew to be an elderly woman; and this I did not desire.

I had read and heard enough of the travels of others to be able to continue my descriptions of foreign countries for an indefinite period; but I had determined, from the first, that nothing should go into my book except my own actual experiences, and therefore I could not rely upon other books for the benefit of mine. But, in considering the matter, I concluded that, if my material should be entirely my own, it would answer my purpose to make that material what I pleased; and thus it happened that I determined to weave a story into my narrative. This plan, I assured myself, would be in perfect harmony with the design of my work. The characters could be drawn from the people whom I had met in my travels. The scenes could be those which I had visited, and the plot and tone of the story could be made to aid the reader in understanding the nature of the country and the people of which it was told. More than all, I could make the story as long as I pleased.

This was a capital idea, and I began immediately to work upon it. I managed the story very deftly; at least that was my opinion. My two principal characters made their appearance in Sicily, and at first were so intermingled with scenery and incidents as not to be very prominent; then they came more to the front, and other characters introduced themselves upon occasion. As these personages appeared and reappeared, I hoped that they would gradually surround themselves with an interest which would steadily increase the desire to know more and more about them. Thus, as I went on, I said less and less about Sicily, and more and more about my characters, especially the young man and the young woman, the curious blending of whose lives I was endeavoring to depict.

This went on very smoothly for a few days, and then, about eleven o'clock one morning, my nun suddenly leaned back in her chair and laid down her pen.

"I cannot write any more of this," she said, looking out of the window.

I was so astonished that I could scarcely ask her what she meant.

"This is love-making," she continued, "and with love-making the sisters of the House of Martha can have nothing to do. It is one of our principal rules that we must not think about it, read about it, or talk about it; and of course it would have been forbidden to write about it, if such a contingency had ever been thought of. Therefore I cannot do any more work of that kind."

In vain I expostulated; in vain I told her that this was the most important part of my book; in vain I declaimed about the absurdity of such a regulation; in vain I protested; in vain I reasoned. She shook her head, and said there was no use talking about it; she knew the rules, and should obey them.

I had been standing near the grating, but now I threw myself into a chair, and sat silent, wondering what I should do. Must I give up this most admirable plan of carrying on my work, simply because those foolish sisters had made absurd rules for themselves? Must I wind up my book for want of material? Not for a moment did I think of getting another secretary, or of selecting some other sort of that stuff which literary people call padding, for the purpose of prolonging my pleasant labors. I was becoming interested in the love-story I had begun, and I wanted to go on with it, and I believed also that it would be of great advantage to my book; but, on the other hand, it was plain that my nun would not write this story, and it was quite as plain to me that I could not insist upon anything which would cause her to leave me.

"Don't you think," she said presently, still looking towards the window, "that we had better do some sort of work for the rest of the morning? It is not right for me to sit here idle. Suppose you try to supply some of the words which were left out of the manuscript, in the first days of my writing for you."

"Very well," said I; and, taking up her memoranda, she began to look for the vacant spaces which she had left in the manuscript pages. I supplied very few words, for to save my life I could not at this moment bring my mind to bear upon such trifles; but it was pretense of work, and better than embarrassing idleness. Before my secretary left me I must think of something to say to her in regard to the work for to-morrow; but what should I say? Should I tell her I would drop the story, or that I would modify it so as to make it feasible for her to write? Something must quickly be decided upon, and while I was tumultuously revolving the matter in my mind twelve o'clock and the sub-mother came. My secretary went away, with nothing but the little bow which she was accustomed to make when leaving the room.

XVII

REGARDING THE ELUCIDATION OF NATIONAL CHARACTERISTICS

I was left in my study in a very unpleasant state of mind. I was agitated and apprehensive. Perhaps that young woman would not come any more. I had not told her that I was going to stop writing about love, and there was every reason to suppose she would not return. What an imbecile I had been! I had done nothing, because I could not think of exactly the right thing to do.

I now felt that I must ask the advice of somebody in regard to this embarrassing and important affair. For a moment I thought of my grandmother, but she would be sure to begin by advising me to change my secretary. She seldom urged me to do what I did not want to do, but if I offered her a chance to give me advice on this occasion I knew what would be uppermost in her mind.

So I put on my hat and went to Walkirk, at the inn. I found him at work on a mass of accounts, dating back for years, which I had given him to adjust. With great circumspection I laid before him this new affair.

"You see," said I, "she is a first-class secretary. She has learned to do my work as I like it done, and I do not wish to make a change, and, on the other hand, I do not care to alter the plan of my book."

Walkirk was always very respectful, but he could not restrain a smile at the situation.

"It does seem to me," he said, "a very funny thing to dictate a love-story to one of the sisters of the House of Martha. Of course they are not nuns, they are not even Roman Catholics, but they are just as strict and strait-laced about certain things as if their house were really a convent. So far as I can see, there is but one thing to do, and that is to confine yourself to descriptions of travel; and perhaps it would be well to let your secretary know in some way that you intend to do so; otherwise I think she may throw up the business, and that would be a pity."

It sometimes surprises me to discover what an obstinate person I am. When I want to do a thing, it is very difficult for me to change my mind.

"She must not throw up the business," I said, "and I do not see how I can leave out the story. I have planned it far ahead, and to discard it I should have to go back and cut and mangle a great deal of good work that I have done."

Walkirk reflected.

"I admit," he replied, "that that would be very discouraging. Perhaps we can think of some plan of getting out of the difficulty."

"I hope you can do that," said I, "for I cannot."

"How would this do?" he asked presently. "Suppose I go and see Mother Anastasia this afternoon, and try and make her look at this matter from a strictly business point of view.

I can tell her that the sort of thing you are doing is purely literature, that you can't keep such things out of literature, and that the people who engage in the mechanical work of literature cannot help running against those things at one time or another. I can try to make her understand what an advantageous connection this is, and what a great injury to the House of Martha it would be if it should be broken off. I can tell her that it is not improbable that you may take to writing as a regular business, and that you may give profitable employment to the sisters for years and years. There are a good many other things I might say, and you may be sure I shall do my very best."

"Go," I said, "but be very careful about what you say. Don't make her think that I am too anxious to retain this particular sister, but make her understand that I do not wish to begin all over again with another one. Also, do not insist too strongly on my desire to write a love-story, but put it to her that when I plan out work of course I want to do the work as I have planned it. Try to keep these important points in your mind; then you can urge common sense upon her as much as you please."

I sent a note to my grandmother saying that I should not be home to luncheon, and after having taken a bite at the inn I set out for a long walk. It was simply impossible for me to talk about common things until this matter was settled.

It was about the middle of the afternoon when I returned to the inn, and Walkirk had not come back. I went away again, took a turn through the woods, and on approaching the inn I saw him walking down the shady road which led from the House of Martha. I hurried to meet him.

So soon as he was near enough, Walkirk, with a beaming face, called out:—

"All right, sir. I have settled that little matter for you."

"How? What?" I exclaimed. "What have you done?"

We had now reached each other, and stood together by the side of the road.

"Well," said my under-study, "I have seen Mother Anastasia, and I have found her a very sensible woman,—an admirable woman, I assure you. She was a good deal surprised when I told her my errand, for that was the first she had heard of the love-story; in fact, I suppose your secretary had not had time to tell her about it. She commended the sister highly for her refusal to write it, saying that her action was in strict accordance with the spirit of their rules. When she had finished saying all she had to say on that point, I presented your side of the question; and I assure you, sir, that I clapped on it a very bright light, so that if she did not see its strong points the fault must be in her own eyes. As the event proved, there was nothing the matter with her eyes. I shall not try to repeat what I said, but I began by explaining to her the nature of your work, and showed her how impossible it was for you to write about foreign countries without referring to their people, and how you could not speak of the people without mentioning their peculiar manners and customs, and that this story was nothing more nor less than an interweaving of some of the characteristics of the people of Sicily with the descriptions of the country. Thus much I inferred from your remarks about the story.

"I persisted that, although such characteristics had no connection with the life of the sisters of the House of Martha, they were a part of the world which you were describing, and that it could be no more harm for a sister, working for wages and the good of the cause, to assist in that description than it would be for one of them to make lace to be worn at a wedding, a ceremony with which the sisters could have nothing to do, and which in connection with themselves they could not even think about. This point made an impression on Mother Anastasia, and, having thought about it a minute or two, she said there was a certain force in it.

"Then she asked me if this narrative of yours was a strongly accentuated love-story. Here she had me at a disadvantage, for I have not heard it; but I assured her that, knowing the scope and purpose of your work, I did not believe that you would accentuate any portion of it more than was absolutely necessary.

"After some silent consideration, Mother Anastasia said she would go and speak with the sister who had been doing your work. She was gone a good while,—at least it seemed so to me; and when she came back she said that she had been making inquiries of the sister, and had come to the conclusion that there was no good reason why the House of Martha should not continue to assist you in the preparation of your book."

"Did she say she would send the same sister?" I asked quickly.

"No, she did not," answered Walkirk; "but not wishing to put the question too pointedly, I first thanked her, on your behalf, for the kindly consideration she had given the matter. I then remarked—without intimating that you said anything about it—that I hoped nothing would occur to retard the progress of the work, and that the present arrangement might continue without changes of any kind, because I knew that when you were dictating your mind was completely absorbed by your mental labors, and that any alteration in your hours of work, or the necessity of explaining your methods to a new amanuensis, annoyed and impeded you. To this she replied it was quite natural you should not desire changes, and that everything should go on as before."

"Walkirk," I exclaimed, "you are a trump!" In my exuberant satisfaction I would have clapped him on the back; but it would not do to be so familiar with an under-study, and besides I did not wish him to understand the extent of my delight at the result of his mission. That sort of thing I liked to keep to myself.

XVIII

AN ILLEGIBLE WORD

Every morning there seemed to be some reason or other why I should anticipate with an animated interest the coming of my secretary, and on the morning after what I might call her "strike" the animation of said interest was very apparent to me, but I hope not to any one else. Over and over I said to myself that I must not let my nun see that I was greatly pleased with Walkirk's intervention. It would be wise to take the result as a matter of course.

As the clock struck nine, she and Sister Sarah entered the anteroom, and the latter advanced to the grating and looked into my study, peering from side to side. I did not like this sister's face; she looked as if she had grown unpleasantly plump on watered milk.

"Is it necessary," she asked, "that you should smoke tobacco during your working hours?"

"I never do it," I replied indignantly,—"never!"

"Several times," she said, "I have thought I perceived the smell of tobacco smoke in this sister's garments."

"You are utterly mistaken!" I exclaimed. "During the hours

of work these rooms are perfectly free from anything of the sort."

She gave a little grunt and departed, and when she had locked the door I could not restrain a slight ejaculation of annoyance.

"You must not mind Sister Sarah," said the sweet voice of my nun behind the barricade of her bonnet; "she is as mad as hops this morning."

"What is the matter with her?" I asked, my angry feelings disappearing in an instant.

"She and Mother Anastasia have had a long discussion about the message you sent in regard to my keeping on with the story. Sister Sarah is very much opposed to my doing your writing at all."

"Well, as she is not the head of your House, I suppose we need not trouble ourselves about that," I replied. "But how does the arrangement suit you? Are you satisfied to continue to write my little story?"

"Satisfied!" she said. "I am perfectly delighted;" and as she spoke she turned toward me, her eyes sparkling, and her face lighted by the most entrancing smile I ever beheld on the countenance of woman. "This is a thousand times more interesting than anything you have done yet, although I liked the rest very much. Of course I stopped when I supposed it was against our rules to continue; but now that I know it is all right I am—But no matter; let us go on with it. This is what I last wrote," and she read: "'Tomaso and the pretty Lucilla now seated themselves on the rock, by a little spring. He was trying to look into her lovely blue eyes, which were slightly turned away from him and veiled by their long lashes. There was something he must say to her, and he felt he could wait no longer. Gently he took the little hand which lay nearest him, and'—There is where I stopped," she said; and then, her face still bright, but with the smile succeeded by an air of earnest consideration, she asked, "Do you object to suggestions?"

"Not at all," said I; "when they are to the point, they help me."

"Well, then," she said, "I wouldn't have her eyes blue. Italian girls nearly always have black or brown eyes. It is hard to think of this girl as a blonde."

"Oh, but her eyes are blue," I said; "it would not do at all to have them anything else. Some Italian girls are that way. At any rate, I couldn't alter her in my mind."

"Perhaps not," she replied, "but in thinking about her she always seems to me to have black eyes; however, that is a matter of no importance, and I am ready to go on."

Thus, on matters strictly connected with business, my nun and I conversed, and then we went on with our work. I think that from the very beginnings of literature there could have been no author who derived from his labors more absolute pleasure than I derived from mine: never was a story more interesting to tell than the story of Tomaso and Lucilla. It proved to be a very long one, much longer than I had supposed I could make it, and sometimes I felt that it was due to the general character of my book that I should occasionally insert some description of scenery or instances of travel.

My secretary wrote as fast as I could dictate, and sometimes wished, I think, that I would dictate faster. She seldom made comments unless she thought it absolutely necessary to do so, but there were certain twitches and movements of her head and shoulders which might indicate emotions, such as pleasant excitement at the sudden development of the situation, or impatience at my delay in the delivery of interesting passages; and I imagined that during the interpolation of descriptive matter she appeared to be anxious to get through with it as quickly as possible, and to go on with the story.

It was my wish to make my book a very large one; it was therefore desirable to be economical with the material I had left, and to eke it out as much as I could with fiction; but upon considering the matter I became convinced that it could not be very long before the material which in any way could be connected with the story must give out, and that therefore it would have to come to an end. How I wished I had spent more time in Sicily! I would have liked to write a whole book about Sicily.

Of course I might take the lovers to other countries; but I had not planned anything of this kind, and it would require some time to work it out. Now, however, a good idea occurred to me, which would postpone the conclusion of the interesting portion of my work. I would have my secretary read what she had written. This would give me time to think out more of the story, and it is often important that an author should know what he has done before he goes on to do more. We had arrived at a point where the narrative could easily stop for a while; Tomaso having gone on a fishing voyage, and the middle-aged innkeeper, whose union with Lucilla was favored by her mother and the village priest, having departed for Naples to assume the guardianship of two very handsome young women, the daughters of an old friend, recently deceased.

When I communicated to my nun my desire to change her work from writing to reading, she seemed surprised, and asked if there were not danger that I might forget how I intended to end the story. I reassured her on this point, and she appeared to resign herself to the situation.

"Shall I begin with the first page of the manuscript," said she, "or read only what I have written?"

"Oh, begin at the very beginning," I said. "I want to hear it all."

Then she began, hesitating a little at times over the variable chirography of my first amanuensis. I drew up my chair near to the grating, but before she had read two pages I asked her to stop for a moment.

"I think," said I, "it will be impossible for me to get a clear idea of what you are reading unless you turn and speak in my direction. You see, the sides of your bonnet interfere very much with my hearing what you say."

For a few moments she remained in her ordinary position, and then she slowly turned her chair toward me. I am sure she had received instructions against looking into my study, which was filled with objects calculated to attract the attention of an intelligent and cultivated person. Then she read the manuscript, and as she did so I said to myself, over and over again, that for her to read to me was a thousand times more agreeable than for me to dictate to her.

As she read, her eyes were cast down on the pages which she held in her hand; but frequently when I made a correction they were raised to mine, as she endeavored to understand exactly what I wanted her to do. I made a good many alterations which I think improved the work very much.

Once she found it utterly impossible to decipher a certain word of the manuscript. She scrutinized it earnestly, and then, her mind entirely occupied by her desire properly to

Frank R. Stockton

read the matter, she rose, and came close to the grating, holding the page so that I could see it.

"Can you make out this word?" she asked. "I cannot imagine how any one could write so carelessly."

I sprang to my feet and stood close to the grating. I could not take the paper from her, and it was necessary for her to hold it. I examined the word letter by letter. I gave my opinion of each letter, and I asked her opinion. It was a most illegible word. A good many things interfered with my comprehension of it. Among these were the two hands with which she held up the page, and another was the idea which came to me that in the House of Martha the sisters were fed on violets. I am generally quite apt at deciphering bad writing, but never before had I shown myself so slow and obtuse at this sort of thing.

Suddenly a thought struck me. I glanced at the clock in my study. It wanted ten minutes of twelve.

"It must be," said I, "that that word is intended to be 'heaven-given,'—at any rate, we will make it that; and now I think I will get you to copy the last part of that page. You can do it on the back of the sheet."

She was engaged in this writing when Sister Sarah came in.

XIX

GRAY ICE

During the engagement of my present secretary, a question had frequently arisen in my mind, which I wished to have answered, but which I had hesitated to ask, for fear the sister should imagine it indicated too much personal interest in her. This question related to her name, and now it was really necessary for me to know it. I did not wish any longer to speak to her as if she were merely a principle; she had become a most decided entity. However harsh and gray and woolly her name might be, I wanted to know it and to hear it from her own lips. The next morning I asked her what it was.

She was sitting at the table arranging the pages she was going to read, and at the question she turned toward me. Her face was flushed, but not, I think, with displeasure.

"Do you know," she said, "it has seemed to me the funniest thing in the world that you have never cared the least bit to know my name."

"I did care," I replied, "in fact it was awkward not to know it; but of course I did not want to—interfere in any way with the rules of your establishment."

"Ah," she said, "I have noticed your extreme solicitude in regard to our rules, but there is no rule against telling our names. Mine is Sister Hagar."

"Hagar!" I exclaimed. "You do not mean that is your real name?"

"It is the name given me by the House of Martha," she answered. "There is a list of names by which the sisters must be called, and as we enter the institution we take the names in their order on the list. Hagar came to me."

"I shall not call you by that," said I, "and we may as well go on with our work."

I was anxious to have her read, and to forget that she was called Hagar.

She was a long time arranging the manuscript and putting the pages in order. I did not hurry her, but I could not see any reason for so much preparation. Presently she said, still arranging the sheets, and with her head bent slightly over her work: "I don't know whether or not I ought to tell you, but I dislike to be called Hagar. The next name on the list is Rebecca, and I am willing to take that, but the rules of the House do not allow us to skip an unappropriated name, and permit no choosing. However, Mother Anastasia has not pressed the matter, and, although I am entered as Sister Hagar, the sisters do not call me by that name."

"What do they call you?"

"Oh, they simply use the name that was mine before I entered the House of Martha," said she.

"And what is that?" I asked quickly.

"Ah," said my nun, pushing her sheets into a compact pile, and thumping their edges on the table to make them even, "to talk about that would be decidedly against the rules of the institution;—and now I am ready to read."

Thus did she punish me for what she considered my want of curiosity or interest; I knew it as well as if she had told me so. I accepted the rebuff and said no more, and she went on with her reading.

On this and the following day I became aware how infinitely more pleasant it was to listen than to be listened to,—at least under certain circumstances. I considered it wonderfully fortunate to be able to talk to such an admirable listener as Walkirk: but to sit and hear my nun read; to watch the charming play of her mouth, and the occasional flush of a smile when she came to something exciting or humorous; to look into the blue of her eyes, as she raised them to me while I considered an alteration, was to me an overwhelming rapture,—I could call it nothing less. But by the end of the third morning of reading my good sense told me that this sort of thing could not go on, and it would be judicious for me to begin again my dictation, and to let my secretary confine herself to her writing. The fact that on any morning I had not allowed her to read until the hour of noon was an additional proof that my decision was a wise one.

The story of Tomaso and Lucilla now went bravely on, with enough groundwork of foreign land for the characters to stand on, and I tried very hard to keep my mind on the writing of my book and away from its writer. Outwardly I may have appeared to succeed fairly well in this purpose, but inwardly the case was different. However, if I could suppress any manifestations of my emotions, I told myself, I ought to be satisfied.

Frank R. Stockton

A few mornings after the recommencement of the dictation I was a little late in entering my study, and I found my secretary already at the table in the anteroom. In answer to my morning salutation she merely bowed, and sat ready for work. She did not even offer to read what she had last written. This surprised me. Was she resenting what she might look upon as undue stiffness and reserve? If so, I was very sorry, but at the same time I would meet her on her own ground. If she chose to return to her old rigidity, I would accept the situation, and be as formal as she liked.

More than this, I began to feel a little resentment. I would revert not only to my former manner, but to my former matter. I would wind up that love-story, and confine myself to the subject of foreign travel.

Acting on this resolution, I made short work of Tomaso and Lucilla. The former determined not to think of marriage until he was several years older, and had acquired the necessary means to support a wife; and Lucilla accepted the advice of her mother and the priest, and obtained a situation in a lace-making establishment in Venice, where she resolved to work industriously until the middle-aged innkeeper had made up his mind whether or not he would marry one of the handsome girls to whom he had become guardian.

To this very prosaic conclusion of the love-story I added some remarks intended as an apology for introducing such a story into my sketches of travel, and showing how the little narrative brought into view some of the characteristics of the people of Sicily. After that I discoursed of the present commerce of Italy as compared with that of the Middle Ages.

My secretary took no notice whatever of my change of subject, but went on writing as I dictated. This apathy at last became so annoying to me that, excusing myself, I left my study before the hour of noon.

It is impossible for me to say how the events, or rather the want of events, of that morning disturbed my mind. By turns I was angry, I was grieved, I was regretful, I was resentful. It is so easy sometimes for one person, with the utmost placidity, to throw another person into a state of mental agitation; and this I think is especially noticeable when the placid party is a woman.

As the day wore on, my disquiet of mind and body and general ill humor did not abate, and, wishing that other people should not notice my unusual state of mind, I took an early afternoon train to the city; leaving a note for Walkirk, informing him that his services as listener would not be needed that evening. The rest of that day I spent at my club, where, fortunately for my mood, I met only a few old fellows who could not get out of town in the summer, and who had learned, from long practice, to be quite sufficient unto themselves. Seated in a corner of the large reading-room, I spent the evening smoking, holding in my hand an unread newspaper, and asking myself mental questions.

I inquired why in the name of common sense I allowed myself to be so disturbed by the conduct of an amanuensis, paid by the day, and, moreover, a member of a religious order. I inquired why the fates should have so ordered it that this perfectly charming young woman should suddenly have become frozen into a mass of gray ice. I inquired if I had inadvertently done or said anything which would naturally wound the feelings or arouse the resentment of a sister of the House of Martha. I inquired if there could be any reasonable excuse for a girl who, on account of an omission or delay in asking her name, would assume a manner of austere rudeness to a gentleman who had always treated her with scrupulous courtesy. Finally I asked myself why it was that I persisted, and persisted, and persisted in thinking about a thing like this, when my judgment told me that I should instantly dismiss the whole affair from my mind, and employ my thoughts on something sensible; and to this I gave the only answer which I made to any of the inquiries I had put to myself. That was that I did not know why this was so, but it was so, and there was no help for it.

Walking home from the station quite late at night, the question which had so much troubled me suddenly resolved itself, and I became convinced that the change in the manner of my secretary was due to increased pressure of the rules of the House of Martha. I would not, I could not, believe that a fit of pique, occasioned by my apparent want of interest in her, could make her thus cold and even rude. She was not the kind of girl to do this thing of her own volition. It was those wretched rules; and if they were to be enforced in this way, the head of the House of Martha should know that I considered the act a positive discourtesy, if nothing more.

I was angry,—that was not to be wondered at; but it was a great relief to me to feel that I need not be angry with my secretary.

XX

TOMASO AND I

The next day my amanuensis bade me good-morning in her former pleasant manner, but without turning toward me seated herself quickly at the table, and took the manuscript from the drawer. "Oh, ho!" I thought, "then you can speak; and it was not the rules which made you behave in that way, but your own pique, which has worn off a little." I glanced at her as she intently looked over the work of the day before, and I was considering whether or not it would be fitting for me to show that there might be pique on one side of the grating as well as on the other, when suddenly my thoughts were interrupted by a burst of laughter,—girlish, irrepressible laughter. With the manuscript in her hands, my nun actually leaned back in her chair and laughed so heartily that I wonder my grandmother did not hear her.

"I declare," she said, turning to me, her eyes glistening with tears of merriment, "this is the funniest thing I ever saw. Why, you have actually separated those poor lovers for life, and crushed every hope in the properest way. And then all the rest about commerce! I wouldn't have believed you could do it."

"What do you mean?" I exclaimed. "You showed no surprise when you wrote it."

Frank R. Stockton

Again she laughed.

"Wrote it!" she cried. "I never wrote a line of it. It was Sister Sarah who was your secretary yesterday. Didn't you know that?"

I stood for a moment utterly unable to answer; then I gasped, "Sister Sarah wrote for me yesterday! What does it mean?"

"Positively," said she, pushing back her chair and rising to her feet, "this is not only the funniest, but the most wonderful thing in the world. Do you mean truly to say that you did not know it was Sister Sarah who wrote for you yesterday?"

"I did not suspect it for an instant," I answered.

"It was, it was!" she exclaimed, clasping her hands in her earnestness, and stepping closer to the grating. "When we came here yesterday, and found you were not in your room, a sudden idea struck her. 'I will stay here myself, this morning,' she said, 'and do his writing. I want to know what sort of a story this is that is being dictated to a sister of our House;' and so she simply turned me out and told me to go home. You don't know how frightened I was. I was afraid that, as we dress exactly alike, you might not at first notice that Sister Sarah was sitting at the table, and that you might begin with an awfully affectionate speech by Tomaso; for I knew that something of that kind was just on the point of breaking out, and I knew too that if you did it there would be lively times in the House of Martha, and perhaps here also. I fairly shivered the whole morning, and my only hope was that she would begin to snap at you as soon as you came in, and you would then know whom you had to deal with, and that you would have to put a lot of water into your love-making if you wanted any more help from the sisters. But if I had known that you would not find out that she was writing for you, I should certainly have died. I couldn't have stood it. But how in the world could you have kept on thinking that that woman was I? She is shorter and fatter, and not a bit like me, except in her clothes; and if you thought I was writing for you, why did you dictate that ridiculous stuff?"

I stood confounded. Here were answers to devise.

"Of course the dress deceived me," I said presently, "and not once did she turn her face toward me; besides, I did not imagine for a moment that any one but you could be sitting at that table."

"But I cannot understand why," she pursued, "if you didn't know it was Sister Sarah, you made that sudden change in your story."

For a moment I hesitated, and then I saw I might as well speak out honestly. When a man sees before him a pair of blue eyes like those which were then fixed upon me, the chances are that he will speak out honestly.

"The fact is," I said, "that I'm a little—well, sensitive; and when you, or the person I thought was you, did not speak to me, nor look at me, nor pay any more heed to me than if I had been a talking-machine worked with a crank, I was somewhat provoked, and determined that if you suddenly chose to freeze in that way I would freeze too, and that you should have no more of that story in which you were so interested; and so I smashed the loves of Tomaso and Lucilla and took up commerce, which I was sure you would hate."

At this there was a quick flash in her eyes, and the first tremblings of a smile at the corners of her mouth.

"Oh!" she said, and that was all she did say, as she returned to the table and took her seat.

"Is my explanation satisfactory?" I asked.

"Oh, certainly," she answered; "and if you will excuse me for saying so, I think you are a very fortunate man. In trying to punish me you protected yourself,—that is, if you care to have secretaries from our institution."

As I could not see her face, I could not determine what answer I should make to this remark, and she continued, as she turned over the sheets:—

"What are you going to do with the pages which were written yesterday?"

"Tear them up," I replied, "and throw them into the basket. I wish to annihilate them utterly."

She obeyed me, and tore Sister Sarah's work into very small pieces.

"Now we will go on with the original and genuine story," I said. "And as the occurrences of yesterday are entirely banished from my mind, and as all recollection of the point where we left off has gone, will you kindly read two or three pages of what you last wrote?"

Several times I had perceived, or thought I had perceived, symptoms of emotion in the back of my secretary's shawl, and these symptoms, if such they were, were visible now. She occupied some minutes in selecting a suitable point at which to begin, but when she had done this she read without any signs of emotion, either in her shawl or in her face.

The story of the Sicilian young people progressed slowly, not because of any lack of material, but because I was anxious to portray the phases as clearly and as effectively as I could possibly do it; and whenever I could prevent myself from thinking of something else, I applied my mind most earnestly to this object. I flatter myself that I did the work very well, and I am sure there were passages the natural fervor of which would have made Sister Sarah bounce at least a yard from her chair, had they been dictated to her, but my nun did not bounce in the least.

Before the hour at which we usually stopped work I arose from my chair, and stated that that would be all for the day. My secretary looked at me quickly.

"All for to-day?" she asked, a little smile of disapprobation upon her brow. "It cannot be twelve o'clock yet."

"No," I answered, "it is not; but it is not easy to work out the answer which Lucilla ought now to make to Tomaso, and I shall have to take time for its consideration."

"I shouldn't think it would be easy," said she, "but I hoped you had it already in your mind."

"Then you are interested in it?" I asked.

"Of course I am," she answered,—"who wouldn't be? And just at this point, too, when everything depends on what she says; but it is quite right for you to be very careful about what you make her say," and she gathered her sheets together to lay them away.

Now I wanted to say something to her. I stopped work for that purpose, but I did not know what to say. An apology for my conduct of the day before would not be exactly in order, and an explanation of it would be exceedingly

Frank R. Stockton

difficult. I walked up and down my study, and she continued to arrange her pages. When she had put them into a compact and very neat little pile, she opened the table drawer, placed them in it, examined some other contents of the drawer, and finally closed it, and sat looking out of the window. After some minutes of this silent observation, she half turned toward me, and without entirely removing her gaze from the apple-tree outside, she asked:—

"Do you still want to know my name?"

"Indeed I do!" I exclaimed, stepping quickly to the grating.

"Well, then," she said, "it is Sylvia."

At this moment we heard the footsteps of Sister Sarah in the hall, at least two minutes before the usual time.

When they had gone, I stood by my study table, my arms folded and my eyes fixed upon the floor.

"Horace Vanderley," I said to myself, "you are in love;" and to this frank and explicit statement I answered, quite as frankly, "That is certainly true; there can be no mistake about it."

XXI

LUCILLA AND I

A Saturday afternoon, evening, and night, the whole of a Sunday and its night, with some hours of a Monday morning, intervened between the moment at which I had acknowledged to myself my feelings toward my secretary and the moment at which I might expect to see her again, and nearly the whole of this time was occupied by me in endeavoring to determine what should be my next step. To stand still in my present position was absolutely impossible: I must go forward or backward. To go backward was a simple thing enough; it was like turning round and jumping down a precipice; it made me shudder. To go forward was like climbing a precipice with beetling crags and perpendicular walls of ice.

The first of these alternatives did not require any consideration whatever. To the second I gave all the earnest consideration of which I was capable, but I saw no way of getting up. The heights were inaccessible.

In very truth, my case was a hard one. I could not make love to a woman through a grating; and if I could, I would not be dishonorable enough to do it, when that woman was locked up in a room, and could not get away in case she did not wish to listen to my protestations. But between the girl I

Frank R. Stockton

loved and myself there was a grating compared with which the barrier in the doorway of my study was as a spider's web. This was the network of solemn bars which surrounded the sisters of the House of Martha,—the vows they had made never to think of love, to read of it or speak of it.

To drop metaphors, it would be impossible for me to continue to work with her and conceal my love for her; it would be stupidly useless, and moreover cowardly, to declare that love; and it would be sensible, praiseworthy, and in every way advantageous for me to cease my literary labors and go immediately to the Adirondacks or to Mount Desert. But would I go away on Saturday or Sunday when she was coming on Monday? Not I.

She came on Monday, surrounded by a gray halo, which had begun to grow as beautiful to my vision as the delicate tints of early dawn. When she began to read what she had last written, I seated myself in a chair by the grating. When she had finished, I sat silent for a minute, got up and walked about, came back, sat down, and was silent again. In my whole mind there did not seem to be one crevice into which an available thought concerning my travels could squeeze itself. She sat quietly looking out of the window at the apple-tree. Presently she said:—

"I suppose you find it hard to begin work on Monday morning, after having rested so long. It must be difficult to get yourself again into the proper frame of mind."

"On this Monday morning," I answered, "I find it very hard indeed."

She turned, and for the first time that day fixed her eyes upon me. She did not look well; she was pale.

"I had hoped," she said, with a little smile without any

brightness in it, "that you would finish the story of Tomaso and Lucilla; but I don't believe you feel like composing, so how would you like me to read this morning?"

"Nothing could suit me better," I answered; and in my heart I thought that here was an angelic gift, a relief and a joy.

"I will begin," she said, "at the point where I left off reading." She took up a portion of the manuscript, she brought her chair within a yard of the grating, she sat down with her face toward me, and she read. Sometimes she stopped and spoke of what she was reading, now to ask a question, and now to tell something she had seen in the place I described. I said but little. I did not wish to occupy any of that lovely morning with my words,—words which were bound to mean nothing. As she read and talked, some color came into her face; she looked more like herself. What a shame to shut up such a woman in a House where she never had anything interesting to talk about, never anybody interested to talk to!

After the reading of half a dozen pages during which she had not interrupted herself, she laid the manuscript in her lap, and asked me the time. I told her it wanted twenty minutes of twelve. She made no answer, but rose, put the manuscript in the drawer, and then returned with a little note which she had taken from her pocket.

"Mother Anastasia desired me to give you this," she said, folding it so that she could push it through one of the interstices of the grating; "she told me to hand it to you as I was coming away, but I don't think she would object to your reading it a little before that."

I took the note, unfolded it, and read it. Mother Anastasia wrote an excellent hand. She informed me that it had been decided that the sister of the House of Martha who had been acting as my amanuensis should not continue in that position, but should now devote herself to another class of work. If, however, I desired it, another sister would take her place.

I stood unable to speak. I must have been as pale as the white paint on the door-frame near which I stood.

"You see," said Sylvia, and from the expression upon her face I think she must have perceived that I did not like what I had read, "this is the work of Sister Sarah. I might as well tell you that at once, and I am sure there is no harm in my doing so. She has always objected to my writing for you; and although the morning she spent with you would have satisfied any reasonable person that there could be no possible objection to my doing it, she has not ceased to insist that I shall give it up, and go to the Measles Refuge. That, however, I will not do, but I cannot come here any more. Mother Anastasia and I are both sure that if I am not withdrawn from this work she will make no end of trouble. She has consented that I should go on until now simply because this day ends my month."

I was filled with amazement, grief, and rage.

"The horrible wretch!" I exclaimed. "What malignant wickedness!"

"Oh," said Sylvia, holding up one finger, "you mustn't talk like that about the sister. She may think she is right, but I don't see how she can; and perhaps she would have some reason on her side if she could see me standing here talking about her, instead of attending to my work. But I determined that I would not go away without saying a word. You have always been very courteous to us, and I don't see why we should not be courteous to you."

"Are you sorry to go?" I asked, getting as close to the grating as I could. "If they would let you, would you go on writing for me?"

"I should be glad to go on with the work," she said; "it is just what I like."

"Too bad, too bad!" I cried. "Cannot it be prevented? Cannot I see somebody? You do not know how much I— how exactly you"—

"Excuse me," said Sylvia, "for interrupting you, but what time is it?"

I glanced at the clock. "It wants four minutes of twelve," I gasped.

"Then I must bid you good-by," she said.

"Good-by?" I repeated. "How can you bid me good-by? Confound this grating! Isn't that door open?"

"No," she replied, "it's locked. Do you want to shake hands with me?"

"Of course I do!" I cried. "Good-by like this! It cannot be."

"I think," she said quickly, "that if you could get out of your window, you might come to mine and shake hands."

What a scintillating inspiration! What a girl! I had not thought of it! In a moment I had bounded out of my window, and was standing under hers, which was not four feet from the ground. There she was, with her beautiful white hand already extended. I seized it in both of mine.

"Oh, Sylvia," I said, "I cannot have you go in this way. I

Frank R. Stockton

want to tell you—I want to tell you how"—

"You are very good," she interrupted, endeavoring slightly to withdraw her hand, "and when the story of Tomaso and Lucilla is finished and printed I am going to read it, rules or no rules."

"It shall never be finished," I exclaimed vehemently, "if you do not write it," and, lifting her hand, I really believe I was about to kiss it, when with a quick movement she drew it from me.

"She is coming," she said; "good-by! good-by!" and with a wave of her hand she was gone from the window.

I did not return to my study. I stood by the side of the house, with my fists clenched and my eyes set. Then, suddenly, I ran to the garden wall; looking over it, I saw, far down the shaded village street, two gray figures walking away.

XXII

I CLOSE MY BOOK

By the rarest good fortune my grandmother started that afternoon for a visit to an old friend at the seashore, and, in the mild excitement of her departure, I do not think she noticed anything unusual in my demeanor.

"And so your amanuensis has left you?" she remarked, as she was eating a hasty luncheon. "Sister Sarah stopped for a moment and told me so. She said there was another one ready to take the place, if you wanted her."

I tried to suppress my feelings, but I must have spoken sharply.

"Want her!" I exclaimed. "I want none of her!"

My grandmother looked at me for a moment.

"I shall be sorry, Horace," she said, "if you find that the sisters do not work to suit you. I hoped that you might continue to employ them, because the House of Martha is at such a convenient distance, and offers you such a variety of assistance to choose from; and also because you would contribute to a most worthy cause. You know that all the money they may make is to go to hospitals and that sort of thing."

"I was a little afraid, however," she continued, after a pause, "that the sister you engaged might not suit you. She was so much younger than the others that I feared that, away from the restraints of the institution, she might be a little frivolous. Was she ever frivolous?"

"Not in the least," I answered; "not for an instant."

"I am very glad to hear that," she remarked,—"very glad indeed. I take an interest in that sister. Years ago I knew her family, but that was before she was born. I remember that I was intending to speak to you about her, but in some way I was interrupted."

"Well," I asked, "tell me now, who is she?"

"She *is*," said my grandmother, "Sister Hagar, of the House of Martha. She *was* Sylvia Raynor, of New Haven. I think that in some way her life has been darkened. Mother Anastasia takes a great interest in her, and favors her a good deal. I know there was opposition to her entering the House, but she was determined to do it. You say you are not going to engage another sister? Who is to be your amanuensis?"

"No one," I answered. "I shall stop writing for the present. This is a very good time. I've nearly reached the end of—a sort of division of the book."

"An excellent idea," said my grandmother, with animation. "You ought to go to the sea or the mountains. You have been working very hard. You are not looking well."

"I shall go, I shall go," I answered quickly; "fishing, probably, but I can't say where. I'll write to you as soon as

I decide."

"Now that is very pleasant," said my grandmother, as she rose from the table, "very pleasant indeed; and if you write that you will be away fishing for a week or two, I shall stay at the Bromleys' longer than I intended,—perhaps until you return."

"A week or two!" I muttered to myself.

Walkirk had sharper eyes than those of my grandmother. I am sure that when he came that evening he saw immediately that something was the matter with me,—something of moment. He was a man of too much tact to allude to my state of mind; but in a very short time I saved him all the trouble of circumspection, for I growled out that I could not talk about travels at present, and then told him that I could not write about them, either, for I had lost my secretary. His countenance exhibited much concern.

"But you can get another of the sisters," he said.

What I replied to this I do not remember, but I know I expressed myself so freely, so explicitly, and with such force that Walkirk understood very well that I wanted the secretary I had lost, that I wanted none other, and that I wanted her very much indeed. In fact, he comprehended the situation perfectly.

I was not sorry. I wanted somebody to whom I could talk about the matter, in whom I could confide. In ten minutes I was speaking to Walkirk in perfect confidence.

"But you can't do anything," said he, when there came a pause. "This is a case in which there is nothing to do. My advice is that you go away for a time, and try to get over it."

"I am going away," I replied.

"You could do nothing better," Walkirk remarked. "I am altogether in favor of that, although of course such counsel is against my own interests."

"Not at all," said I, catching his meaning, "for I shall take you with me."

After a considerable pause in the conversation Walkirk inquired if I had decided where I would go.

"No," I answered, "that is your affair. My desire is to get away from every place where there is any chance of seeing a woman. I wish to obliterate from my mind all idea of the female human being. In fact, I think I should like to take lodgings near a monastery, and have the monks come and write for me,—a different one every day."

Walkirk smiled. "Since you wish me to select your retreat," he said, "I am bound to have an opinion regarding it. I might advise a visit to the Trappists of Kentucky, or to some remote fishing and hunting region; but it strikes me that a background made up of exclusive association with men would be very apt to bring out in strong relief any particular female image which you might have in your mind. I should say that the best way of getting rid of such an image would be to merge it in a lot of other female images."

"Away with the idea!" I cried. "Walkirk, I will neither merge nor relieve. I will go with you to some place where we shall see neither men nor women; where we can hunt, fish, sail, sleep, read, smoke, and banish the world. I don't wish you to take a servant. We can do without service, and if necessary I can cook. I put the whole matter in your hands, Walkirk, and when you have decided on our destination let me know."

The next afternoon Walkirk found me at my club in the city, and informed me that he had selected a place which he thought would suit my purposes.

"No people?" I asked.

"None but ourselves," replied he.

"Very good," said I. "When can we start?"

"I shall be ready to-morrow afternoon," he answered, "and I will call for you at your house."

Frank R. Stockton

XXIII

RACKET ISLAND

We traveled all night, and early in the morning alighted at a small station, on the shore of a broad bay. Here we found moored a cat-rigged sailboat, of which Walkirk took possession, and we stowed therein the valises, guns, and fishing tackle which we had brought with us. I examined the craft with considerable interest. It was about twenty feet long, had a small cabin divided into two compartments, and appeared to be well stocked with provisions and other necessaries.

"Is it to be a long cruise?" I said to Walkirk; "and do you know how to sail a boat?"

"With this wind," he answered, "we should reach our destination in a couple of hours, and I consider myself a very fair skipper."

"Up sail, then," I cried, "and I am not in the least hurry to know where I am going."

Walkirk sailed a boat very well, but he did it in rather an odd way, as if he had learned it all out of a book, and never had handled a tiller before. I am not a bad amateur sailor myself, but I gave no consideration to the management of our craft. Walkirk had said that he knew where he was going, and was able to sail there, and I left the matter entirely to him; and whether or not this were his first essay in sailing, in due time we ran upon a low beach, and he exclaimed:—

"Here we are!"

I rose to my feet and looked about me. "Now, then," said I, "I shall ask you, where are we?"

"This is Racket Island," he replied, "and as soon as we get the boat pulled up and the sail down I will tell you about it."

"Racket Island," said Walkirk, a short time afterwards, as we stood together on a little sandy bluff, "was discovered two years ago by me and a friend, as we were sailing about in this bay. I suppose other people may have discovered it before, but as I have seen no proof of this I am not bound to believe it. We named it Racket Island, having found on the beach an old tennis racket, which had been washed there by the waves from no one knows where. The island is not more than half a mile long, with a very irregular coast. The other end of it, you see, is pretty well wooded. We stayed here for three days, sleeping in our boat; and so far as solitude is concerned, we might as well have been on a desert island in the midst of the Pacific. Now I propose that we do the same thing, and stay for three days, or three weeks, or as long as you please. This is the finest season of the year for camping out, and we can moor the boat securely, and cook and sleep on board of it. There is plenty of sand and there is plenty of shade, and I hope you will like it."

"I do!" I cried. "On Racket Island let us settle!"

For two days I experienced a sort of negative enjoyment. If I could not be at home dictating to my late secretary, or, better still, looking at her, as she sat close to the grating, reading to me, this was the next best thing I could do. I could walk over the island; I could sail around it; I could watch Walkirk fish; I could lie on the sand, and look at the sky; and I could picture Sylvia with her hair properly arranged, and attired in apparel suited to her. In my fancy I totally discarded the gray garb of the sisters of the House of Martha, and dressed my nun sometimes in a light summer robe, with a broad hat shading her face, and again in the richest costumes of silks and furs. Sometimes Walkirk interrupted these pleasant reveries, but that, of course, was to be expected.

In several directions we could see points of land, but it did not interest me to know what these were, or how far away they were. Walkirk and I had Racket Island to ourselves. My grandmother was happy with her friends, and where the rest of the world happened to stow themselves I did not care. Several times I said this to myself, but it was a mistake. I cared very much where Sylvia stowed herself. Philosophize as I might, I thought of her continually in that doleful House of Martha; and as I thought of her there I cried out against the shortcomings of civilization.

We had pitched a small tent in the shelter of a clump of trees on the higher part of the island; and near this, on the morning of our third day, I was sitting, smoking, and trying the effect of Sylvia's face under a wide black hat heavy with ostrich plumes, when Walkirk approached me, carrying a string of freshly caught fish.

"I am sorry to say," said he, "that in coming here to escape the society of women we have made a failure, for one of them is sitting on the beach, on the other side of the island."

I sprang to my feet with an abrupt exclamation.

"How did the woman get here?" I cried. "I thought this place was deserted."

"It is; I know every inch of it. No one lives here, but this female person came in a small sailboat. I saw it tied up, not far from where she is sitting."

"If women come here," I said, "I want to go, and you may as well get ready to leave."

"I think," remarked Walkirk, "that it would be well not to be in too great a hurry to leave. I know of no place where we are less likely to be disturbed, and so long as these dry nights continue there can be no pleasanter camping place. She may now be sailing away, and the chances are we shall never see her again."

"I'll go and look into the matter," said I.

I walked over the ridge of the little island, and soon caught sight of a female figure sitting on the sandy beach. Near by was the boat which Walkirk had mentioned. As soon as I saw her I stopped; but she must have heard my approach, for she turned toward me. I had come merely to make an observation of her, but now I must go on. As I approached her I turned as if I were about to walk along the shore, and as I passed her I raised my hat. She was a lady of middle age, of a reddish blonde complexion, and her hair was negligently put up under a plain straw hat. Her large blue eyes, her slightly uplifted brows, and the general expression of her rather thin face gave me the idea that she was a pleasantly disposed woman, who was either very tired or not in good health.

"Good-morning, sir," she said. "On desert islands, you know, people speak to each other without ceremony."

I stopped, and returned her salutation. "Excuse me," I remarked, "but this does not seem to be a desert island. May I be permitted to ask if it is a place of much resort?"

"Of course you may," she answered. "People sometimes come here; but would you like it better if they did not? You need not answer; I know you would."

This was a very free and easy lady, but if she liked that mood it suited me very well.

"Since you will have it," I replied, "I will admit I came here because I thought my companion and I would have the island to ourselves."

"And now you are disappointed," she said, with a smile.

She was surely a person of very pleasant humor.

"Good lady," said I, "you must not corner me. I came here because I thought it would be a good place in which to stop awhile and grumble undisturbed; and as you say it is proper to be unceremonious, may I ask how you happen to be here, and if you sail your boat yourself?"

"I am here," she answered, "because I like this island. I take an interest in it for two reasons: one is that it is a good island, and the other is that I own it."

"Really!" I exclaimed, in sudden embarrassment, "you must pardon me! I assure you I did not know that."

"Don't apologize," she said, raising her hand. "Scarcely any one knows, or at least remembers, that I own this island. I bought it a good many years ago, intending to build upon it; but it was considered too remote from the mainland, and I have established a summer home on the island which you can just see, over there to the west; so this island is perfectly free to respectable seekers after solitude or fish. I may add that I do not sail my boat, but came here this morning with my brother and another gentleman. They have now gone up the beach to look for shells."

"Madam," said I, "I feel that I am an intruder; but to assure you that I am a respectable one, allow me to introduce myself," and I presented my card.

"No, thank you," she replied, with a smile, as she gently waved back my card; "we don't do that sort of thing here; as far as possible we omit all ordinary social customs. We come here to rid ourselves, for a time, of manners and customs. My other island is called the 'Tangent,' because there we fly off from our accustomed routine of life. We dress as we please, and we live as we please. We drop all connection with society and its conventions. We even drop the names by which society knows us. I am known as the 'Lady Who Sits on the Sand,' commonly condensed to the 'Sand Lady.' My brother, who spends most of his time in his boat, is the 'Middle-Aged Man of the Sea,' and his scientific friend is the 'Shell Man.' When we have stayed on the Tangent as long as the weather and our pleasure induce us, we return to our ordinary routine of life. Now, if you have any title which is characteristic of you, I shall be glad to hear it, as well as that of your companion. We consider ourselves capable of forming unbiased opinions in regard to what is generally known as respectability."

It struck me as a very satisfactory thing to look upon this pleasant lady solely and simply as a human being. It is so seldom that we meet any one who can be looked upon in that light.

"Madam," I said, "I greatly like your plan for putting yourselves out of the world for a time, but I find it difficult

Frank R. Stockton

properly to designate myself."

"Oh, anything will do," she said; "for instance, your reason for desiring to seclude yourself."

"Very well, then," said I, "you may call me a 'Lover in Check.'"

"Excellent!" she exclaimed,—"just the sort of person for this place; and what is the other one?"

"Oh, he is an Understudy," I replied.

"Delightful," she said; "I never saw one. And here come my brother and the Shell Man."

I was now introduced formally by my new title to the Middle-Aged Man of the Sea, a hearty personage, with a curling beard, and to the Shell Man, who was tall, and wore spectacles.

When my presence was explained, the brother was as cordial as the lady had been, and proffered any assistance which I might need during my sojourn on the island. When they took their leave, the Sand Lady urged me to inhabit her island as long as I pleased, and hoped that I and the Understudy would sometimes sail over to them, and see what it was to be on a Tangent. At this I shook my head, and they all laughed at me; but it was easy to see that they were people of very friendly dispositions.

When I reported my interview to Walkirk, he remarked, "It is impossible to get away from people, but in all probability these folks will not come here again."

"Perhaps not," I answered, and dropped the subject.

XXIV

THE INTERPOLATION

"They did not seem in the least surprised to find us here," I said to Walkirk, as we were eating our dinner.

"Who?" he asked. "Oh, the people who came over this morning? Quite likely they saw us when we were sailing this way. We passed their island at no great distance. There is no reason why they should object. Your soft hat and flannel shirt would not prevent them from seeing that you were a gentleman."

I nodded, and sat silent for a time.

"Walkirk," said I, "suppose we sail over to those people this afternoon? It might be interesting."

"Very good," he answered, turning suddenly to watch a sea gull, which had made a great swoop toward us, as if attracted by the odors of our meal; "that will be an excellent thing to do."

In making our way, that afternoon, in the direction of the Tangent, our course was not mathematically correct, for the wind did not favor us, and it was impossible to sail in a right line; but the sun was still high when we reached the larger island, and made the boat fast to a little pier.

This island was much more attractive than the one on which we were camping. The ground receded from the beach in rolling slopes covered with short grass, and here and there were handsome spreading trees. On a bluff, a few hundred yards from the pier, stood a low, picturesque house, almost surrounded by a grove. The path to the house was plainly marked, and led us along the face of a little hill to a jutting point, where it seemed to make an abrupt turn upward. As we rounded this point, we saw on a rocky ledge not far ahead of us a lady dressed in white. She was standing on the ledge, looking out over the water, and apparently very much engaged with her own thoughts, for she had not yet perceived our approach.

At the first glance I saw that the figure before us was not the Sand Lady. This was a tall and graceful woman, carrying no weight of years. She held her hat in her hand, and her dark hair was slightly blown back from a face which, seen in profile against the clear blue sky, appeared to me to be perfect in its outline. We stopped involuntarily, and at that moment she turned toward us. Her face was one of noble beauty, with great dark eyes, and a complexion of that fine glow which comes to women who are not quite brunettes.

Walkirk started, and seized my arm. "Good heavens," he whispered, "it is Mother Anastasia!"

As we now advanced toward the lady, I could scarcely believe what I had heard; certainly I could not comprehend it. Here was one of the most beautiful women I had ever beheld, dressed in a robe of soft white flannel, which, though simple, was tasteful and elegant. She had a bunch of wild flowers in her belt, and at her neck a bow of dark yellow ribbon. I particularly noticed these points, in my amazement at hearing Walkirk say that this was the Mother

Superior of the House of Martha.

As we approached, she greeted us pleasantly, very much as if she had expected our coming, and then, addressing Walkirk, she said, with a smile:

"I see, sir, that you recognize me, and I suppose you are somewhat surprised to find me here, and thus," glancing at her dress.

"Surprised, madam!" exclaimed Walkirk. "I am astounded."

"Well," said she, "that sort of thing will happen occasionally. The people on this island have been expecting a visit from you gentlemen, but I really do not know where any of them are. It is not always easy to find them, but I will go and see if the Sand Lady is in the house, and if so I will tell her of your arrival. Of course," she continued, now turning to me, "you both will remember that in this place we put ourselves outside of a good many of the ordinary conventions, and are known by our characteristics instead of our names."

I assured her we understood this, and considered it an admirable idea.

"As you, sir," turning to Walkirk, "have met me before, I will immediately state that I am known on this island only as the 'Interpolation.'"

She turned to walk toward the house, but stopped. "We are all here to enjoy ourselves, and it is against the rules to worry each other with puzzles. I therefore will at once say, in explanation of my name, that I have briefly thrust myself into the life of my friends; and of my appearance, that the Middle-Aged Man of the Sea, who is a very self-willed person, caused the costume which I ordinarily wear, and in which I arrived, to be abstracted and hidden, so that I am obliged, while here, to wear clothes belonging to others. Now, you see, Mr. Understudy, everything is as plain as daylight."

"They have been talking about us," I remarked, as the lady rapidly walked away, "and of course, having recognized you, she must know who I am."

"Know you? There is no doubt of it," he answered. "She must have seen you often in the village, although you may never have noticed her."

"I certainly never have," said I; "in fact, I make it a point not to look under the bonnets of those gray-garbed women."

"When you meet them in the street?" he asked.

"Yes," I replied.

"She knows us both," said Walkirk, "and she has now gone to the house to tell the people who we are; and yet I am surprised that she met us so serenely. She could not possibly have known that the two men on that little island were her neighbors in the village of Arden."

I made no answer. I was strangely excited. I had flown to an uninhabited island to get away from Sylvia, and, if my conscience could be made to work properly, to get away from all thoughts of her; and here I had met, most unexpectedly and suddenly, with one who was probably the most intimate connection of the girl from whom I was flying. I was amazed; my emotion thrilled me from head to foot.

"It is just like women," remarked Walkirk, as we slowly

walked toward the house, "to put on disguises to conceal their identities, but they have no respect for our identities. Without doubt, at this moment Mother Anastasia is telling the lady of the house all about you and your grandmother, your position in society, and the manner in which you were furnished with a secretary from the House of Martha."

Still I did not reply. "Mother Anastasia!" I said to myself. "Here is a gray-garbed sister transformed into a lovely woman. Why should not another sister be so transformed? Why should not Sylvia be here, in soft white raiment, with flowers and a broad hat? If one can be thus, why not the other?" The possibility fevered me.

We found the mistress of the house—the same who was called the Sand Lady—upon a piazza. Her demeanor had been pleasant enough when we had seen her before, but now she greeted us as cordially as if we had been old friends. It was plain enough that Mother Anastasia had told her all about us. Her brother and the Shell Man were also there, and the first was friendly and the latter polite. The Mother Superior was on the piazza, but keeping a little in the background, as if she felt that she had had her turn.

"And now, Mr. Lover in Check and Mr. Understudy," said the Sand Lady, "I present you with the freedom of this island, as I have already presented you with the freedom of the other. If what we happen to be doing interests you, join us. If it does not, interest yourselves as you please. That is our custom here."

The mention of the name which I had applied to myself gave me a little shock. Under the circumstances I did not like it. It was possible that the Mother Superior of the House of Martha might know what it meant; and whether she knew it now, or ever should come to know it, I did not wish the knowledge to come to her in that way.

"There is still another one of our family," said the Sand Lady; "but she is very independent, and may not care for me to present you just now. I will go and ask her."

She stepped off the piazza, and went to a lady who was reading in a hammock, under a tree near by. In a minute or two this lady arose, and, with her book in her hand, came toward us. She was a woman of good figure, and with a certain air of loftiness. Her dress was extremely simple, and she may have been thirty years old. Approaching us, she said:—

"I wish to introduce myself. I am a 'Person.' In this place that is all I am. It is my name. It denotes my characteristics. Your titles have been mentioned to me. The ceremony is over," and, with a little nod, she returned to her hammock.

"Now," said the Man of the Sea, "who could prune away conventionalities better than that?" He then announced that in half an hour the tide would serve for fishing,—that he was going out in his boat, and would take any one who cared to accompany him; and this announcement having been made, he settled himself upon the piazza to talk to us. The conversation was interesting and lively. The people at this house were well worth knowing.

The Sand Lady and Walkirk went in the boat to fish. The latter had been very prompt to accept the invitation. I do not know whether the Shell Man went with them or not. At all events, he disappeared, and Mother Anastasia and myself were left upon the piazza. It surprised me that events had so quickly shaped themselves to my advantage.

"Do you insist," I said, when we were left alone, "on being called an Interpolation?"

"Of course I do," she answered; "that is what I am."

"You like plain speech."

"I am very fond of it," was her reply.

During the general conversation I had determined that as soon as an opportunity offered I would speak very plainly to this lady. I looked about me. The occupant of the hammock was not far away. I surmised that she could readily hear me if I spoke in my ordinary tone.

"Plain speech appears difficult to you," remarked my companion.

I still looked about me. "It strikes me," said I, "that beyond the other side of the house there is a bluff from which one might get a view of the mainland. Would you like to go and find out whether that is so or not?"

"I have seen that view several times," she answered; and then, after a little pause, she added, "But I don't mind in the least seeing it again." Together we walked to the bluff. There we found two rude seats which had been made for the convenience of viewers, and on one of these she seated herself.

"Now," said she, "please sit down, and you may immediately begin to ask me about Sister Ha—"

"Oh, do not call her by that name!" I cried.

She laughed. "Very well, then," said she, "what shall I call her?"

"Sylvia," I replied.

She opened her eyes. "Upon my word," she exclaimed, "this is progress! How did you come to know that her name is Sylvia?"

"She told me," I answered. "But why do you think I want to ask you about Sylvia?"

"I knew there was no other reason for your wishing to have a private talk with me; but I must admit that I would not have felt warranted to act upon my assumptions had you not announced yourself in this place as a Lover in Check."

"But could not some one else have held me in check?" I asked.

"No, sir," said she. "I have heard of the manner in which you parted from your late secretary."

This conversation was getting to be plainer than I desired it to be. I was willing to declare my position, but I did not care to have it declared for me. I was silent for a minute.

"I did not suppose," I then said, "that you were so well informed. You think that I am a lover held in check by the circumstances surrounding the lady you designated my late secretary?"

"I do."

"May I ask," I continued, with a little agitation, "if Sylvia considers me in this light, and if she has—expressed any opinion on the subject?"

"Those are pretty questions," said the lady, fixing her dark eyes upon me. "She has said nothing about the light in which she considers you. In fact, all she has told me about you has been in answer to questions I have put to her; but had she spoken of you as a lover, checked or unchecked, of course you would have been none the wiser for me. Sylvia is a simple-hearted, frank girl, and I have thought that she might not have suspected the nature of your very decided liking for her; but now that I have found out that she let you know her as Sylvia I am afraid she is deeper than I thought her. I should not be surprised if you two had flirted dreadfully."

"I never flirt," I answered emphatically.

"That is right," said she. "Never do it."

"But why," I asked, "did you allow her to continue to come to me, if you thought I had a decided liking for her, and all that?"

"Because I chose to do it," she replied, with not the ripple of a smile nor the furrow of a frown upon her face.

I looked at her in amazement.

"Madam," said I, "Interpolation, Mother Anastasia, or whatever name you give yourself, begin now and tell me about Sylvia, and speak to me freely, as I speak to you. I love her with all my heart. If I can, I intend to marry her, Martha or no Martha. I care not what may be the odds against me. Now you see exactly where I stand, and as far as I am concerned you may speak without restraint."

"You are certainly very clear and explicit," she said, "and I shall be glad to tell you about Sylvia."

XXV

ABOUT SYLVIA

"Before I begin," continued my companion, slanting her hat so as to prevent the sun from meddling with the perfect tones of her complexion, "tell me what you already know about this young lady. I do not wish to waste any information."

"All I know," said I, "is that her family name is Raynor,—my grandmother told me that,—that she is absolutely, utterly, and even wickedly out of place in the House of Martha, and that I want her for my wife."

"Very good," said my companion, with a smile. "Now I know what not to tell you. I am very fond of Sylvia. In fact, I believe I love her better than any other woman in the world"—

"So do I," I interrupted.

She laughed. "For a lover in check you are entirely too ready to move. For years I have looked upon her as a younger sister, and there is no good thing which I would not have lavished upon her had I been able, but instead of that I did her an injury. At times I have thought it a terrible injury."

"You mean," I asked, "that you have allowed her to enter the House of Martha?"

"Your quickness is wonderful," she said, "but you do not put the case quite correctly. Had it been possible for me to prohibit her joining our sisterhood, I should have done so; but she was perfectly free to do as she pleased, and my advice against it was of no avail. It was my example which induced her to enter the House of Martha. She had had trouble. She wished to retire from the world, and devote herself to good works which should banish her trouble. I had so devoted myself. She loved me, and she followed me. I talked to her until I made her unhappy, and then I let her go her way. But the great object of my life for nearly a year has been to make that girl feel that her true way is out of the House of Martha."

"Then she is not bound by vows or promises?" I asked, with some excitement.

"Not in the least," said she. "She can leave us when she pleases. I do not think she likes her life or her duties, unless, indeed, they lead her in the direction of dictated literature; but she has a firm will, and, having joined us, has never shown the slightest sign of a desire to leave us. She always asserts that, when the proper time arrives, she shall vow herself a permanent member of our sisterhood."

"What preposterous absurdity!" I exclaimed. "She will never conform to your rules. She hates nursing. She has too much good sense to insult her fine womanly nature by degrading and unnecessary sacrifices."

"How delightfully confidential she must have been!—but I assure you, sir, that she never said that sort of thing to me. There were things she liked and things she did not like, but she showed no signs of rebellion."

"Which was wise," I said, "knowing that you thought she ought not to be there, any way."

"Oh, but she is a little serpent," exclaimed my companion, "and so wise to confide in you, and without flirting! It must have been charming to see."

I did not reply to this remark, which I considered flippant, and my mind was not inclined to flippancy.

"It may appear strange to you," she continued, "and would probably appear strange to any one who did not understand the case, that I should have allowed her to become your amanuensis, but this whole affair is a very peculiar one. In the first place, it is absolutely necessary that Sylvia should work. It is not only her duty as a sister, but without it she would fall into a morbid mental condition. She is not fitted in any way for the ordinary labors of our House, so I was glad to find something which would not only suit her, but would so interest her that it would help to draw her away from us, and back into the world, to which she rightfully belongs. This must appear an odd desire for a mother superior of a religious body, but it is founded on an earnest and conscientious regard for the true welfare of my young friend.

"And then there was another reason for my allowing her to come to you. You would smile if you could picture to yourself the mental image I had formed of you, which was founded entirely on your grandmother's remarks when she came to see me about engaging one of our sisters as your secretary. Before this matter was discussed I may have seen you in the village, but I never had known you even by sight, and from what that good lady said of you I supposed that you were decidedly middle-aged in feeling, if not in years; that you were extremely grave and studious, and wished, when engaged upon literary composition, to be entirely oblivious of your surroundings; and that you desired an amanuensis who should be simply a writing-machine,—who would in no way annoy you by intruding upon you any evidence that she possessed a personality. A sister from our House, your grandmother urged, would be the very person you needed, and infinitely better suited to the position than the somewhat frivolous young women who very often occupy positions as amanuenses.

"It was for these reasons that I sent Sylvia to write at the dictation of the sedate author of the forthcoming book on European travel. Even when I heard that a love-story had been introduced into the descriptions of countries, I concluded, after consideration, not to interfere. I did not think that it would be of any disadvantage to Sylvia if she should become a little interested in love affairs; but that you should become interested in a love affair, such as that you have mentioned to me, I did not imagine in the remotest degree."

"I am sure," said I, "that your motives as far as Sylvia was concerned, and your action as far as I am concerned, were heaven-born. And now, as we are speaking plainly here together, let me ask you if you do not think you would be fulfilling what you consider your duty to Sylvia by aiding me to make her my wife! There can surely be no better way for her to fill her proper place in the world than to marry a man who loves her with his whole heart. I know that I love her above all the world; I believe that I am worthy of her."

She answered me in a tone which was grave, but gentle. "Do you not know you are asking me to do something which is entirely impossible? In the first place, my official position precludes me from taking part in affairs of this nature; and although I am willing to admit that I see no reason why you might not be a suitable partner for Sylvia, I must also admit that, on the other hand, I have no reason to believe that

Sylvia would be inclined to accept you as such a partner. I have no doubt that she has made herself very agreeable to you,—that is her nature; I know that she used to make herself very agreeable to people. You must remember that, even should Sylvia leave us, your chances may be no better than they are now."

"Madam," I said, leaning toward her, and speaking with great earnestness, "I will take all possible chances! What I ask and implore of you is, that if you should ever be able to do the least little thing which would give me the opportunity to plead my own suit before Sylvia, you would do it. I can give her position and fortune. I think I am suited to her, and if love can make me better suited, I have love enough. Now tell me, will you not do this thing? If you have the opportunity, and see no reason against it, will you not help me?"

"This is a hard position for me," she said, after a pause, "and all I can promise you is this: I love Sylvia, and I am going to do whatever I think will be of the greatest advantage to her."

"Then," I asserted with continued earnestness, "it shall be my labor to prove that to love the man who loves her as I do will be her greatest good! If I do that, will you be on my side?"

She smiled, looked at me a few moments, and then answered, "Yes."

"Your hand upon it!" I cried, leaning still farther forward. She laughed at the enthusiastic warmth of my manner, and gave me her hand.

"It is a promise!" I exclaimed, and was about to raise her fingers to my lips when she quickly drew them away.

"I declare," she said, rising as she spoke, "I did not suppose that you would forget that I am the Mother Superior of the House of Martha."

"Excuse me," I replied, "but you are not that; with your own mouth you have assured me that you are an Interpolation, and there is nothing in a social or moral law which forbids a suitable expression of gratitude to an Interpolation."

"Sir," said she, "I think I have seen quite as much as is necessary of the view which you asked me here to look upon."

XXVI

MOTHER ANASTASIA

In the half hour during which I remained alone upon the bluff, awaiting the return of Walkirk and the fishing party, I thought as much of the lady with whom I had been talking as the lady of whom I had been talking.

"How is it possible," I asked myself, "that this gentlewoman, warm with her rich blooded beauty, alive with ripe youth, born to delight the soul of man and fire his heart, should content herself to be a head nurse in a hospital; to wander in an unsightly disguise among dismal sick-beds; to direct the management of measles-refuges; to shut herself up in a bare-floored, cold-walled institution with narrow-minded Sister Sarahs; to be, in a word, the Mother Superior of the House of Martha?"

That she should occupy this position seemed to me a crime. There were many women in the world who could do all she was doing, but there were few who could take her place in the world of full, true life.

When the fishing party returned, I went to the house to take leave of our new friends.

"You must go?" said the Sand Lady. "And where, may I ask,

is it imperative that you should go?"

"To the island where you have so kindly allowed us to sojourn," I replied.

"You sleep in the cabin of your boat, I believe?" she said; and I answered that we did.

"Very well, then," continued she, "why not bring your floating home to this island? It is in every way better than that. I will give you exclusive rights over a little bay and an adjoining dell. There you can cook your own meals when you like, or you can come to us when you like; we always have more than enough for all who inhabit this island. In the evening you can sit alone on the beach and think of the far-away loved one, or you can come up to the house and play whist or twenty questions. The Understudy can go fishing with my brother; they suit each other admirably. What do you say?"

"I say, madam," I replied, with a bow, "the sands of which you are the lady are the dust of diamonds, and your invitation is a golden joy."

"Bless me," she exclaimed, "what must you be out of check!"

That evening we sailed to Racket Island, brought away our belongings, and established ourselves in the land-locked little bay, about a quarter of a mile from the house of the Sand Lady.

Early the next morning I walked around to a pier where I had noticed a good-sized yacht was moored. It was still there; apparently no one had left the island. After our breakfast on the beach I told Walkirk to devote himself to independent occupations, and walked up to the house. I found the lady who had called herself a Person and the one of whom I did not like to think as an Interpolation sitting together upon the piazza. I joined them.

"Wouldn't you be very much obliged to me," asked the Person, after a scattering conversation, in which I suppose I appeared as but a perfunctory performer, "if I were to go away and leave you alone with this lady?"

"As this is an island of plain speaking," I replied, "I will say, yes."

Both ladies laughed, and the Person retired to her hammock.

"Now, then," asked Mother Anastasia, "what is the meaning of this alarming frankness?"

"I wish to talk to you of Sylvia," I answered.

"If you imagine," she said, "that I intend to spend the short time I shall remain upon this island in talking of Sylvia, you are very much mistaken."

"Then let us talk of yourself," I replied.

She turned upon me with a frown and a laugh.

"If I had known," she said, "your habits of ingenuousness and candor, I should have made you dictate to Sylvia through a speaking-tube. You have known me less than a day. You have known her for a month. Can it be possible that you talk to her as freely as you talk to me?"

"Madam," I exclaimed, "I love Sylvia, and therefore could not speak freely to her."

"Your distinctions are wonderfully clear-cut," she said; "but why do you wish to talk of me? I suppose you want to know why I am Mother Superior of the House of Martha?"

"Yes," I answered, "that is a thing I cannot understand; but of course I should not feel justified in even alluding to it if, yesterday, you had not so kindly given me your confidence in regard to yourself and Sylvia."

"It seems to me," she remarked, "that, as you decline to recognize the name given to that young woman by our institution, you should call her Miss Raynor; but I will say no more of that."

"It would be well," said I. "She is Sylvia to me. You must remember that I never met her in the circles of conventionalism."

She laughed. "This whole affair is certainly very independent of conventionalism; and as to your curiosity about me, that is very easily gratified. Nearly five years ago I connected myself with the House of Martha. Although there were sisters older than myself, I was chosen Mother Superior, because I possessed rather more administrative abilities than any of the others. I think I have governed the House fairly well, even if, in regard to the matter of furnishing secretaries to literary men, there has been some dissatisfaction."

"You allude to Sister Sarah?" said I.

"Yes," she answered; "and had she been head of the House, your peace of mind would not have been disturbed. But what I did in that case I did conscientiously and with good intent."

"And you are not sorry for it?" I asked.

"It may be that I shall be sorry for you," she replied, "but that is all I have to say on that point. In a very short time I shall return to my duties and to my sombre bonnet and gown, and these interpolated days, which in a manner have been forced upon me, should be forgotten."

"But one thing you must not forget," I exclaimed: "it was in this time that you promised me"—

"You selfish, selfish man," she interrupted, "you think only of yourself. I shall talk no more of yourself, of myself, or of Sylvia. My friends are at the other side of the house, and I am going to them." And she went.

While Walkirk and I were sailing that afternoon, he managing the boat and I stretched upon some cushions, I told him of my conversations with Mother Anastasia. I considered him worthy of my confidence, and it was pleasant to give it to him.

"She is a rare, strange woman," said he. "I thought her very handsome when I visited her at the House of Martha; but since I have seen her here, dressed in becoming clothes, I consider that she possesses phenomenal attractions."

"And I hope," I remarked, "that she may be phenomenally good-natured, and give me some chances of seeing Sylvia Raynor."

"That would indeed be phenomenal," said Walkirk, laughing, "considering that she is a Mother Superior, and the young lady is a member of the sisterhood. But everything relating to the case is peculiar, and in my opinion Mother Anastasia is more peculiar than anything else."

That evening we were invited to dine at the house of the Sand Lady. It was a delightful occasion. Everybody was in good spirits, and the general tone of the conversation was singularly lively and unrestrained. Mother Anastasia would not play cards, but we amused ourselves with various sprightly social games, in which the lady who preferred to be called a Person showed a vivacious though sometimes nipping wit. I had no opportunity for further private talk with Mother Anastasia, nor did I desire one. I wished to interest her in my love for Sylvia, but not to bore her with it.

The next day, at about eleven o'clock, the Sand Lady and the Shell Man walked over to our little bay, where they found Walkirk and me fencing upon the level beach.

"Stop your duel, gentlemen," said the lady. "I come to give you the farewells of the Interpolation. She was sorry she could not do this herself, but she went away very early this morning."

"Went away!" I cried, dropping my foil upon the sand. "Where did she go?"

"She sailed in our yacht for Sanford," answered the Sand Lady, "to take the morning train for her beloved House of Martha. My brother accompanied her to the town, but he will be back to-day."

I was surprised and grieved, and showed it.

"We are all sorry to have her go," said the Sand Lady, "and sorry to see her wearing that doleful gray garb, which my brother allowed her to assume this morning."

"I am glad," I exclaimed, "that I did not see her in it!"

The lady looked at me with her pleasant, quiet smile.

"You seem very much interested in her."

"I am," I replied, "very much interested, both directly and indirectly, and I am exceedingly sorry that she departed without my knowing it."

This time the Sand Lady laughed. "Good-morning, gentlemen," said she. "Go on with your duel."

XXVII

A PERSON

I fenced no more. "Walkirk," I cried, "let us get our traps on board, and be off!"

My under-study looked troubled,—more troubled than I had ever seen him before.

"Why do you think of this?" he asked. "Where do you propose to go?"

"Home," said I, "to my own house. That is the place where I want to be."

Walkirk stood still and looked at me, his face still wearing an air of deep concern.

"It is not my place to advise," he said, "but it seems to me that your return at this moment would have a very odd appearance, to say the least. Every one would think that you were pursuing Mother Anastasia, and she herself would think so."

"No," said I, "she will not suppose anything of the kind. She will know very well on whose account I came. And as for the people here, they might labor under a mistake at

Frank R. Stockton

first, because of course I should not offer them any explanation, but they would soon learn the real state of the case; that is, if they correspond with the Mother Superior."

"You propose, then," said Walkirk, "to lay siege to the House of Martha, and to carry away, if you can, Miss Sylvia Raynor?"

"I have made no plans," I answered, "but I can look after my interests better in Arden than I can here. I do not like this sudden departure of the Mother Superior. I very much fear that something has induced her to withdraw the good will with which she previously seemed to look upon my attachment to Miss Raynor. Were this not so, she would have advised with me before she left. Nothing could have been more natural. Now I believe she has set herself against me, and has gone away with the intention of permanently separating Sylvia and myself."

"Have you any reason," asked Walkirk, "to impute such an intention to her?"

"Her sudden flight indicates it," I replied; "and besides, you know, although she is not a Roman Catholic, she is at the head of a religious house, and persons in that position are naturally averse to anybody marrying the sisters under their charge. Even if she does not approve of Miss Raynor's remaining in the House, she may not want her to date a love affair from the establishment. If I remain here, Miss Raynor may be spirited entirely out of my sphere of action."

"It strikes me," said Walkirk, "the way to get her spirited out of your sight and knowledge is for you to go home at this juncture. In that case, Mother Anastasia would be bound, in duty to the young lady and her family, to send her away. Do you not agree with me that if you were to reach Arden in the natural course of events, so to speak, and especially if you got there after your grandmother had returned, you would avoid a great deal of undesirable complication, and perhaps actual opposition?"

"You are right," I answered; "it would not look well for me to start away so suddenly. We will wait a day or two, and then drop off naturally."

Walking toward the house, in the afternoon, I met the Person. She advanced toward me, holding out her hand with an air of peremptory friendliness.

"I am heartily glad to see you. I want you to amuse me. I could not ask this of you so long as that fascinating abbess was on the island."

I was a little surprised at this salutation, and not at all pleased. I did not fancy this lady. She had an air as if she were availing herself of her right to be familiar with her inferiors.

"I fear it is not in my power to do anything to amuse you," said I.

"Entirely too modest," she answered. "Let us walk over to this bench in the shade. You are not desired at the house; everybody is taking a nap."

I went with her to the bench she had pointed out, and we sat down.

"Now, then," said she, turning toward me, "will you do me the favor to flirt with me? Say for twenty-five minutes," looking at her watch; "that will bring us to four o'clock, when I must go indoors."

At first I thought the woman was insane, but a glance at her

Frank R. Stockton

face showed that there was no reason for fear of that kind.

"That sounds crazy, doesn't it?" she asked, "but it isn't. It is an honest expression of a very natural wish. Hundreds of ladies have doubtless looked at you and had that wish; but social conventions forbade their expressing it. Here we have no conventions, and I speak my mind."

"Madam," said I, "or miss, there are few things I hold in such abhorrence as flirtation." As I said this I looked at her severely, and she looked at me quizzically. She had gray eyes, which were capable of a great variety of expressions, and her face, suffused by the light of a bantering jocularity, was an attractive one. I was obliged to admit this, in spite of my distaste for her.

"I like that," she said; "it sounds so well, after your vigorous flirtation with our abbess. If I had not seen a good deal of that, I should not have dared to ask you to flirt with me. I thought you liked it, and now that she is gone might be willing to take up with some one else."

I was irritated and disquieted. I had been very earnest in my attentions to Mother Anastasia. Perhaps this lady had seen me attempt to kiss her hand. I must set myself right.

"You are utterly mistaken," said I. "What I had to say to Mother Anastasia related entirely to another person."

"One of the sisters in her institution?" she asked. "She had nothing to do with any other persons, so far as I know. Truly, that is a capital idea!" she exclaimed, without waiting for response from me. "In order to flirt with a member of the sisterhood, a gentleman must direct his attentions to the Mother Superior who represents them, and the flirting is thus done by proxy. Now don't attempt to correct me. The idea is entirely too delightful for me to allow it to be destroyed by any bare statements or assertions."

"I suppose," I answered, "that Mother Anastasia has taken you into her confidence?"

"Thank you very much for that most gratifying testimony to my powers of insight!" she cried. "The Mother Superior gave me no confidences. So you have been smitten by a gray-gown. How did you happen to become acquainted with her? I do not imagine they allow gentleman visitors at the House of Martha?"

"Madam, you know, or assume to know, so much of my affairs," said I, "that in order to prevent injurious conjectures regarding the House of Martha, its officers and inmates, I shall say that I became acquainted in a perfectly legitimate manner with a young lady living therein, who has not yet taken the vows of the permanent sisterhood, and I intend, as soon as circumstances will permit, to make her an offer of marriage. I assure you, I regret extremely that I have been obliged to talk in this way to a stranger, and nothing could have induced me to do it but the fear that your conjectures and surmises might make trouble. I ask as a right that you will say no more of the matter to any one."

"Would you mind telling me the lady's name?" she asked.

"Of course I shall do no such thing," I answered, rising from my seat, with my face flushing with indignation.

"This is odd flirting, isn't it?" said she, still retaining her seat,—"a quarrel at the very outset. I shall not be prevented from informing you why you ought to tell me the name of the lady. You see that if you don't give me her name my ungovernable curiosity will set me to working the matter out for myself, and it is quite as likely as not that I shall go to the House of Martha, and ask questions, and pry, and

Frank R. Stockton

watch, and make no end of trouble. If a blooming bride is to be picked from that flock of ash-colored gruel-mixers, I want to know who it is to be. I used to be acquainted with a good many of them, but I haven't visited the House for some time."

I had never known any one assume toward me a position so unjustifiable and so unseemly as that in which this lady had deliberately placed herself. I could find no words to express my opinion of her conduct, and was on the point of walking away, when she rose and quickly stepped to my side.

"Don't go away angry," she said. "On this island we don't get angry; it is too conventional. I am bound to find out all about this affair, because it interests me. It is something quite out of the common; and although you are in a measure right in saying that I have nothing to do with your affairs, you must know you have in a measure mixed yourself up with my affairs. I am one of the original subscribers to the House of Martha, and used to take a good deal of interest in the establishment, as was my right and privilege; but the sisters bored me after a time, and as I have been traveling in Europe for more than a year I now know very little of what has been going on there. But if there is a young woman in that House who prefers marriage to hospital life and tailor-made costumes to ash-bags, I say that she has mistaken her vocation, and ought to be helped out of it; and although I know you to be a pretty peppery gentleman, I am perfectly willing to help her in your direction, if that is the way she wants to go. I offer myself to you as an ally. Take me on your side, and tell me all about it. It would be perfectly ridiculous to let me go down there imagining that this or that underdone-griddle-cake-faced young woman was your lady-love. I might make mistakes, and do more harm than good."

"Madam," I replied, "let us have done with this. I have

never said one word to the young lady in question of my feelings toward her, and it is in the highest degree improper and unjust that she should be discussed in connection with them. I have laid the matter before Mother Anastasia, as she stands in position of parent to the young lady; but with no one else can I possibly act, or even discuss the subject," and I bowed.

"I don't like this," she said, without noticing that I had taken leave of her. "Mother Anastasia did not intend to leave here until to-morrow, and she went away early this morning. She has some pressing business on hand, and ten chances to one she has gone to fillip your young lady out of your sight and hearing. Don't you see that it would not look at all well for one of her sisters to marry, or even to receive the attentions of a gentleman, immediately after she had left the institution?"

This suggestion, so like my own suspicions, greatly disturbed me.

"Are you in earnest," said I, "or is all this chaffer? What reasonable interest can you take in me and my affairs?"

"I take no interest whatever," said she, "excepting that I have heard you are both eccentric and respectable, and that I have found you amusing, and in this class of people I am always interested. But I will say to you that if there is a woman in that House who might make a suitable and satisfactory marriage, if an opportunity were allowed her, I believe she should be allowed the opportunity, and, acting upon general principles of justice and a desire to benefit my fellow-mortals, I should use my influence to give it to her. So you see that I should really be acting for the girl, and not for you, although of course it would amount to the same thing. And if Mother Anastasia has gone to pull down the curtain on this little drama, I am all the more anxious to jerk it up again. Come, now, Mr. Lover in Check,—and when I first heard your name I had no idea how well it fitted,—confide in me. It would delight me to be in this fight; and you can see for yourself that it would be a very humdrum matter for me to join your opponents, even if I should be of their opinion. They do not need my help."

This argument touched me. I needed help. Should Mother Anastasia choose to close the doors of the House of Martha against me, what could I do? It might divert this lady to act on my behalf. If she procured an interview for me with Sylvia, I would ask no more of her. There was nothing to risk except that Sylvia might be offended if she heard that she had been the object of compacts. But something must be risked, otherwise I might be simply butting my head against monastic brickwork.

"Madam," said I, "whatever your motives may be, I accept your offer to fight on my side, and the sooner the battle begins the better. The young lady to whom I wish to offer myself in marriage, and with whom I am most eager to meet, is Miss Sylvia Raynor, a novice, or something of the kind, in the House of Martha."

With her brows slightly knitted, as if she did not exactly understand my words, my companion looked at me for an instant. Then her eyes sparkled, her lips parted, and a flush of quick comprehension passed over her face. She put back her head and laughed until she almost lost her breath. I looked upon her, shocked and wounded to the soul.

"Pardon me," she said, her eyes filled with the tears of laughter, "but it can't be helped; I withdraw my offer. I cannot be on your side, at least just now. But I shall remain neutral,—you can count on that," and, still laughing, she went her way.

Any one more disagreeably unpleasant than this woman I had never met. When I told Walkirk what had happened I could not restrain my burning indignation, and I declared I would not remain another hour on the island with her. He listened to me with grave concern.

"This is very unfortunate," he said, "but do not let us be precipitate."

XXVIII

THE FLOATING GROCERY

I now positively decided that the next day I would leave this island, where people flew off at such disagreeable tangents; but as I was here on invitation, I could not go away without taking leave of my hostess. Accordingly, in the evening Walkirk and I went up to the house.

The Sand Lady was manifestly grieved when she heard of our intended departure, and her brother was quite demonstrative in his expressions of regret; even the Shell Man, who had discovered in Walkirk some tastes similar to his own, demurred at our going. The Person, however, made no allusion to the subject, and gave us, indeed, as little of her society as she apparently did of her thoughts.

In order not to produce the impression that I was running after Mother Anastasia, as Walkirk had put it, I announced that we should continue our cruise for an indefinite time. I was sorry to leave these good people, but to stay with that mocking enigma of a woman was impossible. She had possessed herself, in the most crafty and unwarrantable manner, of information which she had no right to receive and I had no right to give, and then contemptuously laughed in my face. My weakness may have deserved the contempt, but that made no difference in my opinion of the woman who had inflicted it upon me. I was glad, when we bade good-night and farewell to the little party, that the Person was not present.

But early the next morning, just as we were hoisting sail on our boat, this lady appeared, walking rapidly down to our beach. She was dressed in a light morning costume, with some sort of a gauzy fabric thrown over her head, and if I had not hated her so thoroughly I should have considered her a very picturesque and attractive figure.

"I am glad I am in time," she called out. "I don't want you to go away with too bad an opinion of me, and I came to say that what you have confided to me is just as safe with me as it would be with anybody else. Do you think you can believe that if you try?"

It was impossible for me to make any answer to this woman, but I took off my hat and bowed. The sail filled, and we glided away.

Walkirk was not in good spirits. It was plain enough that he liked the Tangent Island and wanted to stay; and he had good reason, for he had found pleasant company, and this could not always be said to be the case when sailing in a small boat or camping out with me. My intention was to sail to a town on the mainland, some thirty miles distant, there leave our boat, and take a train for Arden. This, I considered, was sacrificing to appearances as much time as I could allow.

But the breeze was light and fitful, and we made but little progress, and about the middle of the forenoon a fog came slowly creeping up from the sea. It grew thicker and heavier, until in an hour or two we were completely shut out from all view of the world about us. There was now no wind. Our sail hung damp and flabby; moisture, silence, and obscurity were upon us.

The rest of the day we sat doleful, waiting for the fog to lift and the wind to rise. My fear was that we might drift out to sea or upon some awkward shoals; for, though everything else was still, the tide would move us. What Walkirk feared, if anything, I do not know, but he kept up a good heart, and rigged a lantern some little distance aloft, which, he said, might possibly keep vessels from running into us. He also performed, at intervals, upon a cornet which he had brought with him. This was a very wise thing to do, but, for some reason or other, such music, in a fog, depressed my spirits; however, as it seemed quite suitable to the condition of my affairs I did not interfere, and the notes of Bonnie Doon or My Old Kentucky Home continued to be soaked into the fog.

Night came on; the fog still enveloped us, and the situation became darker. We had our supper, and I turned in, with the understanding that at midnight I was to take the watch, and let Walkirk sleep. It was of no use to make ourselves any more uncomfortable than need be.

It was between two and three o'clock when I was called to go on watch; and after I had been sitting in the stern smoking and thinking for an hour or more, I noticed that the light on the mast had gone out. It was, however, growing lighter, and, fancying that the fog was thinner, I trusted to the coming of the day and a breeze, and made no attempt to take down and refill the lantern.

Not long after this my attention was attracted by something which appeared like the nucleus of a dark cloud forming in the air, a short distance above the water, and not far away on our port quarter. Rapidly the cloud grew bigger and blacker. It moved toward us, and in a few moments, before I had time to collect my thoughts and arouse Walkirk, it was almost upon us, and then I saw that it was the stern of a vessel, looming high above my head.

I gave a wild shout; Walkirk dashed out of his bunk; there was a call from above; then I felt a shock, and our boat keeled over on her starboard side. In a moment, however, she receded from the other vessel, and righted herself. I do not know that Walkirk had ever read in a book what he ought to do in such an emergency, but he seized a boat hook and pushed our boat away from the larger vessel.

"That's right!" cried a voice from above. "I'll heave ye a line. Keep her off till we have drifted past ye, and then I'll haul ye in."

Slowly the larger vessel, which was not very large, but which drifted faster than our little boat, floated past us, until we were in tow at her bow. We could now see the form of a man leaning over the rail of the vessel, and he called out to us to know if we were damaged, and if we wanted to come aboard. I was about to reply that we were all right, and would remain where we were, when Walkirk uttered an exclamation.

"We are taking in water by the bucketful," said he; "our side has been stove in."

"Impossible!" I exclaimed. "We were not struck with enough force for that."

But examination proved that he was correct. One or more of our planks had been broken just below the water line and our boat was filling, though not rapidly.

"Stoved in, eh?" shouted the voice from above. "Well, ye needn't sink. I'll haul yer bowline taut, and I'll heave ye another to make fast to yer stern. That'll keep yer little craft afloat until ye can unlade her; and the quicker ye get yer traps up here the better, if ye don't want 'em soaked."

Acting upon these suggestions, Walkirk and I went vigorously to work, and passed up our belongings as rapidly as possible to the man above, who, by leaning over the rails, could easily reach them. When everything movable had been taken out of our boat, the man let down a ladder and I climbed on board the larger vessel, after which he came down to our boat, detached the boom, gaff, and sail, and unshipped the mast; all of which we afterwards hoisted on board his vessel by means of a block and tackle.

"Now, then," said our new companion, "ye're safe, and yer boat can capsize if it's a mind to, but it can't sink; and when it's better daylight, and Abner's on deck, perhaps we'll rig out a couple of spars and haul her up at the stern; but there's time enough to settle all that. And now I'd like to know how ye came to be driftin' around here with no light out."

I explained, but added I had not seen any light on his vessel.

"Well," said the man, looking upward, "that light's out, and ten to one it was out when we run inter ye. I'spect Abner didn't calkerlate for fillin' it for day work and night work too."

The speaker was a grizzled man, middle-aged, and rather too plump for a sailor. He had a genial, good-natured countenance, and so far as I could see was the only occupant of the vessel.

His craft was truly a peculiar one. It was sloop-rigged, and on the after part of the deck, occupying about one third of the length of the vessel, was a structure resembling a small one-storied house, which rose high above the rest of the deck, like the poop of an old-fashioned man-of-war. In the gable end of this house, which faced upon the deck, there was a window and a door. The boom of the mast was rigged high enough to allow it to sweep over the roof.

"I reckon you gents think this is a queer kind of a craft," said the man, with a grin of pleasure at our evident curiosity; "and if ye think that, ye are about right, for there isn't jist such another one as far as I know. This is a floating grocery, and I am captain of the sloop or keeper of the store, jist as it happens. In that house there is a good stock of flour, sugar, feed, trimmings, notions, and small dry goods, with some tinware and pottery, and a lot of other things which you commonly find in a country grocery store. I have got the trade of about half the families in this bay; all of them on the islands, and a good many of them on the mainland, especially sech as has piers of their own. I have regular days for touching at all the different p'ints; and it is a mighty nice thing, I can tell ye, to have yer grocery store come round to ye instead of yer having to go to it, especially if ye live on an island or out in the country."

Walkirk and I were very much interested in this floating grocery store, which was an entirely novel thing to us, and we asked a good many questions about it.

"There's only me and Abner aboard," said the grocer-skipper, "but that's enough, for we do a good deal more anchorin' than sailin'. Abner, he's head clerk, and don't pretend to be no sailor at all; but he lays a hold of anythin' I tell him to, and that's all I ask of him in the sailorin' line. But he is first class behind the counter, I can tell ye, and in keepin' the books I couldn't find nobody like Abner,—not in this State. Now it may strike ye, gents, that I am not much of a sailor neither, to be driftin' about here at night in this fog instead of anchorin' and tootin' a foghorn; but ye see, I did anchor in the fore part of the night, and after

Abner had gone to his bunk—we don't keep regular watches, but kinder divide the night between us, when we are out on the bay, which isn't common, for we like to tie up at night, and do our sailin' in the daytime—it struck me that as the tide was runnin' out we might as well let it take us to Simpson's Bar, which, if ye don't know this bay, is a big shallow place, where there is always water enough for us, bein' a good deal on the flat-bottomed order, but where almost any steamin' craft at low tide would stick in the mud before they could run into us. So thinks I, If we want to get on in the direction of Widder Kinley's (whose is the last house I serve down the bay), and to feel safe besides, we had better up anchor, and I upped it. But I had ought to remembered about that light; it wasn't the square thing to be driftin' about without the light, no more fur me than fur ye. I've sounded a good many times, but we don't seem to have reached the bar yet. It must be pretty near time for Abner to turn out," and he looked at his watch.

"Your assistant must be a sound sleeper," I remarked.

"Yes, he is," replied the man. "He needs lots of sleep, and I make it a p'int to give it to him. If it isn't positively necessary, I don't wake him up until the regular time. Of course, if it had been our boat that had been stoved in, and she had been like to sink, I'd have called Abner; but as it was yer boat, and none of us was in no danger, I didn't call him. Here he is, though, on time."

At this, a tall, lean man, not quite so much grizzled as the other, made his appearance on deck. He gazed from one to the other of us, and upon our various belongings, which were strewn upon the deck, with undisguised amazement.

His companion laughed aloud. "I don't wonder, Abner," he cried, "that ye open yer eyes; 't ain't often two gentlemen come on board in the night, bag and baggage; but these two stoved in their boat agin our rudder, and here they are, with their craft triced up to keep her from sinkin'."

Abner made no answer, but walked to the side of the vessel, looked over, and satisfied himself that this last statement was correct.

"Capt'n Jabe," said he, turning to the other, "we can't sail much, can we, with that thing hangin' there?"

"Well, now, Abner," replied the captain, "we are not sailin' at the present time,—we are driftin'; for it is my idee to drop anchor as soon as we get to Simpson's Bar, and this tide is bound to carry us over it if we wait long enough, so we must keep soundin', and not slip over without knowin' it."

"It strikes me," said Abner, "that we should save a lot of trouble if we should put the anchor out and let it hang; then, when we come to the bar, she'll ketch and fetch us up without our havin' it on our minds."

"You see, gents," said Captain Jabe to us, "Abner don't pretend to be no sailor, but he's got his idees about navigation, for all that."

Abner took no notice of this remark. "Capt'n," said he, "does these gents want to turn in?"

"Not till they have had some breakfast," replied Captain Jabe, and we assented.

"All right," said Abner, "I'll tackle the grub," and, opening the door of the grocery store, he went inside. In a few minutes he reappeared. "Capt'n," said he, in a voice which he intended to be an aside, "are you goin' to count 'em as mealers, or as if they was visitin' the family?"

Frank R. Stockton

Captain Jabe laughed. "Well, Abner," said he, "I guess we will count them as mealers, though I don't intend to make no charge."

Abner nodded, and again entered the little house.

"What are mealers?" I asked of the captain.

"In this part of the country," he answered, "there's a good many city folks comes for the summer, and they take houses; but they don't want the trouble of cookin', so they make a contract with some one livin' near to give them their meals regular, and this sort of folks goes by the general name of mealers. What Abner wanted to know fur was about openin' the cans. You see, most of our victuals is in cans, and if Abner knowed you was regular payin' mealers he would open fresh ones; but if you was visitin' the family, he'd make you help eat up what was left in the cans, just as we do ourselves."

It was not long before the thrifty Abner had given us a substantial breakfast; and then Walkirk and I were glad to take possession of a spare couple of bunks, for we were tired and sleepy, and the monotonous fog still hung around us.

It was about noon when I waked and went on deck, where I found Walkirk, Captain Jabe, and Abner engaged in consultation. There was a breeze blowing, and every particle of fog had disappeared.

"We've been considerin'," said the captain, addressing me, "what's the best thing to do with yer boat; there's no use tryin' to tinker her up, for she has got a bad hole in her, and it is our fault, too. One of the iron bands on our rudder got broke and sprung out a good while ago, and it must have been the sharp end of that which punched into yer boat when we drifted down on her. We ain't got no tackle

suitable to h'ist her on board, and as to towin' her—a big
boat like that, full of water,—'t ain't possible. We've lost a
lot of time already, and now there's a good wind and we are
bound to make the best of it; so me and Abner thinks the
best thing ye can do is to sink yer boat right here on the bar
where we are now anchored, having struck it all right, as ye
see, and mark the spot with an oil-cag. Anybody that knows
this bay can come and git her if she is on Simpson's Bar,
buoyed with an oil-cag."

I was sorry that we should not be able to repair our boat and
continue our trip in her, but I saw that this would be
impossible, and I asked Captain Jabe if he could take us to
Brimley.

"I can do that," he answered, "but not straight. I have got
fust to sail over to Widder Kinley's, which is on that p'int
which ye can just see over there on the edge of the water,
and where I was due yesterday afternoon. Then I've got to
touch at three or four other places along the east shore; and
then, if this wind holds, I guess I can git across the bay to
my own house, where I have got to lay up all day to-
morrow. The next day is Saturday, and then I am bound to
be in Brimley to take in stock. There ye two gents can take
the cars for wherever ye want to go; and if ye choose to give
me the job of raisin' yer boat and sendin' it to its owners, I'll
do it for ye as soon as I can fix things suitable, and will
charge ye just half price for the job, considerin' that nuther
of us had our lights out, and we ought to share damages."

I agreed to the proposed disposition of our boat, and asked
Captain Jabe if I could not hire him to take us direct to
Brimley.

"No, sir!" he answered. "I never pass by my customers,
especially Widder Kinley, for she is the farthest off of any of
them."

"And she must be lookin' out sharp for us, too," said Abner, "for she bakes Thursdays, and she ought to sot her bread last night."

"And I am a great deal afeard," continued Captain Jabe, "that her yeast cakes won't be any too fresh when she gits 'em; and the quicker that boat's down to the bottom and our anchor up off the bottom, the better it will be for the Widder Kinley's batch of bread."

In the course of half an hour an empty oil-keg was moored over the spot where our boat lay upon the sandy bar, and we were sailing as fast as such an unwieldy vessel, with her mainsail permanently reefed above the roof of her grocery store, could be expected to sail. Our tacks were long and numerous, and although Walkirk and I lent a hand whenever there was occasion for it, and although there was a fair wind, the distant point rose but slowly upon our horizon.

"I hope," I remarked to Captain Jabe, "that the Widow Kinley will buy a good bill of you, after you have taken all this trouble to get to her."

"Dunno," said he; "she don't generally take more than she has ordered the week before, and all she has ordered this time is two yeast cakes."

"Do you mean," exclaimed Walkirk, "that you are taking all this time and trouble to deliver two yeast cakes, worth, I suppose, four cents?"

"That's the price on 'em," said the captain; "but if the Widder Kinley didn't git 'em she wouldn't do no bakin' this week, and that would upset her housekeepin' keel up."

Late in the afternoon we delivered the yeast cakes to the Widow Kinley, whom we found in a state of nervous agitation, having begun to fear that another night would pass without her bread being "sot." Then we coasted along the shore, tying up at various little piers, where the small farmers' and fishermen's families came on board to make purchases.

Now Abner was in his glory. Wearing a long apron made of blue-and-white bed-ticking, he stood behind the counter in the little house on deck, and appeared to be much more at ease weighing sugar, coffee, and flour than in assisting to weigh anchor. I seated myself in the corner of this floating grocery, crowded, shelves, floor, and counter, with such goods as might be expected to be found at an ordinary country store.

It seemed to me that nearly every one who lived near the points at which we touched came on board the floating grocery, but most of them came to talk, and not to buy. Many of those who did make purchases brought farm produce or fish, with which to "trade." It was an interesting spectacle, and amused me. During our slow progress from one place to another, Captain Jabe told me of an old woman who once offered him an egg which she wished to take out in groceries, half in tea and half in snuff.

"We don't often do business down as fine as that," said the captain; "but then, on the other hand, we don't calkerlate to supply hotels, and couldn't if we wanted to."

Walkirk appeared uneasy at the detentions which still awaited us.

"Couldn't you take us straight on to Brimley," he asked of the captain, "and sail back to your home in the morning?"

"No, sir!" answered Captain Jabe, with much decision. "My old woman 'spects me to-night,—in p'int of fact, she 'spected me a good deal before night,—and I am not goin' to have her thinkin' I am run down in a fog, and am now engaged in feedin' the sharks. There is to be a quiltin' party at our house to-morrer arternoon, and there's a lot to be done to get ready for it. Abner and me will have to set up pretty late this night, I can tell yer!"

"Is there no way of getting to the railroad," I asked, "but by your boat?"

"No," said Captain Jabe, "I can't see that there is. Pretty nigh all the folks that will be at the bee to-morrow will come in boats. None of them live nigh to a railroad station, and if they did, and could take ye back with 'em, they wouldn't leave early enough for ye to ketch the last train: so the best thing ye can do is to stick by me, and I'll guarantee to git ye over to Brimley in time for the mornin' train on Saturday."

XXIX

FANTASY?

We reached Captain Jabe's house a little after nightfall, and received a hearty welcome and a good supper from his wife. Walkirk and I slept on board the floating grocery, as also did Abner; that is to say, if he slept at all, for he and the captain were busy at the house when we retired. The quilting party, we were informed, was expected to be a grand affair, provided, of course, there were no signs of rain; for country people are not expected to venture out for pleasure in rainy weather.

Captain Jabe's house, as we saw it the next morning, was a good-sized waterside farmhouse, wide-spreading and low-roofed. The place had a sort of amphibious appearance, as if depending for its maintenance equally upon the land and the water. The house stood a little distance back from the narrow beach, and in its front yard a net was hung to dry and to be mended; a small boat, in course of repair, lay upon some rude stocks, while bits of chain, an old anchor, several broken oars, and other nautical accessories were scattered here and there.

At the back of the house, however, there was nothing about the barn, the cow-yard, the chicken-yard, and the haystacks to indicate that Captain Jabe was anything more than a thrifty small-farmer. But, farmer and sailor as he was, Captain Jabe was none the less a grocer, and I think to this avocation he gave his chief attention.

He took me into a small room by the side of his kitchen, and showed me what he called his "sinkin' fund stock."

"Here, ye see," said he, "is canned fruit and vegetables, smoked and salted meat and fish, cheeses, biscuits, and a lot of other things that will keep. None of these is this year's goods. Some of them have been left over from last year, some from the year before that, and some is still older. Whenever I git a little short, I put a lot of these goods on board and sell 'em with the discount off,—twenty per cent for last year's stock, forty per cent off for the year before that, and so on back. So, ye see, if I have got anythin' on hand that is five years old, I am bound to give it away for nothin', if I stick to my principles. At fust me and my old woman tried eatin' what was left over; but discount isn't no good to her, and she wants the best victuals that is goin'. Did ye ever think, sir, what this world would be without canned victuals?"

I assured him that I never had, but would try to do so if possible.

The day proved to be a very fine one, and early in the afternoon the people invited to the quilting party began to arrive, and by two o'clock the affair was in full swing. The quilting frame was set up in a large chamber at the right of the parlor, the "comfortable" to be quilted was stretched upon it, and at the four sides sat as many matrons and elderly maidens as could crowd together, each with needle in hand. Long cords rubbed with chalk were snapped upon the surface of the quilt to mark out the lines to be stitched; wax, thread, and scissors were passed from one to another; and every woman began to sew and to talk as fast as she could.

I stood in the doorway and watched this scene with considerable interest, for I had never before seen anything of the kind. The quilting ladies, to every one of whom I had been presented, cordially invited me to enter and take a seat with them; some of the more facetious offering to vacate their places in my favor, and, more than that, to show me how to thread and use a needle. I found from their remarks that it was rather an unusual thing for a man to take an interest in this part of the proceedings at a quilting party.

After a time I went into the parlor, which room was then occupied by the young men and young women. It was ever so much pleasanter out-of-doors than in this somewhat gloomy and decidedly stuffy parlor; but as these people were guests at a quilting party, they knew it was proper to enjoy themselves within the house to which they had been invited.

The young folks were not nearly so lively and animated as their elders in the next room, but they had just begun to play a game which could be played in the house, and in which every one could participate, and as the afternoon wore on they would doubtless become warmed up. Walkirk was making the best of it, and had entered the game; but I declined all invitations to do so.

Before long there was some laughing and a good deal of romping, and I fancied that the girls, some of whom were not at all bad looking, would have been pleased if I had joined in the sport. But this did not suit me; I still was, as I declared myself, a Lover in Check, and the society of young women was not attractive to me.

I went outside, where a group of elderly men were discussing the tax rates; and after remaining a few minutes with them, I came to the conclusion that the pleasantest thing I could do would be to take a stroll over the country.

I made my way over some rolling meadow land, where three or four of Captain Jabe's cows were carefully selecting the edible portions of the herbage, and, having passed the crest of a rounded hill, I found myself on the edge of a piece of woodland, which seemed to be of considerable extent. This suited my mood exactly, and I was soon following the curves and bends of a rude roadway, in places almost overgrown by vines and bushes, which led me deeper and deeper into the shadowed recesses of the woods. It was now about four o'clock in the afternoon. The sun was still well up, and out in the open the day was warm for an up-and-down-hill stroll; but here in the woods it was cool and quiet, and the air was full of the pleasant summer smells that come from the trees, the leaves, and the very earth of the woods.

It was not long before I came upon a stream of a character that somewhat surprised me. It was not very wide, for at this spot the trees met above it, darkening its waters with their quivering shadows; but it was evidently deep, much deeper than the woodland streams of its size to which I had been accustomed. I would have liked to cross it and continue my walk, but I saw no way of getting over. With a broken branch I sounded the water near the shore, and found it over two feet deep; and as it was no doubt deeper toward the middle, I gave up the idea of reaching the other side. But as I had no particular reason for getting over, especially as I should be obliged to get back again, I contented myself easily with my present situation, and, taking a seat on the upheaved root of a large tree, I lighted a cigar, and gave myself up to the delights of this charming solitude. I was glad to be away from everybody, even from Walkirk, the companion I had chosen for my summer journey.

There were insects gently buzzing in the soft summer air; on the other side of the stream, in a spot unshadowed by the trees, the water was sparkling in the sunlight, and every little puff of the fitful breeze brought to me the smell of wild grapes, from vines which hung from the trees so low that they almost touched the water. It was very still in these woods. I heard nothing but the gently rustling leaves, the faint buzzing in the air, and an occasional tiny splash made by some small fish skimming near the surface of the stream. When I sat down on the root of the tree, I intended to think, reflect, make plans, determine what I should do next; but I did nothing of the sort. I simply sat and drank in the loveliness of this woodland scene.

The stream curved away from me on either hand, and the short stretch of it which I could see to the left seemed to come out of the very heart of the woods. Suddenly I heard in this direction a faint regular sound in the water, as if some animal were swimming. I could not see anything, but as the sounds grew stronger I knew that it must be approaching. I did not know much of the aquatic animals in this region; perhaps it might be an otter, a muskrat, I knew not what. But, whatever it was, I wanted to see it, and, putting down my cigar, I slipped softly behind the tree at whose foot I had been sitting.

Now the swimming object was in view, coming rapidly toward me down the middle of the stream. There was but little of it above the water, and the shadows were so heavy that I could see nothing but a dark point, with a bright ripple glancing away from it on either side. Nearer and nearer it came into the better lighted portion of the stream. It was not a small animal. The ripples it made were strong, and ran out in long lines; its strokes were vigorous; the head that I saw grew larger and larger. Steadily it came on; it reached the spot in the clear light of the sun. It was the head of a human swimmer. On the side nearest me, I could see, under the water, the strokes of a dark-clad arm. Above the water was only a face, turned toward me and upward. A mass of long hair swept away from it, its blue eyes gazed dreamily into the treetops; for a moment the sunbeams touched its features. My heart stopped beating,—it was the face of Sylvia.

Another stroke and it had passed into the shadow. The silvery ripples came from it to me, losing themselves against the shore. It passed on and on, away from me. I made one step from behind the tree; then suddenly stopped. On went the head and upturned face, touched once more by a gleam of light, and then it disappeared around a little bluff crowned with a mass of shrubbery and vines. I listened, breathless; the sounds of the strokes died away. All was still again.

For some minutes I stood, bewildered, dazed, doubting whether I had been awake or dreaming. My mind could not grasp what had happened,—even my imagination could not help me. But one thing I knew: whether this had all been real, or whether it had been a dream, I had seen the face of Sylvia. This I knew as I knew I lived.

Slowly I came away, scarcely knowing how I walked or where I emerged from the woods, and crossed the open country to the house of Captain Jabe.

XXX

A DISCOVERY

I found the quilting party at supper. I could see them through the open windows of the large living-room, and I heard their chatter and laughing when I was still a considerable distance from the house. With my mind quivering with the emotions excited by what had happened in the woods, it was impossible for me to join a party like this. I walked around the barn and into a little orchard, where, between two gnarled apple-trees, there hung an old hammock, into which I threw myself.

There I lay, piling conjecture and supposition high upon each other; but not at all could I conjecture how it was that the face which I had last seen in my own home, under the gray bonnet of a sister of Martha, should flash upon my vision in this far-away spot, and from the surface of a woodland stream.

It was growing dusky, when I heard a loud whistle, and my name was called. I whistled in return, and in a few moments Walkirk came running to me.

"I was beginning to get frightened," he said. "I have been looking everywhere for you. We have had supper, and the party is breaking up. There is no moon to-night, and the people must start early for their homes."

"Let them all get away," I replied; "and when they are entirely out of sight and hearing let me know, and I'll go in to supper."

"I am afraid," said Walkirk, hesitating, "that they will not like that. You know these country people are very particular about leave-taking, and all that sort of thing."

"I can't help it," I answered. "I don't feel at all like seeing people at present. You can go and bid them good-by in my name."

"As an under-study?" said he, smiling. "Well, if I can tell them you are out of condition and not feeling like yourself, that will make it all right, and will also explain why you kept yourself away all the afternoon." With this he left me, promising to return when the guests had departed. It was a long time before he came back, and it was then really dark.

"Your supper is awaiting you," he announced, "and I am afraid that Mrs. Jabe is contemplating a hot footbath and some sort of herb tea; and we ought to turn in pretty early to-night, for Captain Jabe has announced that he will sail between four and five o'clock in the morning."

"Walkirk," said I, sitting up in the hammock, "I have no intention of sailing to-morrow. I prefer to stay here for a time; I don't know for how long."

"Stay here!" exclaimed Walkirk. "What on earth can you do here? What possible attraction can this place have?"

"My good Walkirk," I said, rising and walking toward the house, "I am here, and here I want to stay. Reasons are the most awkward things in the world. They seldom fit; let us drop them. Perhaps, if Captain and Mrs. Jabe think I did not treat their company with proper courtesy, they may feel that I am making amends by desiring to stay with them. Any way, I am going to stay."

Captain Jabe and his wife were very much surprised when I announced my intention of remaining at their place for a day or two longer, but, as I had surmised, they were also flattered.

"This is a quiet place," said the captain, "but as ye ain't very well, and seem to like to keep to yerself, I don't see why it shouldn't suit ye. There's plenty o' good air, and fishin' if ye want it, and we can accommodate ye and give ye plenty to eat. I shall be back to-morrow night, and expect to stay home over Sunday myself."

Walkirk was very much dissatisfied, and made a strong attempt to turn me from my purpose. "If you intend to do anything in regard to Miss Raynor," he said, "I really think you ought to get home as soon as you can. Mother Anastasia is now having everything her own way, you know."

"Walkirk," said I, "you blow hot and cold. If it had not been for you, I should be home this minute; but you dissuaded me from a hot chase after Mother Anastasia, and now my ardor for the chase has cooled, and I am quite inclined to let that sport wait."

Walkirk looked at me inquiringly. It was evident that he did not understand my mood.

The next morning I found myself in a quandary. I had determined to make a long tramp inland, and if necessary to ford or swim streams, and I could not determine whether or not it would be wise to take Walkirk with me. I concluded at last to take him; it would be awkward to leave him behind, and he might be of use. We provided ourselves with fishing rods and tackle and two pairs of wading-boots, as well as with a luncheon basket, well filled by Mrs. Jabe, and started on our expedition. I felt in remarkably good spirits.

I had formed no acceptable hypothesis in regard to what I had seen the day before, but I was going to do something better than that; I was going to find out if what had occurred could possibly be real and actual. If I should be convinced that this was impossible, then I intended to accept the whole affair as a dream which had taken place during an unconscious nap.

When we reached the woodland stream, Walkirk gazed about him with satisfaction. "This looks like sport," he said. "I see no reason why there should not be good fishing in this creek. I did not suppose we should find such pleasant woods and so fine a stream in Captain Jabe's neighborhood."

"You must know," said I, "that I have a talent for exploration and discovery. Had it not been for this stream, I should not have thought of such a thing as allowing Captain Jabe and Abner to sail off by themselves this morning."

"Really," replied Walkirk, "you care much more for angling than I supposed."

Truly I cared very little for angling, but I had discovered that Walkirk was an indefatigable and patient fisherman. I had intended that he should cross the stream with me, but it now occurred to me that it would be far better to let him stay on this side, while I pursued my researches alone. Accordingly I proposed that he should fish in the part of the stream which I had seen the day before, while I pressed on farther. "In this way," I remarked artfully, "we shall not interfere with each other." Had I supposed that there was the slightest possibility of the appearance on the stream of the apparition of the day before, I should have requested Walkirk to fish from the top of a distant tree. But I had no fears on this score. If what I had seen had been a phantasm, my under-study would have to doze to see it, and I knew he would not do that; and if what I had seen was real, it would not appear this morning, for the water was too low for swimming. The creek, as I now perceived, was affected by the tide, and its depth was very much less than on the preceding afternoon.

I turned to the right, and followed the stream for some distance; now walking by its edge, and now obliged, by masses of undergrowth, to make a detour into the woods. At last I came to a spot where the stream, although wide, appeared shallow. In fact, even in the centre I could see the stones at the bottom. I therefore put on my wading-boots and boldly crossed. The woods here were mostly of pine, free from undergrowth, and with the ground softened to the foot by a thick layer of pine needles.

Now that I was on the other side of the creek, I desired to make my way out of the woods, which could not, I imagined, be very extensive. To discover a real basis for yesterday's vision, I believed that it would be necessary to reach open country. Leaving the stream behind me, it was not long before I came to a rude pathway; and although this seemed to follow the general direction of the creek, I determined to turn aside from the course I was taking and follow it. After walking for nearly a mile, sometimes seeing the waters of the stream, and sometimes entirely losing sight of them, I found the path making an abrupt turn, and in a few minutes was out of the woods.

The country before me was very much like that about Captain Jabe's residence. There were low rolling hills covered with coarse grass and ragged shrubbery, with here and there a cluster of trees. Not a sign of human habitation was in sight. Reaching the top of a small hill, I saw at my right, and not very far before me, a wide expanse of water. This I concluded must be the bay, although I had not expected to see it in this direction.

I went down the hill toward the shore. "If what I seek is in reality," I said to myself, "it will naturally love to live somewhere near the water." Near the beach I struck a path again, and this I followed, my mind greatly agitated by the thoughts of what I might discover, as well as by the fear that I might discover nothing.

After a walk of perhaps a quarter of an hour I stopped suddenly. I had discovered something. I looked about me, utterly amazed. I was on the little beach which the Sand Lady had assigned to Walkirk and me as a camping ground.

I sat down, vainly endeavoring to comprehend the situation. Out of the mass of wild suppositions and conjectures which crowded themselves into my mind there came but one conviction, and with that I was satisfied: Sylvia was here.

It mattered not that the Sand Lady had said that hers was the only house upon the island; it mattered not that Captain Jabe had said nothing of his neighbor; in truth, nothing mattered. One sister of the House of Martha had come to this place; why not another? What I had seen in the woods had been no fantasy. Sylvia was here.

XXXI

TAKING UP UNFINISHED WORK

My reasons for believing that Sylvia was on this island were circumstantial, it is true, but to me they were entirely conclusive, and the vehement desire of my soul was to hasten to the house and ask to see her. But I did not feel at all sure that this would be the right thing to do. The circumstances of this case were unusual. Sylvia was a sister of a religious house. It was not customary for gentlemen to call upon such sisters, and the lady who was the temporary custodian of this one might resent such an attempt.

It was, however, impossible for me entirely to restrain my impulses, and without knowing exactly what I intended to do I advanced toward the house. Very soon I saw its chimneys above the trees which partly surrounded it. Then, peeping under cover of a thicket, I went still nearer, so that, if there had been any people in the surrounding grounds, I could have seen them; but I saw no one, and I sat down on a log and waited. It shamed me to think that I was secretly watching a house, but despite the shame I continued to sit and watch.

There was the flutter of drapery on a little porch. My heart beat quickly, my eyes were fixed upon the spot; but nothing appeared except a maid who brought out some towels, which she hung on a bush to dry. Then again I watched and watched.

After a time four people came out from the house, two of them carrying colored parasols. I knew them instantly. There was the Middle-Aged Man of the Sea, and his friend the Shell Man; and there was the Sand Lady, and my enemy who called herself a Person. They went off toward the little pier. Sylvia was not with them, nor did she join them. They entered their boat and sailed away. They were going fishing, as was their custom. The fact that Sylvia was not with them, and that no one of them had stayed behind to keep her company, caused my heart to fall. In cases like mine, it takes very little to make the heart fall. The thought forced itself into my mind that perhaps, after all, I had seen a vision, and had been building theories on dreams.

Suddenly the shutter of an upper window opened, and I saw Sylvia!

It was truly Sylvia. She was dressed in white, not gray. Her hair was massed upon her head. There was no gray bonnet. She looked up at the sky, then at the trees, and withdrew.

My heart was beating as fast as it pleased. My face was glowing, and shame had been annihilated. I sat and watched. Presently a door opened, and Sylvia came out.

Now I rose to my feet. I must go to her. It might not be honorable to take her at this disadvantage, but there are moments when even honor must wait for a decision upon its case. However, there was no necessity for my going to Sylvia; she was coming to me.

As she walked directly to the spot where I stood, I saw Sylvia as I had seen her in my day-dreams,—a beautiful girl, dressed as a beautiful girl should dress in summer time. In one hand she carried a portfolio, in the other a little leathern case. As she came nearer, I saw that she was attired exactly as Mother Anastasia had been dressed when I met her here. Nearer she came, but still she did not see me. I was not now concealed, but her eyes seemed fixed upon the path in which she was walking.

When she was within a hundred feet of the thicket through which her path would lead, I advanced to meet her. I tried to appear cool and composed, but I am afraid my success was slight. As for Sylvia, she stopped abruptly, and dropped her leathern case. I think that at first she did not recognize me, and was on the point of screaming. Suddenly to come upon a man in the midst of these solitudes was indeed startling.

Quickly, however, I made myself known, and her expression of fright changed to one of amazement. I am happy to say that she took the hand I offered her, though she seemed to have no words with which to return my formal greeting. In cases like this, the one who amazes should not impose upon the amazed one the necessity of asking questions, but should begin immediately to explain the situation.

This I did. I told Sylvia how I had been accidentally brought to Captain Jabe's house, how I had strolled off in this direction, and how delighted I was to meet her here. In all this I was careful not to intimate that I had suspected her presence in this region. While speaking, I tried hard to think what I should say when she should remark, "Then you did not know I was here?" But she did not make this remark. She looked at me with a little puzzled wrinkle on her brow, and said, with a smile:—

"It is absolutely wonderful that you should be here, and I should not know it; and that I should be here, and you should not know it."

Ever since my meeting with Mother Anastasia it had been my purpose, as soon as I could find or make an opportunity, to declare to Sylvia my love for her. Apart from my passionate yearning in this direction, I felt that what I had done and attempted to say when I had parted from my secretary made it obligatory on me, as a man of honor, to say more, the moment I should be able to do so.

Now the opportunity had come; now we were alone together, and I was able to pour out before her the burning words which so often, in my hours of reverie, had crowded themselves upon my mind. The fates had favored me as I had had no reason to expect to be favored, but I took no advantage of this situation. I spoke no word of love. I cannot say that Sylvia's demeanor cooled my affection, but I can say that it cooled my desire for instantaneous expression of it. After her first moments of astonishment, her mind seemed entirely occupied with the practical unraveling of the problem of our meeting. I endeavored to make this appear a very commonplace affair. It was quite natural that my companion and I should come together to a region which he had before visited.

"Yes," said she, "I suppose all out-of-the-way things can be made commonplace, if one reasons long enough. As for me, of course it is quite natural that, needing a change from the House of Martha, I should come to my mother's island."

"Your mother!" I stammered.

"Yes," she answered. "Mrs. Raynor, who spends her summers in that house over there, is my mother. Her brother is here, too, and she has some friends with her. Mother Anastasia was away recently on a little jaunt, and when she came back she said that I looked tired and wan, and that I ought to go to my mother's for a fortnight. So I came. That was all simple enough, you see."

Simple enough! Could anything be more extraordinary, more enigmatical? I did not know what to say, what course to pursue; but in the midst of my surprise I had sense enough to see that, until I knew more, the less I said the better. Sylvia did not know that I had visited her mother's island and her mother's house. It is possible that she did not know that Mother Anastasia had been here. I must decide whether or not I would enlighten her on these points. My disposition was to be perfectly open and frank with her, and to be thus I must enlighten her. But I waited, and in answer to her statement merely told her how glad I was that she had a vacation and such a delightful place to come to. She did not immediately reply, but stood looking past me over the little vale beyond us.

"Well, here I am," she said presently, "and in a very different dress from that in which you used to see me; but for all that, I am still a sister of the House of Martha, and so"—

"So what?" I interrupted.

"I suppose I should go back to the house," she answered.

Now I began to warm up furiously.

"Don't think of it!" I exclaimed. "Now that I have met you, give me a few moments of your time. Let me see you as you are, free and undisguised, like other women, and not behind bars or in charge of old Sister Sarah."

"Wasn't she horrid?" said Sylvia.

"Indeed she was," I replied; "and now cannot you walk a little with me, or shall we sit down somewhere and have a talk?"

She shook her head. "Even if mother and the rest had not gone away in the boat, I could not do that, you know."

If she persisted in her determination to leave me, she should know my love in two minutes. But I tried further persuasion.

"We have spent hours together," I said; "why not let me make you a little visit now?"

Still she gently shook her head, and looked away. Suddenly she turned her face toward me. Her blue eyes sparkled, her lips parted, and there was a flush upon her temples.

"There is one thing I would dearly like," she said, "and I think I could stay for that. Will you finish the story of Tomaso and Lucilla?"

"I shall be overjoyed to do it!" I cried, in a state of exultation. "Come, let us sit over there in the shade, at the bottom of this hill, and I will tell you all the rest of that story."

Together we went down the little slope.

"You can't imagine," she said, "how I have longed to know how all that turned out. Over and over again I have finished the story for myself, but I never made a good ending to it. It was not a bit like hearing it from you."

I found her a seat on a low stone near the trunk of a tree, and I sat upon the ground near by, while my soul bounded up like a loosened balloon.

"Happy thought!" she exclaimed. "I came out here to write letters, not caring for fishing, especially in boats; how would you like me to write the rest of the story from your dictation?"

Like it! I could scarcely find words to tell her how I should like it.

"Very well, then," said she, opening her portfolio and taking out some sheets of paper. "My inkstand is in that case which you picked up; please give it to me, and let us begin. Now this is a very different affair. I am finishing the work which the House of Martha set me to do, and I assure you that I have been very much dissatisfied because I have been obliged to leave it unfinished. Please begin."

"I cannot remember at this moment," I said, "where we left off."

"I can tell you exactly," she answered, "just as well as if I had the manuscript before me. Tomaso held Lucilla by the hand; the cart was ready in which he was to travel to the sea-coast; they were calling him to hurry; and he was trying to look into her face, to see if he should tell her something that was in his heart. You had not yet said what it was that was in his heart. There was a chance, you know, that it might be that he felt it necessary for her good that the match should be broken off."

"How did you arrange this in the endings you made?" I asked. "Did you break off the match?"

"Don't let us bother about my endings," she said. "I want to know yours."

XXXII

TOMASO AND LUCILLA

On this happy morning, sitting in the shade with Sylvia, I should have much preferred to talk to her of herself and of myself than to dictate the story of the Sicilian lovers; but if I would keep her with me I must humor her, at least for a time, and so, as well as I could, I began my story.

The situation was, however, delightful: it was charming to sit and look at Sylvia, her portfolio in her lap, pen in hand, and her blue eyes turned toward me, anxiously waiting for me to speak; it was so enchanting that my mind could with difficulty be kept to the work in hand. But it would not do to keep Sylvia waiting. Her pen began to tap impatiently upon the paper, and I went on. We had written a page or two when she interrupted me.

"It seems to me," she said, "that if Tomaso really starts for Naples it will be a good while before we get to the end of the story. So far as I am concerned, you know, I would like the story just as long as you choose to make it; but we haven't very much time, and it would be a dreadful disappointment to me if I should have to go away before the story is ended."

"Why do you feel in a hurry?" I asked. "If we do not finish

this morning, cannot I come to you to-morrow?"

"Oh, no, indeed," she answered. "It's only by the merest chance, you know, that I am writing for you this morning, and I couldn't do it again. That would be impossible. In fact, I want to get through before the boat comes back. Not that I should mind mother, for she knows that I used to write for you, and I could easily explain how I came to be doing it now; and I should not care about Uncle or Mr. Heming; but as for Miss Laniston,—that is the lady who is visiting us,—I would not have her see me doing this for anything in the world. She hates the House of Martha, although she used to be one of its friends, and I know that she would like to see me leave the sisterhood. She ridicules us whenever she has a chance, and to see me here would be simply nuts to her."

"Is she a bad-tempered lady?" I asked. "Do you know her very well? Could you trust her in regard to anything important?"

"Oh, I know her well enough," said Sylvia. "She has always been a friend of the family. She is wonderfully well educated, and knows everything and has never married, and travels all about by herself, and is just as independent as she can be. She has very strong opinions about things, and doesn't hesitate to tell you them, no matter whether she thinks you like it or not. I have no doubt she is perfectly trustworthy and honorable, and all that; but if you knew her, I do not think you would like her, and you can easily see why I shouldn't want her to see me doing this. It would give her a chance for no end of sneers at the work of the sisters."

"Has she never said anything about your acting as my amanuensis?" I asked.

"No, indeed," replied Sylvia. "You may be sure she never heard of that, or she would have made fun enough of it."

It was impossible for me to allow this dear girl to remain longer in ignorance of the true state of affairs.

"Miss Raynor," I said,—how I longed to say "Sylvia"!—"I am ashamed that I have allowed you to remain as long as this under a misunderstanding, but in truth I did not understand the case myself. I did not know that the lady of this house was your mother, but I have met her, and have been kindly entertained by her. I did not know Miss Laniston's name, but I have also met her, and talked to her about you, and she knows you used to write for me, and I do not like her."

Sylvia answered not a word, but, as she sat and looked at me with wide-open eyes, I told her what had happened since my companion and I had landed at Racket Island. I omitted only my confidences to Mother Anastasia and Miss Laniston.

"Mother Anastasia has been here," repeated Sylvia, "and she never told me! That surpasses all. And mother never mentioned that you had been here, nor did any one." She gazed steadfastly upon the ground, a little pale, and presently she said, "I think I understand it, but it need not be discussed;" and, closing her portfolio, she rose to her feet.

"Sylvia," I exclaimed, springing up and stepping nearer to her, "it must be discussed! Ever since I parted from you at the window of your writing-room I have been yearning to speak to you. I do not understand the actions of your family and friends, but I do know that those actions were on your account and on mine. They knew I loved you. I have not in the least concealed the fact that I loved you, and I hoped, Sylvia, that you knew it."

She stood, her closed portfolio in one hand, her pen in the other, her eyes downcast, and her face grave and quiet. "I cannot say," she answered presently, "that I knew it, although sometimes I thought it was so, but other times I thought it was not so. I was almost sure of it when you took leave of me at the window, and tried to kiss my hand, and were just about to say something which I knew I ought not to stay and hear. It was when thinking about that morning, in fact,—and I thought about it a great deal,—that I became convinced I must act very promptly and earnestly in regard to my future life, and be true to the work I had undertaken to do; and for this reason it was that I solemnly vowed to devote the rest of my life to the House of Martha, to observe all its rules and do its work."

"Sylvia," I gasped, "you cannot keep this vow. When you made it you did not know I loved you. It cannot hold. It must be set aside."

She looked at me for a moment, and then her eyes again fell. "Do not speak in that way," she said; "it is not right. Of course I was not sure that you loved me, but I suspected it, and this was the very reason why I took my vow."

"It is plain, then," I exclaimed bitterly, "that you did not love me; otherwise you would never have done that!"

"Don't you think," said she, "that considering the sister-hood to which I belong, we have already talked too much about that?"

If she had exhibited the least emotion, I think I should have burst out into supplications that she would take the advice of her Mother Superior; that she would listen to her friends; that she would do anything, in fact, which would cause her to reconsider this step, which condemned me to misery and her to a life for which she was totally unfitted,—a career in her case of such sad misuse of every attribute of mind and body that it wrung my heart to think of it. But she stood so quiet, so determined, and with an air of such gentle firmness that words seemed useless. In truth, they would not come to me. She opened her portfolio.

"I will give you these sheets that I have written," she said; "by right they belong to you. I am sorry the story was interrupted, for I very much want to hear the end of it, and now I never shall."

I caught at a straw. "Sylvia," I cried, "let us sit down and finish the story! We can surely do that. Come, it is all ready in my mind. I will dictate rapidly."

She shook her head. "Hardly," she answered, "after what has been said. Here are your pages."

I took the pages she handed me, because she had written them.

"Sylvia," I exclaimed, "I shall finish that story, and you shall hear it! This I vow."

"I am going now," she responded. "Good-by."

"Sylvia," I cried, quickly stepping after her as she moved away, "will you not say more than that? Will you not even give me your hand?"

"I will do that," she replied, stopping, "if you will promise not to kiss it."

I took her hand, and held it a few moments without a word. Then she gently withdrew it.

"Good-by again," she said, "I don't want you to forget me;

but when you think of me, always think of me as a sister of the House of Martha."

As I stood looking after her, she rapidly walked toward the house, and I groaned while thinking I had not told her that if she ever thought of me she must remember I loved her, and would love her to the end of my life. But in a moment I was glad that I had not said this; after her words to me it would have been unmanly, and, besides, I knew she knew it.

When I lost sight of her in the grove by the house, I turned and picked up the pages of the story of Tomaso and Lucilla, which I had dropped. In doing so I saw her inkstand, with its open case near by it, on the ground by the stone on which she had been sitting. I put the inkstand in its case, closed it, and stood for some minutes holding it and thinking; but I did not carry it away with me as a memento. Drawing down a branch of the tree, I hung the little case securely by its handles to a twig, where it would be in full view of any one walking that way.

XXXIII

THE DISTANT TOPSAIL

I found Walkirk still fishing near the place where I had left him.

"I was beginning to be surprised at your long absence," he said, "and was thinking of going to look for you. Have you had good luck?"

This was a hard question to answer. I smiled grimly. "I have not been fishing," I answered. "I have been dictating my story to my nun."

The rod dropped from the relaxed fingers of my under-study, and he stood blankly staring at me, and waiting for an explanation. I gave it.

Depressed as I was, I could not help feeling interested in the variety of expressions which passed over Walkirk's face, as I related what had happened since I had seen him. When I told him how near we were to our old camp on the Sand Lady's island, he was simply amazed; his astonishment, when he heard of the appearance of Sylvia on the scene, was almost overpowered by his amusement, as I related how she and I had continued the story of Tomaso and Lucilla, in the shade of the tree. But when I informed him of Sylvia's determination to devote her life to the work of the House of Martha, without regard to what I told her of my love, he was greatly moved, and I am sure sincerely grieved.

"This is too bad, too bad," he said. "I did not expect it."

"Miss Raynor is young," I answered, "but the strength and integrity of her soul are greater, and her devotion to what she believes her duty is stronger, than I supposed. Her character is marked by a simple sincerity and a noble dignity which I have never seen surpassed. I think that she positively dislikes the life of the sisterhood, but, having devoted herself to it, she will stand firmly by her resolutions and her promise no matter what happens. As regards myself, I do not suppose that her knowledge of my existence has any influence on her, one way or the other. I may have interested and amused her, but that is all. If I had finished the Italian love-story I had been telling her, I think she would have been satisfied never to see me again."

Walkirk shook his head. "I do not believe that," he said; "her determination to rivet the bonds which hold her to her sisterhood shows that she was afraid of her interest in you; and if it gave her reason to fear, it gives you reason to hope."

"Put that in the past tense, please," I replied; "whatever it may have given, it gives nothing now. To hope would be absurd."

"Mr. Vanderley," exclaimed Walkirk, "I would not give up in that way. I am certain, from what I know, that Miss Raynor's interest in you is plain not only to herself, but to her family and friends; and I tell you, sir, that sort of interest cannot be extinguished by promises and resolutions. If I were you, I would keep up the fight. She is not yet a vowed sister."

"Walkirk," said I, offering him my hand; "you are a good fellow, and, although I cannot believe what you say, I thank you for saying it."

It was now long past noon, and we were both ready for the luncheon which we had brought with us. Walkirk opened the basket, and as he arranged its contents on the broad napkin, which he spread upon the grass, he ruminated.

"I think," he remarked, as we were eating, "that I begin to understand the situation. At first I could not reconcile the facts with the Sand Lady's statement that no one lived on her island but her family, but now I see that this creek must make an island of her domain; and so it is that, although Captain Jabe is her neighbor, her statement is entirely correct."

Having finished our meal, I lighted my pipe and sat down under a tree, while Walkirk, with his rod, wandered away along the bank of the stream. After a while he returned, and proposed that we try fishing near the eastern outlet of the creek, where, as the tide was coming in, we might find better sport.

"That will be a very good thing for you to do," said I, "but I shall not fish. I am going to Mrs. Raynor's house."

"Where?" exclaimed Walkirk.

"I am going to speak to Mrs. Raynor," I answered, "whom I have known only as the Sand Lady, but whom I must now know as Sylvia's mother. I have determined to act boldly and openly in this matter. I have made suit to Mrs. Raynor's daughter. I have told other people of the state of my affections, and I think I should lose no time, having now the opportunity, in conferring with Mrs. Raynor herself."

Walkirk's face was troubled.

"You do not approve of that?" I asked.

"Since you ask me," he answered, "I must say that I do not think it a wise thing to do. If I properly understand Miss Raynor's character, her mother knows that you are here; and if she is willing to have you visit her, under the circumstances, she will make a sign. In fact, I now think that she will make some sort of sign, by which you can see how the land lies. Perhaps Mrs. Raynor is on your side; but I am afraid that if you should visit the house where Miss Raynor is, it would set her mother against you. I imagine she is a woman who would not like that sort of thing."

"Walkirk," said I, "your reasoning is very good; but this is not a time to reason,—it is a time to act; and I am going to see Mrs. Raynor this day."

"I hope it may all turn out well," he replied, and walked away gravely.

I did not start immediately for the Sand Lady's house. For a long time I sat and thought upon the subject of the approaching interview, planning and considering how I should plead my case, and what I should answer, and how I should overcome the difficulties which would probably be pointed out to me.

At last, like many another man when in a similar predicament, I concluded to let circumstances shape my plan of action, and set forth for Mrs. Raynor's house. The walk was a long one, but I turned in order to pass under the tree where I had begun to dictate to Sylvia; and glad I was that I did so, for to the twig on which I had hung the case containing her inkstand there was now attached a half sheet of note paper. I ran to the tree, eagerly seized the paper, and read these few words that were written on it:—

"Thank you very much for taking such good care of my little case."

"Now, then," said I to myself, proudly gazing at these lines, "this is only a small thing, but the girl who would write it, and who would expect me to read it, must be interested in me. She believes that I would not fail to come here again; therefore she believes in me. That is a great point."

For a moment I felt tempted to write something in reply, and hang it on the tree twig. But I refrained; what I would write to Sylvia must be read by no one but herself. That tree was in a very conspicuous position, and my tamest words to her must not hang upon it. I carefully folded the paper and put it in my pocket, and then, greatly encouraged, walked rapidly to the house.

On the front piazza I found an elderly woman, with a broom. She knew me, for she had frequently seen me during the time that I was encamped upon the island. She was now greatly surprised at my appearance on the scene.

"Why, sir," she exclaimed, without waiting for me to speak, "have you come back to your camp? It is too bad."

I did not like this salutation. But, making no answer to it, I asked quickly, "Can I see Mrs. Raynor?"

"No, indeed," said she; "they've gone, every one of them, and not an hour ago. What a pity they did not know you were here!"

"Gone!" I cried. "Where?"

"They've gone off in their yacht for a cruise," returned the woman. "The vessel has been at Brimley for more than a week, being repaired, and she got back this morning; and as she was all ready to sail, they just made up their minds that they'd go off in her, for one of their little voyages they are so fond of; and off they went, in less than two hours."

"How long do they expect to be gone?" I asked.

"Mrs. Raynor told me they would be away probably for a week or two," the woman answered, "and she would stop somewhere and telegraph to me when she was coming back. Of course there isn't any telegraph to this island, but when messages come to Brimley they send them over in a boat."

Having determined to speak to Mrs. Raynor, and having set out to do so, this undertaking appeared to me the most important thing in the world, and one in which I must press forward, without regard to obstacles of any kind.

"Are they going to any particular place?" I said. "Are they going to stop anywhere?"

"There is only one place that I know of," she answered, "and that's Sanpritchit, over on the mainland. They expect to stop there to get provisions for the cruise, for there was but little here that they could take with them. They wanted to get there before dark, and I don't doubt but that, with this wind, they'll do it. If you'll step to this end of the piazza, sir, perhaps you can see their topsail. I saw it just before you came, as they were beginning to make the long tack."

"Yes, there it is," she continued, when we reached the place referred to, from which a vast stretch of the bay could be seen, "but not so much of it as I saw just now."

"Their topsail!" I ejaculated.

"Yes, sir," she said. "You can't see their mainsail, because they are so far away, and it's behind the water, in a manner."

I stood silent for a few minutes, gazing at the little ship. Suddenly a thought struck me. "Do you think they will sail on Sunday?" I asked.

"No, sir," she replied; "Mrs. Raynor never sails on Sunday. And that's why I wondered, after they'd gone, why they'd started off on a Saturday. They will have to lay up at Sanpritchit all day to-morrow; and it seems to me it would have been a great deal pleasanter for them to stay here Sunday, and to have started on Monday. There's no church at Sanpritchit, or anything for them to do, so far as I know, unless Miss Raynor reads sermons to them, which she never did here, though she's a religious sister, which perhaps you didn't know, sir."

"Sanpritchit over Sunday," I repeated to myself.

"It's the greatest pity," said the woman, "that they didn't know you and the other gentleman—that is, if he is with you—were coming back to-day, for I am sure they would have been glad to take you with them. There's room enough on that yacht, and will be more; for Mr. Heming, the gentleman that collects shells, is not coming back with them. They are to put him off somewhere, and he is going home. I have an idea, though I wasn't told so, that Miss Raynor is not coming back with the rest. She brought very little baggage with her, but she took a lot of things on board the yacht, and that looks as if she wasn't coming back. But, bless me, they went off in such a hurry I didn't have time to ask questions."

I now turned to go, but the woman obliged me to inform her that I had not come to camp on the island, and that I was staying with Captain Jabe.

"When they go off in this way," she said, "they take the maids, and leave me and my husband in charge; and if you should fancy to come here and camp again, I know that Mrs. Raynor would wish me to make things as comfortable for you as I can, which, too, I'll be very glad to do."

I thanked her, and went away. "This good woman," said I to myself, "is the person who would have read my message to Sylvia, had I been foolish enough to hang one to the twig of the tree."

XXXIV

THE CENTRAL HOTEL

Captain Jabez did not return until late that Saturday evening; but as soon as he set foot on shore I went to him and asked him if he could, in any way, get us to Sanpritchit that night, offering to pay him liberally for the service.

"I've got a sailboat," said he, "and ye'd be right welcome to it if it was here; but it ain't here. I lent it to Captain Neal, of Brimley, having no present use for it, and he won't bring it back till next week some time. There's a dory here, to be sure; but Sanpritchit's twenty-five miles away, and that's too far to go in a dory, especially at night. What's your hurry?"

"I have very important business in Sanpritchit," I answered, "and if it is possible I must go there to-night."

"Sanpritchit's a queer place to have business in," said Captain Jabe; "and it's a pity ye didn't think of it this mornin', when ye might have gone with me and took the train to Barley, and there's a stage from there to Sanpritchit."

"Captain Jabez," said I, "as there seems to be no other way for me to do this thing, I will pay you whatever you may think the service worth, if you will take me to Sanpritchit in your grocery boat, and start immediately. It will be slow work traveling, I know, but I think we can surely get there before morning."

The grocer-captain looked at me for a moment, with his eyes half shut; then he set down on the pier a basket which had been hanging on his arm, and, putting both hands in his pockets, stared steadfastly at me.

"Do you know," he remarked presently, "that that 'ere proposition of yours puts me in mind of a story I heard of a California man and a New York man. The California man had come East to spend the winter, and the New York man was a business acquaintance o' his. The California man called at the New York man's office before business hours; and when he found the New York man hadn't come down town yet, he went up town to see him at his house. It was a mighty fine house, and the New York man, being proud of it, took the California man all over it. 'Look here,' said the California man, 'what will you take for this house, furniture and all, just as it stands?' 'I'll take a hundred and twenty thousand dollars,' said the New York man. 'Does that include all the odds and ends,' asked the California man,— 'old magazines, umbrellas, needles and pins, empty bottles, photographs, candlesticks, Japanese fans, coal ashes, and all that kind of thing, that make a house feel like a home? My family's comin' on from California with nothin' but their clothes, and I want a house they can go right into and feel at home, even to the cold victuals for a beggar, if one happens to come along.' 'If I throw in the odds and ends, it will be one hundred and twenty-five thousand,' said the New York man. 'That's all right,' said the California man, 'and my family will arrive, with their clothes, on the train that gets here at 6.20 this afternoon; so if your family can get out of the house before that time, I'm ready to pay the money, cash down.' 'All right,' said the New York man, 'I'll see that they do it.' And at ten minutes after six the New York family went out with their clothes to a hotel, and at twenty minutes of seven the California family came to the house with their clothes, and found everything all ready for 'em, the servants havin' agreed to stay at California wages.

"Now, then," continued Captain Jabez, "I don't want to hurt nobody's feelin's, and I wouldn't say one word that would make the smallest infant think less of itself than it did afore I spoke, but it does strike me that that there proposition of yours is a good deal like the California man's offer to the New York man."

"Well," said I, "that turned out very well. Each got what he wanted."

"Yes," replied Captain Jabez, "but this ain't New York city. No, sir, not by a long shot. I am just as willin' to accommodate a fellow-man, or a fellow-woman, for that matter, as any reasonable person is; but if the President of the United States, and Queen Victoria, and the prophet Isaiah was to come to me of a Saturday night, after I'd just got home from a week's work, and ask me to start straight off and take them to Sanpritchit, I'd tell 'em that I'd be glad to oblige 'em, but it couldn't be done: and that's what I say to ye, sir,—neither more nor less." And with this he picked up his basket and went into the house.

I was not discouraged, however, and when the captain came out I proposed to him that he should take me to Sanpritchit the next day.

"No, sir," said he. "I never have sailed my grocery boat on Sunday, and I don't feel like beginnin'."

I walked away, but shortly afterward joined him on board his vessel, which he was just about to leave for the night.

"Captain," I asked, "when does Sunday end in this part of the country?"

"Well, strictly speaking, it's supposed to end at sunset, or commonly at six o'clock."

"Very well," said I; "if you will start with me for Sanpritchit at six o'clock to-morrow evening, I will pay you your price."

I made this offer in the belief that, with ordinary good fortune, we could reach our destination before the Raynor yacht weighed anchor on Monday morning.

Captain Jabez considered the matter. "I am going to Sanpritchit on Monday, any way," said he; "and if you're in such a hurry to be there the first thing in the morning, I'd just as lieve sail to-morrow evening at six o'clock as not."

It was not much after the hour at which some people in that part of the country, when they have a reason for it, still believe that Sunday comes to an end, that the grocery boat left her pier with Captain Jabez, Abner, Walkirk, and me on board. There was nothing at all exhilarating in this expedition. I wanted to go rapidly, and I knew we should go slowly. I had passed a dull day, waiting for the time to start, and, to avoid thinking of the slow progress we should make, I soon turned in.

I woke very early, and went on deck. I do not know that I can remember a more disagreeable morning. It was day, but the sun was not up; it was not cloudy, but there was a filmy uncertainty about the sky that was more unpleasant than the clouds. The air was cold, raw, and oppressive. There was no one on deck but Abner, and he was at the wheel, which, on account of the grocery store occupying so large a portion of the after part of the vessel, was placed well forward. Only a jib and mainsail were set, and as I came on deck these were fluttering and sagging, as Abner carefully brought the vessel round. Now I saw that we were floating slowly toward the end of a long pier, and that we were going to land.

As I leaned over the side of the vessel, I did not wonder that Captain Jabez thought Sanpritchit was not much of a place to do business in. There were few houses, perhaps a dozen, scattered here and there along a low shore, which rose, at one end of the place, into a little bluff, behind which I saw a mast or two. On the pier was a solitary man, and he was the only living being in sight. It was that dreary time before breakfast, when everything that seems cheerless is more cheerless, everything that is sad more sad, everything that is discouraging more discouraging, and which right-minded persons who are able to do so spend in bed.

Gradually the vessel approached the pier, and Abner, to whom I had not yet spoken, for I did not feel in the least like talking, left the wheel, and, as soon as he was near enough, threw a small line to the man on the pier, who caught it, pulling ashore a cable with a loop in the end, threw the latter over a post, and in a few minutes the grocery boat was moored. The man came on board, and he and Abner went below.

It was too early to go on shore, for nothing could be done at that bleak, unearthly hour; but I was in that state of nervous disquietude when any change is a relief, and I stepped ashore. I was glad to put my feet upon the pier. Now I felt that I was my own master. It was too soon to go on board the yacht, but I could regulate my movements as I pleased, and was very willing to be alone during the hour or two in which I must remain inactive.

I walked over the loose and warped planks of the pier, the dull water rippling and flopping about the timbers beneath me, inhaling that faint smell of the quiet water and soaked logs, which is always a little dispiriting to me even at less dispiriting hours. The crowing of one or two cocks made me understand how dreadfully still everything was. The stillness of the very early morning is quite different from that of the night. During the latter people are asleep, and may be presumed to be happy. In the former they are about to wake up and be miserable. That, at least, was my notion, as I walked into the little village.

Not a creature did I see; not a sound did I hear except my own footsteps. Presently I saw a cat run around the corner of a house, and this was a relief. I walked on past a wide space, in which there were no houses, when I came to a small, irregularly built white house, in front of which hung a sign bearing the inscription "Central Hotel." If anything could have made me more disgusted with the world than I then was, it was this sign. If the name of this miserable little country tavern had been anything suitable to itself and the place, if it had been called The Plough and Harrow, The Gray Horse, or even The Blue Devil, I think I should have been glad to see it. A village inn might have been a point of interest to me, but Central Hotel in this mournful settlement of small farmers and fishermen,—it was ridiculous!

However, the door of the house was open, and inside was a man sweeping the sanded floor. When he saw me, he stopped his work and stared at me.

"Good-mornin'," he said. "Don't often see strangers here so airly. Did ye come on the grocery boat? I saw her puttin' in. Do ye want a room? Time for a good nap before breakfast."

I answered that I did not want a room, but the remark about breakfast made me feel that I should like a cup of coffee, and perhaps I might get it here. It might have been a more natural thing to go back to the boat and ask Abner to make me the coffee, but I did not want to go back to the

Frank R. Stockton

boat. I did not want to wake Walkirk. I did not want to have him with me on shore. I did not want to have him talk to me. My present intention was to go to the yacht as soon as it was reasonable to suppose that its passengers were awake, to see Mrs. Raynor, and say to her what I had to say. I did not feel in the proper spirit for this; but, in the spirit in which I found myself, the less I was trammeled by advice, by suggestions of prudence, and all that sort of thing, the better it would be for me. So I was very glad that my under-study was asleep on the grocery boat, and hoped that he would remain in that condition until I had had my talk with Sylvia's mother.

I put my request to the man and he smiled. "Ye can't get no coffee," he said, "until breakfast time, and that's pretty nigh two hours off. There is people in the place that have breakfast earlier than we do, but we keep boarders, ye know. We've only got Captain Fluke now, but generally have more; and ye couldn't ask a man like Captain Fluke to git up to his breakfast before half past seven. Then ye don't want yer baggage sent fur? Perhaps ye've come ter see friends, an' it's a little airly ter drop in on 'em? Come in, any way, and take a seat."

I accepted the invitation. Sitting indoors might possibly be less dreary than walking out-of-doors.

"Now I tell ye what ye ought to do," continued the man. "Ye ought to take a nip of whiskey with some bitters in it. It's always kinder damp airly in the mornin', and ye must feel it more, bein' in a strange place. I've always thought a strange place was damper, airly in the mornin', than a place ye're used ter; and there's nothin' like whiskey with a little bitters to get out dampness."

I declined to partake of any Central Hotel whiskey, adding that the one refreshment I now needed was a cup of coffee.

"But there's no fire in the kitchen," said he, "and there won't be for ever so long. That's how whiskey comes in so handy; don't have to have no fire. Ye jes' pour it out and drink it, and there's the end of it."

"Not always," I remarked.

"Ye're right there," said he, with a smile. "A good deal depends on how much ye pour." He turned away, but stopped suddenly. "Look here," said he; "if ye say so, I'll make ye a cup of coffee. I've got an alcohol lamp up there that I can boil water with in no time. I'm out of alcohol, but, if you'll pay for it, I'll fill the lamp with whiskey; that'll burn just as well."

I willingly agreed to his proposition, and the man immediately disappeared into the back part of the house.

I sat and looked about the little bar-room, in which there was absolutely nothing of the quaint interest which one associates with a country inn. It was a bare, cold, hard, sandy, dirty room; its air tainted with the stale odors of whiskey, sugar, and wood still wet from its morning mopping. In less than fifteen minutes the man placed before me a cup of coffee and some soda biscuit. The coffee was not very good, but it was hot, and when I had finished it I felt like another man.

"There now," cried the bar-keeper, looking at me with great satisfaction, "don't that take the dampness out of ye? I tell ye there's no such stiffener in the airly mornin' as whiskey; and if ye don't use it in one way, ye can in another."

Truly the world seemed warmer and more cheerful; the sun was brighter. Perhaps now it was not too early to go on board the yacht. At any rate, I would go near where she lay, and judge for myself. I made inquiries of the innkeeper in regard to Mrs. Raynor's yacht.

"Yacht!" he said. "There's no yacht here."

"You must be mistaken!" I cried. "A yacht belonging to Mrs. Raynor sailed for Sanpritchit on Saturday, and it was not to leave here until this morning."

"Sanpritchit!" he exclaimed. "This is not Sanpritchit."

"What do you mean?" I asked in amazement. "That boat was bound direct for Sanpritchit."

"Captain Jabe's boat?" said the man. "Yes, and so she is. She sails fur Sanpritchit every Monday mornin', and generally stops here when she's got any freight ter leave fur the store, though I never knowed her ter come so airly in the mornin'."

"My conscience!" I exclaimed. "I must get on board of her."

"Aboard of her!" said he. "She's been gone more 'n half an hour. She don't often stop here more 'n ten minutes, if she's got the tide with her, which she had this mornin', strong."

XXXV

MONEY MAKES THE MARE GO

I rushed out of the Central Hotel, and looked over the water, but I could see nothing of the grocery boat: she had disappeared beyond the bluff, behind which I had stupidly taken it for granted Mrs. Raynor's yacht was lying.

"Oh, she's clean gone," said the bar-keeper, who had joined me, "an' she's not likely to come back ag'in' wind an' tide. They must have thought you was asleep in your berth."

This was undoubtedly the truth, for there was no reason to suppose that any one on the boat knew I had gone on shore.

"Where can I get a boat to follow them?" I cried.

"Can't say exactly," said the man. "We've got a big catboat, but she's on the stocks gettin' a new stern post put in. You can see her mast stickin' up over the bluff, there. I don't think there's any other sailboat in the place jes' now, and Captain Fluke's havin' his fresh painted. I told him it was a bad time o' the year to do it in; but he's Captain Fluke, and that's all there's to say about it. There's rowboats; but Sanpritchit's eight miles from here, and it's a putty long pull there and back, and I don't know anybody here who'd care to take it. If ye want to go to Sanpritchit, ye ought to go in a wagon. That's lots the easiest way."

"Where can I get a horse and vehicle?" I asked quickly, so much enraged with myself that I was glad to have some one to direct my movements.

"That's more 'n I know, jes' this minute," said the man; "but if ye'll step inside and sit down, I'll go and ask 'em at the store what they can do fur ye. If it ain't open yet, I'll know where ter find 'em. If anybody comes along for a mornin' drink, jes' tell 'em to wait a minute, and I'll be back."

In about fifteen or twenty minutes the bar-keeper returned, and announced that I could not hire the horse at the store, for one of his hind shoes was off, and they wanted to use him any way. He had asked two or three other people, also, for the village was waking up by this time, but none of them could let me have a horse.

"But I'll tell ye what ye can do," said the man, "if ye choose to wait here a little while. The boss of this house went over to Stipbitts last night to see his mother, and I expect him back putty soon, and I guess he'll let ye have his hoss. Ye see the people about here ain't used to hiring hosses, and we is. People as keeps hotels is expected to do it."

There was nothing for me to do but to wait for the return of the landlord of Central Hotel; and for very nearly an hour I walked up and down the main street of that wretched little hamlet, the name of which I neither heard nor asked, cursing my own stupidity and the incapacity of the waterside rustic.

When the "boss" arrived he was willing to let me have his mare and his buckboard, and a boy to drive me; but the animal must be fed first, and of course I would not start off without my breakfast. As I had to wait, and the morning meal was almost ready, I partook of it; but the mare gave a great deal more time to her breakfast than I gave to mine. I hurried the preparations as much as I could, and shortly after eight o'clock we started. My little expedition had the features of a useless piece of trouble, but I had carefully considered the affair, and concluded that I had a good chance of success. Almost any horse could take me eight miles in an hour and a half, even with poor roads, and, from what I knew of the industrial methods of this part of the country, I did not believe that the necessary supplies would be put on the yacht before half past nine: therefore, I did not allow myself to doubt that I should reach Sanpritchit in time to see Mrs. Raynor.

The mare was a very deliberate traveler, and the boy who sat beside me was an easily satisfied driver.

"We must go faster than this," said I, after we had reached what appeared to be a highroad, "or I shall not get to Sanpritchit in time to attend to my business there."

"Ye can't drive a hoss too fast when ye first set out," answered the boy. "Ye'll hurt a hoss if ye do that. After a little while she'll warm up, and then she'll go better. Oh, she can go if she's a mind ter. She's a rattler when she really gets goin'."

"I don't want her to rattle," said I; "but what is her ordinary rate of travel,—how many miles an hour, do you suppose?"

"Don't know as I ever counted," the boy said. "Some miles she goes faster, and some miles she goes slower. A good deal depends on whether it's uphill or downhill."

"Well," said I, taking out my watch, "we must keep her up to six miles an hour, at least, and then we shall do the eight miles by half past nine, with something to spare."

"Eight miles!" repeated the boy. "Eight miles to where?"

"Sanpritchit," replied I. "That's what they told me."

"Oh, that's by water," said the driver; "but this road's got to go around the end of the bay, and after that 'way round the top of the big marsh, and that makes it a good seventeen miles to Sanpritchit. Half past nine! Why, the boss told me, if I didn't get there before twelve, I must stop somewhere and water the mare and give her some oats. I've got a bag of them back there."

I sat dumb. Of course, with this conveyance, and seventeen miles between me and Sanpritchit, it was absurd to suppose that I could get there before the yacht sailed. It was ridiculous to go an inch farther on such a tedious and useless journey.

"Boy," I asked, "where is the nearest railroad station?"

"Stipbitts," said he.

"How far?"

"Five miles."

"Take me there," I said.

The boy looked at me in surprise. "I can't do that. I was told to take you to Sanpritchit: that's where I'm goin', and I'm goin' to bring back a box belongin' to Captain Fluke. That's what I 'm goin' to do."

"I cannot get there in time," I said. "I didn't know it was so far. Take me to Stipbitts, and I will give you a dollar; then you can go along and attend to Captain Fluke's box. I have already paid for the drive to Sanpritchit."

"Have you got as much as a dollar and a half about you?" asked the boy.

I replied that I had.

"All right," said he; "give me that, and I'll take you to Stipbitts."

The bargain was struck, I was taken to Stipbitts, and an hour afterward I was on my way to my home at Arden.

There was one very satisfactory feature about this course of action: it was plain and simple, and needed no planning. To attempt to follow the yacht would be useless. To wait anywhere for Walkirk would be equally so. He would be more apt to find me at my home than anywhere else. It was his business to find me, and there was no doubt that he would do it. I did not like to defer my intended interview with Mrs. Raynor, but it could not be helped. And as for Sylvia, if she had resolved to return to the House of Martha, the best place for me was the neighborhood of that institution.

XXXVI

IN THE SHADE OF THE OAK

I found my home at Arden very empty and dreary. The servants did not expect me, my grandmother had not returned, and the absence of Walkirk added much to my dissatisfaction with the premises.

I was never a man who could sit down and wait for things to happen, and I felt now that it was absolutely necessary that I should do something, that I should talk to somebody; and accordingly, on the morning after my arrival, I determined to walk over to the House of Martha and talk to Mother Anastasia. For a man to consult with the Mother Superior of a religious institution about his love affairs was certainly an uncommon proceeding, with very prominent features of inappropriateness; but this did not deter me, for, apart from the fact that there was no one else to talk to, I considered that Mother Anastasia owed me some advice and explanation, and without hesitation I went to ask for it.

When I reached the House of Martha, and made known my desire to speak to the head of the institution, I was ushered into a room which was barer and harder than I had supposed, from Walkirk's description of it. It did not even contain the religious pictures or the crucifixes which would have relieved the blankness of the walls in a Roman Catholic establishment of the kind.

As I stood gazing about me, with a feeling of indignation that such a place as this should ever have been the home of such a woman as Sylvia, a door opened, and Mother Anastasia entered.

Her appearance shocked me. I had in my mind the figure of a woman with whom I had talked,—a woman glowing with the warmth of a rich beauty, draped in graceful folds of white, with a broad hat shadowing her face, and a bunch of wild flowers in her belt. Here was a tall woman clothed in solemn gray, her face pale, her eyes fixed upon the ground; but it was Mother Anastasia; it was the woman who had talked to me of Sylvia, who had promised to help me with Sylvia.

Still gazing on the floor, with her hands folded before her, she asked me what I wished. At first I could not answer her. It seemed impossible to open my heart to a woman such as this one. But if I said anything, I must say it without hesitation, and so I began.

"Of course," I said, "I have come to see you about Sylvia Raynor. I am in much trouble regarding her. You promised to aid me, and I have come to ask for the fulfillment of that promise. My love for that girl grows stronger day by day, hour by hour, and I have been thwarted, mystified, and I may say deceived. I have come"—

"She of whom you speak," interrupted Mother Anastasia, "is not to be discussed in that way. She has declared her intention to unite herself permanently with our sisterhood, and to devote her life to our work. She can have nothing more to do with you, nor you with her."

"That will not do at all," I said excitedly. "When I last saw you, you did not talk like that, and the opinions you expressed at that time are just as good now as they were then. I want to go over this matter with you. There are things that I have a right to know."

A little frown appeared upon her brow. "This conversation must cease," she said; "the subjects you wish to discuss are forbidden to our sisterhood. You must mention them no more."

I tried hard to restrain myself and speak quietly. "Madam"—said I.

"You must not call me 'madam,'" she broke in. "I am the Mother Superior of this house."

"I understand that," I continued, "and I understand your feeling of duty. But you have other duties besides those you owe to your sisterhood. You made me a promise, which I accepted with an honest and confiding heart. If you cannot do what you promised, you owe it to me to explain why you cannot do it. I do not know what has happened to change your views and her views, and, so far as I am concerned, the whole world. You can set me right; you can explain everything to me."

The frown disappeared, and her face seemed paler. "It is absolutely impossible to discuss anything of the sort in this house. I must insist"—

I did not permit her to finish her sentence. "Very well, then," I exclaimed, "if you cannot talk to me here, talk to me somewhere else. When you desire it, you go outside of these walls, and you speak freely and fully. You have so spoken with me; and because you have done so, it is absolutely necessary that you do it again. Your own heart, your conscience, must tell you that after what you have said to me, and after what I have said to you, it is unjust, to say no more, to leave me in this state of cruel mystification; not to tell me why you have set aside your promise to me, or even to tell me, when we talked together of Sylvia, that we were then at the home of Sylvia's mother."

For the first time she looked at me, straight in my eyes, as a true woman would naturally look at a man who was speaking strongly to her. I think I made her forget, for a few moments at least, that she was a Mother Superior. Then her eyes fell again, and she stood silent.

"Perhaps," she said presently, and speaking slowly, "I ought to explain these things to you. It is a great mistake, as I now see, that I ever said anything to you on the subject; but things were different then, and I did not know that I was doing wrong. Still, if you rely on me to set you right, you shall be set right. I see that this is quite as necessary from other points of view as from your own. I cannot speak with you to-day, but to-morrow, about this time, I shall be on the road to Maple Ridge, where I am going to visit a sick woman."

"I shall join you on the road," I answered, and took my leave.

For the rest of the day I thought of little but the promised interview on the morrow. To this I looked forward with the greatest interest, but also with the greatest anxiety. I feared that Mother Anastasia would prove to me that I must give up all thoughts of Sylvia. In fact, if Sylvia had resolved to devote herself to the service of the House of Martha,—and she had told me herself that she had so resolved,—I was quite sure she would do so. Then what was there for Mother Anastasia to say, or me to do? The case was settled. Sylvia Raynor must be nothing to me.

I greatly wished for Walkirk. I knew he would encourage me, in spite of the obvious blackness of the situation. It was impossible for me to encourage myself. But, however black my fate might be, I longed to know why it had been made black and all about it, and so waited with a savage impatience for the morning and Mother Anastasia.

Immediately after breakfast, the next day, I was on the Maple Ridge road, strolling from our village toward the top of a hill a mile or more away, whence I could see the rest of the road, as it wound through the lonely country, and at last lost itself in the woods. Back again to Arden I came, and had covered the distance between the village and the hilltop five times, when, turning and coming down the hill, I saw, far away, the figure of a woman walking.

I knew it was Mother Anastasia, but I did not hasten to meet her. In fact, I thought the further she was from the village, when our interview took place, the more likely she would be to make it long enough to be satisfactory. I came slowly down the hill, and, reaching a place where a great oak-tree shaded the road, I waited.

She came on quickly, her gray dress appearing heavier and more sombre against the sun-lighted grass and foliage than it had appeared in the dreary room of the House of Martha. As she approached the tree I advanced to meet her.

"You made me come too far," she said reproachfully, as soon as we were near each other. "The lane which leads to the house I came to visit is a quarter of a mile behind me."

"I am sorry," I replied, "that I have made you walk any farther than necessary on such a warm morning, but I did not know that you intended to turn from this road. Let us step into the shade of this tree; we can talk more comfortably there."

She looked at the tree, but did not move. "What I have to say," she remarked, "can be said here; it will not take long."

"You must not stand in the sun," I replied; "you are already heated. Come into the shade," and, without waiting her answer, I walked toward the tree; she followed me.

"Now, then," said I, "here is a great stone conveniently placed, upon which we can sit and rest while we talk."

She fixed her large eyes upon me with a certain surprise. "Truly, you have no regard for conventionalities. It is sufficiently out of the way for a sister of the House of Martha to meet a gentleman in this manner, but to sit with him under a tree would be ridiculously absurd, to say the least of it."

"It does not strike me in that light," I said. "You are tired and warm, and must sit down. You came here on my account, and I regard you, in a manner, as a guest."

She smiled, and looked at the rock which I had pointed out. It was a flat one, about three feet long, and it seemed as if it had been put there on purpose to serve for a seat.

"I am tired," she said, and sat down upon it. As she did so, she gave a look about her, and at the same time made a movement with her right hand, which I often before had noticed in women. It was the involuntary expression of the female soul, longing for a fan. A fan, however, made up no part of the paraphernalia of a sister of the House of Martha.

"Allow me," I said, and, taking off my straw hat, I gently fanned her.

Mother Anastasia laughed. "This is really too much; please stop it. But you may lend me your hat. I did not know the morning would be so warm, and I am afraid I walked too fast. But we are losing time. Will you tell me precisely what it is you wish to know of me?"

"I can soon do that," I answered; "but I must first say that I believe you will suffocate if you try to talk from under that cavernous bonnet. Why don't you take it off, and get the good of this cool shade? You had discarded all that sort of thing when I last talked with you, and you were then just as much a Mother Superior as you are now."

She smiled. "The case was very different then. I was actually obliged, by the will of another, to discard the garb of our sisterhood."

"I most earnestly wish," said I, "that you could be obliged to do partially the same thing now. With that bonnet on, you do not seem at all the same person with whom I talked on Tangent Island. You appear like some one to whom I must open the whole subject anew."

"Oh, don't do that," she said, with a deprecating movement of her hand,—"I really haven't the time to listen; and if my bonnet hinders your speech, off it shall come. Now, then, I suppose you want to know the reason of my change of position in regard to Sylvia and you." As she said this she took off her bonnet; not with a jerk, as Sylvia had once removed hers, but carefully, without disturbing the dark hair which was disposed plainly about her head. I was greatly relieved; this was an entirely different woman to talk to.

"Yes," I replied, "that is what I want to know."

"I will briefly give you my reasons," she said, still fanning herself with my hat, while I stood before her, earnestly listening, "and you will find them very good and conclusive reasons. When I spoke to you before, the case was this:

Sylvia Raynor had had a trouble, which made her think she was the most miserable girl in the whole world, and she threw herself into our sisterhood. Her mother did not object to this, because of course Sylvia entered as a probationer, and she thought a few months of the House of Martha life would do her good. That her daughter would permanently join the sisterhood never occurred to her. As I was a relative, it was a natural thing that the girl should enter a house of which I was the head. I did not approve of the step, but at first I had no fears about it. After a while, however, I began to have fears. She never liked our life and never sympathized with it, and her heart was never enlisted in the cause of the sisterhood; but after a time I found she was endeavoring to conquer herself, and when a woman with a will—and Sylvia is one of these—undertakes in earnest to conquer herself, she generally succeeds. Then it was I began to have my fears, and then it was I wished to divert her mind from the life of the sisterhood, and send her back to the world to which she belongs."

"Then it was you gave me your promise?" I added.

"Yes," she answered; "and I gave it honestly. I would have helped you all I could. I truly believed that in so doing I was acting for Sylvia's good."

"I thank you from the bottom of my heart," I said; "and tell me, did Mrs. Raynor know, when I was on the island, of my affection for Sylvia?"

"She knew as much as I knew," was the answer, "for I went to the island on purpose to consult with her on the subject; and when you confided in me, and I gave you my promise to help you, I also told her about that."

"And did she approve?" I asked anxiously.

"She did not disapprove. She knew all about you and your family, although she had never seen you until you were at her island."

"It is strange," said I, "that I should have happened to go to that place at that time."

"Yes," she continued, "it does seem rather odd. But, as I was going to say, a letter came not more than an hour after we had had our conversation, which totally altered the face of affairs. Sylvia wrote that she had resolved to devote her life to the sisterhood. This was a great blow to her mother and to me, but Mrs. Raynor had firmly resolved not to interfere with her daughter's resolutions in regard to her future life. She had done so once, and the results had been very unfortunate. I was of an entirely different mind, and I resolved, if the thing could be done, to change Sylvia's purpose; but I failed, and that is the end of it. She is not to be moved. I know her well, and her conviction and determination are not to be changed. She is now on a visit to her mother, and when she returns she will enter the House of Martha as an inmate for life."

"Yes," said I, after a little pause, "I know that. I saw her a few days ago, and she told me of her purpose."

"What!" cried Mother Anastasia, "you have seen her! A few days ago! She told you all this! Why did you not say so? Why did you come to me?"

"Do not be displeased," I said, and as I spoke I seated myself beside her on the stone. She made no objections. I think she was too much agitated even to notice it. "I had no intention of keeping anything from you, but I first wanted to hear what you had to tell me. Sylvia did not tell me everything, nor have you."

"Met her, and talked with her!" ejaculated Mother Anastasia. "Will you tell me how this happened?"

She listened with the greatest attention to my story.

"It is wonderful," she said, when I had finished. "It seems like a tantalizing fate. But it is well you did not overtake Mrs. Raynor. It would have been of no good to you, and the interview would have greatly troubled her."

"Now tell me," I asked, "what I most want to know: what was the reason of Sylvia's sudden determination?"

Mother Anastasia fixed her dark eyes on mine; they were full of a tender sadness. "I thought of you nearly all last night," she said, "and I determined that if you should ask me that question to-day I would answer it. It is a hard thing to do, but it is the best thing. Sylvia's resolve was caused by her conviction that she loved you. Feeling assured of that, she unhesitatingly took the path which her conscience pointed out to her."

"Conscience!" I exclaimed.

"Yes," said Mother Anastasia, "it was her conscience. She was far more in earnest than we had thought her. It was conviction, not desire or sympathy, which had prompted her to enter the sisterhood. Now her convictions, her conscience, prompt her to crush everything which would interfere with the life she has chosen. All this she has told me. Her conscience stands between you and her, and you must understand that what you wish is absolutely impossible. You must be strong, and give up all thought of her. Will you promise me to do this?" and as she spoke she laid her hand upon my arm. "Promise it, and I shall feel that I have devoted myself this morning to as true a mission of charity as anything to which our sisters vow themselves."

I did not respond, but sat silent, with bowed head.

"I must go now," said Mother Anastasia. "Reflect on what I have said, and your heart and your practical sense will tell you that what I ask you to do is what you ought to do and must do. Good-by," and she held out her hand to me.

I took her hand and held it. The thought flashed into my mind that when I released that hand the last tie between Sylvia and myself would be broken.

Presently the hand was adroitly withdrawn, Mother Anastasia rose, and I was left alone, sitting in the shadow of the tree.

XXXVII

THE PERFORMANCE OF MY UNDER-STUDY

On the next day, when Walkirk came back, I received him coolly. To be sure, the time of his return was now of slight importance, but my manner showed him that on general principles I blamed his delay.

I did not care to hear his explanations, but proceeded at once to state the misfortunes which had befallen me. I told him in detail all that had happened since I left the floating grocery. I did not feel that it was at all necessary to do this, but there was a certain pleasure in talking of my mishaps and sorrows; I was so dreadfully tired of thinking of them.

As I told Walkirk of my interview with Mother Anastasia on the Maple Ridge road, he laughed aloud. He instantly checked himself and begged my pardon, but assured me that never had he heard of a man doing anything so entirely out of the common as to make an appointment with a Mother Superior to meet him under a tree. At first I resented his laugh, but I could not help seeing for myself that the situation, as he presented it, was certainly an odd one, and that a man with his mind free to ordinary emotions might be excused for being amused at it.

When I had finished, and had related how Mother Anastasia

Frank R. Stockton

had proved to me that all possible connection between myself and Sylvia Raynor was now at an end, Walkirk was not nearly so much depressed as I thought he ought to be. In fact, he endeavored to cheer me, and did not agree with Mother Anastasia that there was no hope. At this I lost patience.

"Confound it!" I cried, "what you say is not only preposterous, but unfeeling. I hate this eternal making the best of things, when there is no best. With me everything is at its worst, and it is cruel to try to make it appear otherwise."

"I am sorry to annoy you," he said, "but I must insist that to me the situation does not appear to be without some encouraging features. Let me tell you what has happened to me since we parted."

I resumed the seat from which I had risen to stride up and down the room, and Walkirk began his narrative.

"I do not know, sir," he said, "that I ever have been so surprised as when I went on deck of the grocery boat, a short time before breakfast, and found that you were not on board. Captain Jabe and his man were equally astonished, and I should have feared that you had fallen overboard, if a man, who had come on the boat at a little pier where we had stopped very early in the morning, had not assured us that he had seen you go ashore at that place, but had not thought it worth while to mention so commonplace an occurrence. I wished to put back to the pier, but it was then far behind us, and Captain Jabe positively refused to do so. Both wind and tide would be against us, he said; and if you chose to go ashore without saying anything to anybody, that was your affair, and not his. I thought it possible you might have become tired with the slow progress of his vessel, and had left it, to hire a horse, to get to Sanpritchit before we did.

"When we reached Sanpritchit and you were not there, I was utterly unable to understand the situation; but Mrs. Raynor's yacht was there, just on the point of sailing, and I considered it my duty, as your representative, to hasten on board, and to apprise the lady that you were on your way to see her. Of course she wanted to know why you were coming, and all that; and as you were not there to do it yourself, I told her the nature of your errand, and impressed upon her the importance of delaying her departure until she had seen you and had heard what you had to say. She did not agree with me that the interview would be of importance to any one concerned, but she consented to wait for a time and see you. If you arrived, she agreed to meet you on shore; for she would not consent to your coming on board the yacht, where her daughter was. I went ashore, and waited there with great impatience until early in the afternoon, when a boy arrived, who said he had started to bring you to Sanpritchit, but that you had changed your mind, and he had conveyed you to a railroad station, where you had taken a western-bound train.

"I went to the yacht to report. I think Mrs. Raynor was relieved at your non-arrival; and as she knew I wished to join you as soon as possible, she invited me to sail with them to a little town on the coast,—I forget its name,—from which I could reach the railroad much quicker than from Sanpritchit."

"She did not object, then," said I, "to your being on the yacht with her daughter?"

"Oh, no," he answered, "for she found that Miss Raynor did not know me, or at least recognize me, and had no idea that I was in any way connected with you. Of course I accepted Mrs. Raynor's offer; but I did not save any time by it, for the wind fell off toward evening, and for hours there was no wind at all, and it was late the next afternoon when we reached the point where I went ashore."

"Did you see anything of Miss Raynor in all that time?" I inquired.

"Yes," he replied; "she was on deck a great deal, and I had several conversations with her."

"With her alone?" I asked.

"Yes," said he. "Mrs. Raynor is a great reader and fond of naps, and I think that the young lady was rather tired of the companionship of her uncle and the other gentleman, who were very much given to smoking, and was glad of the novelty of a new acquaintance. On my part, I felt it my duty to talk to her as much as possible, that I might faithfully report to you all that she said, and thus give you an idea of the state of her mind."

"Humph!" I exclaimed; "but what did she say?"

"Of course," continued Walkirk, "a great deal of our conversation was desultory and of no importance, but I endeavored, as circumspectly as I could, so to turn the conversation that she might say something which it would be worth while to report to you."

"Now, Walkirk," said I, "if I had known you were doing a thing of that sort, I should not have approved of it. But did she say anything that in any way referred to me?"

"Yes, she did," he answered, "and this is the way it came about. Something—I think it was the heat of the windless day—caused her to refer to the oppressive costume of the sisters of the House of Martha, and she then remarked that she supposed I knew she was one of that sisterhood. I replied that I had been so informed, and then betrayed as much natural interest in regard to the vocations and purposes of the organization as I thought would be prudent. I should have liked to bring up every possible argument against the folly of a young lady of her position and prospects extinguishing the very light of her existence in that hard, cold, soul-chilling house which I knew so well, but the circumstances did not warrant that. I was obliged to content myself with very simple questions.

"'How do the sisters employ themselves?' I inquired.

"'In all sorts of ways,' she said. 'Some nurse or teach, and others work for wages, like ordinary people, except that they do not have anything to do with the money they earn, which is paid directly to the house.'"

"'I think,' I then remarked, 'that there are a good many employments which would give the sisters very pleasant occupation, such as decorative art or clerical work.'"

"At this her face brightened. 'Clerical work is very nice. I tried that once, myself.'"

"'Was it book-keeping?' I asked."

"'Oh, no,' she answered; 'I shouldn't have liked that. It was writing from dictation. I worked regularly so many hours every morning. It was a book which was dictated to me,— sketches of travel; that is, it was partly travel and partly fiction. It was very interesting.'"

"'I should think it would be so,' I answered. 'To ladies of education and literary taste, I should say such employment would be highly congenial. Do you intend to devote yourself principally to that sort of thing?'"

"'Oh, no,' said she, 'not at all. I like the work very much, but, for various reasons, I shall not do any more of it.'"

"I endeavored mildly to remonstrate against such a decision, but she shook her head. 'I was not a full sister at the time,' she said, 'and this was an experiment. I shall do no more of it.'"

"Her manner was very decided, but I did not drop the subject. 'If you do not fancy writing from dictation,' I said, 'why don't you try typewriting? I should think that would be very interesting, and it could be done in your own room. The work would not require you to go out at all, if you object to that.' Now this was a slip, because she had not told me that she had gone out, but she did not notice it.

"'A sister does not have a room of her own,' she answered, 'and I do not understand typewriting;' and with that she left me, and went below, looking very meditative."

"But my remark had had an effect. I think it was not half an hour afterward when she came to me."

"'I have been thinking about your suggestion of type-writing,' she said. 'Is it difficult to learn? Do you understand it? What use could I make of a machine in the House of Martha?'"

"I told her that I understood the art, and gave her all the information I could in regard to it, taking care to make the vocation as attractive as my conscience would allow. As to the use she could make of it, I said that at present there was a constant demand for typewritten copies of all sorts of writings,—legal, literary, scientific, everything.

"'And people would send me things,' she asked, 'and I would copy them on the typewriter, and send them back, and that would be all?'"

"'You have put it exactly,' I said. 'If you do not choose, you need have no communication whatever with persons ordering the work.'"

"'And do you know of any one who would want such work done?'"

"'Yes,' I said; 'I know people who would be very glad to send papers to be copied. I could procure you some work which would be in no hurry, and that would be an advantage to you in the beginning.'"

"'Indeed it would,' she said; and then her mother joined us, and the subject of typewriting was dropped. The only time that it was referred to again was at the very end of my trip, when Miss Raynor came to me, just as I was preparing to leave the yacht, and told me that she had made up her mind to get a typewriter and to learn to use it; and she asked me, if I were still willing to assist her in securing work, to send my address to the Mother Superior of the House of Martha, which of course I assured her I would do."

"Why in the name of common sense," I cried, turning suddenly around in my chair and facing Walkirk, "did you put into Miss Raynor's head all that stuff about typewriting? Did you do it simply because you liked to talk to her?"

"By no means," he replied. "I did it solely on your account and for your benefit. If she learns to copy manuscripts on the typewriter, why should she not copy your manuscripts? Not immediately, perhaps, but in the natural course of business. If she should make me her agent, which I have no doubt she would be willing to do, I could easily manage all that. In this way you could establish regular communications with her. There would be no end to your opportunities, and I am sure you would know how to use them with such discretion and tact that they would be very effective."

I folded my arms, and looked at him. "Walkirk," said I, "you are positively, completely, and hopelessly off the track. Mother Anastasia has shown me exactly how I stand with Sylvia Raynor. She has vowed herself to that sisterhood because she thinks it is wrong to love me. She has made her decision, and has taken all the wretched steps which have rendered that decision final, and now I do not intend to try to make her do what she religiously believes is wrong."

"That is not my idea," answered Walkirk. "What I wish is that she shall get herself into such a state of mind that she shall think the sisterhood is wrong, and therefore leave it."

I gave a snort of despair and disgust, and began to stride up and down the room. Presently, however, I recovered my temper. "Walkirk," said I, "I am quite sure that you mean well, and I don't intend to find fault with you; but this sort of thing does not suit me; let us have no more of it."

XXXVIII

A BROKEN TRACE

As soon as my grandmother heard that I was at Arden, she terminated her visit abruptly, and returned home. When she saw me, she expressed the opinion that my holiday had not been of any service to me. She did not remember ever seeing me so greatly out of condition, and was of the opinion that I ought to see the doctor.

"These watering places and islands," she said, "are just as likely to be loaded down with malaria as any other place. In fact, I don't know but it is just as well for our health for us to stay at home. That is, if we live in a place like Arden."

I had no desire to conceal from this nearest and dearest friend and relative the real cause of my appearance, and I laid before her all the facts concerning Sylvia and myself.

She was not affected as I supposed she would be. In fact, my narrative appeared to relieve her mind of some of her anxieties.

"Any way," she remarked, after a moment or two of consideration, "this is better than malaria. If you get anything of that kind into your system, it is probable that you will never get it out, and it is at any time likely to affect your health, one way or another; but love affairs are different. They have a powerful influence upon a person, as I well know, but there is not about them that insidious poison, which, although you may think you have entirely expelled it from your system, is so likely to crop out again, especially in the spring and fall."

To this I made no answer but a sigh. What was the good of saying that, in my present state of mind, health was a matter of indifference to me?

"I am not altogether surprised," continued my grand-mother, "that that secretary business turned out in this way. If it had been any other young woman, I should have advised against it, but Sylvia Raynor is a good match,— good in every way; and I thought that if her working with you had made you like her, and had made her like you, it might be very well; but I am sure it never entered my mind that if you did come to like each other she would choose the sisterhood instead of you. I knew that she was not then a full sister, and I hadn't the slightest doubt that if you two really did fall in love with each other she would leave the House of Martha as soon as her time was up. You must not think, my dear boy," she continued, "that I am anxious to get rid of you, but you know you must marry some day."

I solemnly shook my head. "All that," I said, "is at an end. We need speak no more of it."

My grandmother arose, and gently placed her hand upon my shoulder. "Come! come! Do not be so dreadfully cast down. You have yet one strong ground of hope."

"What is that?" I inquired.

My grandmother looked into my face and smiled. "The girl isn't dead yet," she answered.

I now found myself in a very unsettled and unpleasant state of mind. My business affairs, which had been a good deal neglected of late, I put into the charge of Walkirk, who attended to them with much interest and ability. My individual concerns—that is to say, the guidance and direction of myself—I took into my own hands, and a sorry business I made of it.

I spent a great deal of my time wondering whether or not Sylvia had returned to the House of Martha. I longed for her coming. The very thought of her living within a mile of me was a wild and uneasy pleasure. Then I would ask myself why I wished her to come. Her presence in the neighborhood would be of no good to me unless I saw her, and of course I could not see her. And if this could be so, what would be worse for me, or for her, than our seeing each other? From these abstract questions I came to a more practical one: What should I do? To go away seemed to be a sensible thing, but I was tired of going away. I liked my home, and, besides, Sylvia would be in the neighborhood. It also seemed wise to stay, and endeavor to forget her. But how could I forget her, if she were in the neighborhood? If she were to go away, I might be willing to go away also; but the chances were that I should not know where she had gone, and how could I endure to go to any place where I was certain she was not?

During this mental tangle I confided in no one. There was no one who could sympathize with my varying view of the subject, and I knew there was no one with whose view of the subject I could agree. Sometimes it was almost impossible for me to sympathize with myself.

It suited my mood to take long walks in the surrounding country. One morning, returning from one of these, when about half a mile out of the village, I saw in the road, not very far from me, a carriage, which seemed to be in distress.

It was a four-wheeled, curtained vehicle, of the kind to be had for hire at the railroad stations; and beside the raw-boned horse which drew it stood a man and a woman, the latter in the gray garb of a sister of the House of Martha.

When I recognized this costume, my heart gave a jump, and I hastened toward the group; but the woman had perceived my approach, and to my surprise came toward me. I quickly saw that it was Mother Anastasia. My heart sank; without any good reason, it must be admitted, but still it sank.

The face of the Mother Superior was slightly flushed, as she walked rapidly in my direction. Saluting her, I inquired what had happened.

"Nothing of importance," she answered; "a trace has broken."

"I will go and look at it," I said. "Sometimes that sort of mishap can be easily remedied."

"Oh, no," said she, "don't trouble yourself. It's broken in the middle, and so you cannot cut a fresh hole in it, or do any of those things which men do to broken traces. I have told the boy that he must take out the horse, and ride it back to the stable and get another set of harness. That is the only thing to be done. I shall wait here for his return, and I am very glad to have met you."

Naturally I was pleased at this. "Then you have something to say to me?" I remarked.

"Yes," she answered, "I have a good deal to say. Let us walk on to a more shaded place."

"Now it strikes me," said I, "that the most pleasant place to wait will be in the carriage; there we can sit and talk quite comfortably."

"Oh, no," she said, with a sort of half laugh, "it is stuffy and horrid. I greatly prefer the fresh air. I have reason to suppose you do not object to conversing under a tree. I see a promising bit of shade a little farther on."

"Would it be wise to go so far from the carriage?" I asked. "Have you left in it anything of value?"

Mother Anastasia was more animated than I had ever seen her before when in the uniform of the house.

"Oh, pshaw!" she answered. "You know the people around here do not steal things out of carriages. Let us step on."

"But first," I said, "I will run down and pull the carriage out of the way of passing vehicles. It now stands almost across the road."

With a movement of impatience, she put her hand upon my arm. "Don't trouble yourself about that hack; let it stand where it is. I wish to speak with you, and do not let us waste our time."

I had no objection to speaking with Mother Anastasia, and, giving no further thought to the abandoned vehicle, I walked with her to a spot where a clump of straggling locust-trees threw a scanty shade upon the sidewalk. I could not but feel that my companion had something important to say to me, for she was evidently a good deal agitated. She stepped a little in front of me, and then turned and faced me.

"There is no place to sit down here," she said, "but I'm not tired, are you?"

Frank R. Stockton

I assured her that I was not, and would as soon talk standing as sitting.

"Now, then," she began, "tell me about yourself. What have you been doing? What are your plans?"

"My plans!" I cried. "Of what importance are my plans and actions? I thought you wished to speak to me of Sylvia."

She smiled. "There is really nothing to say about that young person, of whom, by the way, you should not speak as 'Sylvia.' She is now a full member of the sisterhood, and has accepted the name of 'Sister Hagar.' We found that the other sisters would not like it if an exception were made in her favor, in regard to her name."

"'Hagar!'" I groaned. "Horrible!"

"Oh, no," replied Mother Anastasia, "there is nothing horrible about it. 'Hagar' is a little harsh, perhaps, but one soon gets used to that sort of thing."

"I can never get used to it," I said.

"My dear Mr. Vanderley," said the Mother Superior, speaking very earnestly, but with a gentleness that was almost affectionate, "I wish I could impress upon your mind that there is no need of your getting used to the name of our young sister, or of your liking it or disliking it. You ought thoroughly to understand, from what she has told you, and from what I have told you, that she never can be anything to you, and that, out of regard to yourself, if to no one else, you should cease to think of her as I see you do think."

"As long as I live in this world," I replied, "I shall continue to think of her as I do think."

Mother Anastasia gave a sigh. "The unreasonableness of men is something inexplicable. Perhaps you think I am not old enough to give you advice, but I will say that, for your own sake, you ought to crush and obliterate the feelings you have toward our sister; and if you do not choose to do it for your own sake, you ought to do it for her sake and that of our sisterhood. It makes it extremely awkward for us, to say the least of it, to know that there is a gentleman in the village who is in love with one of the sisters of the House of Martha."

"I suppose you would have me exile myself," I replied, "leave forever my home, my grandmother, everything that is dear to me, and all for the sake of the peace and quiet of your sisterhood. Let me assure you I do not care enough for your sisterhood to do that."

The Mother Superior smiled ironically, but not ill-naturedly. "I am very much afraid," she remarked, "that in this matter you care for no one but yourself. There is nothing so selfish as a man in love."

"He needs to be," I answered. "But tell me, is Sylvia here?"

"Sylvia again," said she, half laughing. "Yes, she has returned to the House of Martha, and you can see for yourself that, if you continue in your present state of mind, it will be impossible for her ever to go outside of the house."

"I shall not hurt her," I answered.

"Yes, you will hurt her," quickly replied Mother Anastasia. "You will hurt her very much, if you meet her, and show by your words, looks, or actions that your former attitude toward her is not changed." She came nearer to me, looking into my face with her eyes full of an earnest tenderness, and as she spoke she laid the tips of her fingers gently upon my shoulder. She had a very pleasant way of doing this. "I do wish," she said, "that you would let me prevail upon you to do what your conscience must tell you is right. If you have ever loved the girl who was once Sylvia Raynor, that is the best of reasons why you should cease to love her now. You owe it to her to cease to love her."

I looked steadily into the face of the Mother Superior.

"You promise me that you will do that?" she said, with a smile upon her lips and a light in her eyes which might have won over almost any man to do almost anything. "You promise me that you will allow our young sister, who has hardships enough to bear without any more being thrust upon her, to try to be happy in the way she has chosen, and that you will try to be happy in the way you should have chosen; that you will go out into the world and act your part in life; that you will look upon this affair as something which has vanished into the past; and that you will say to your heart, 'You are free, if not by my will, by the irresistible force of circumstances'?"

I looked at her a few moments in silence, and then answered, very quietly, "I shall do nothing of the kind."

She gave her head a little toss and stepped backward, and then, with a half laugh which seemed to indicate an amused hopelessness, she said: "You are utterly impracticable, and I am certain I do not know what is to be done about it. But I see that the boy has returned with the horse, and I must continue my journey. I am going to the Iron Furnace to see a sick woman. I wish you would think of what I have said, and remember that it was spoken from the depth of my soul. And do not think," she continued, as I turned and accompanied her toward the carriage, "that I do not appreciate the state of your feelings. I understand them thoroughly, and I sympathize with you as perhaps only a woman can sympathize; but still I say to you that there are some things in this world which we must give up, and which we ought to give up promptly and willingly."

"Do you think," said I, "that if Sylvia were to learn typewriting there would be any objection to her copying manuscript for me?"

Mother Anastasia burst into a laugh. "You ought to be ashamed of yourself for making a person of my position behave so giddily in the presence of a hack-driver."

We now reached the carriage, and I assisted her to enter it.

"Good-morning," she said, her face still perturbed by her suddenly checked merriment, "and do not forget the counsels I have given you."

I bowed and stepped back, but the driver did not start. He sat for a moment irresolute, and then, turning toward Mother Anastasia, asked, "Shall I wait for the other sister?"

"Oh, go on!" cried the Mother Superior. "There is no other sister."

The boy, startled by her tone, gave his horse a cut, and the equipage rattled away. I walked slowly homeward, meditating earnestly upon Mother Anastasia's words and upon Mother Anastasia.

XXXIX

A SOUL WHISPER?

My meditations upon the Mother Superior of the House of Martha were not concluded during my homeward walk; the subject occupied my mind for the greater part of the rest of the day. I do not call myself a philosopher, but I am in the habit of looking into the nature and import of what happens about me. My reflections on Mother Anastasia gradually produced in me the conviction that there was something more in her words, her manner, and her actions than would appear to the ordinary observer.

In considering this matter, I went back to the very first of my intercourse with this beautiful woman, who, divested of the dismal disguise of her sisterhood, had produced upon my memory an impression which was so strong that, whenever I now thought of Mother Anastasia, she appeared before my mental vision in a white dress, with a broad hat and a bunch of flowers in her belt. In the character of a beautiful and sensible woman, and not at all in that of a Mother Superior, she had warmly commended my suit of Sylvia Raynor. With our regard for Sylvia as a basis, we had consulted, we had confided, we had shown ourselves to each other in a most frank and friendly manner.

Suddenly she had changed, she had deserted me without a

word of explanation, and the next time I saw her she was totally opposed to my maintaining any connection whatever with Sylvia.

But there had been more than this. This woman, beautiful even in her gray garb, had shown an increasing interest in the subject, which could not be altogether explained by her interest in Sylvia. If she truly believed that that young sister would devote her life to the service of the House of Martha, that matter might be considered as settled; and what was her object in so earnestly endeavoring to impress upon my mind the fact that I could not marry Sylvia? It might be supposed that, in the ordinary course of events, I should be compelled to admit this point. But not only did she continually bring up this view of the subject, but she showed such a growing interest in me and my welfare that it made me uneasy.

It is almost impossible truly to understand a woman; most men will admit this. I could not say that I understood Mother Anastasia. At times I hoped I did not understand her. From what I knew of the constitution of the sisterhood, some of its members were vowed to it for life, and others for a stated period. Putting together this and that which Mother Anastasia had said to me about the organization, it did not appear to me that she felt that devotion to it which a sister for life would naturally feel. She had used all the art of a logician to impress upon me the conviction that Sylvia was a life sister, and could be nothing else. Was it possible—I scarcely dared to ask myself the question—that she had used the arts of a woman to intimate to me that she might be something else? It did not cross my mind for an instant that anything that Mother Anastasia had said to me, or anything that could be deduced from her manner, was in the slightest degree out of the way. A woman has a right to indicate her position in regard to a fellow-being, and in this age she generally does indicate it. If the true nature of Mother Anastasia had so far exerted itself as to impel her, perhaps involuntarily, to let me know that she was as much a woman as she was a Mother Superior, and that in time she would be all of the first and not any of the latter, she had truly done this with a delicate ingenuousness beyond compare. It had not been the exhalation by the flower of inviting perfume or its show of color; it had been the simple opening of the blossom to the free sun and air before my eyes.

My last interview with Mother Anastasia had crystallized in my mind a mist of suppositions and fancies which had vaguely floated there for some time. It is not surprising that I was greatly moved at the form the crystal took.

When Walkirk came, the next day, to make his usual reports, I talked to him of Mother Anastasia. Of course I did not intimate to him how I had been thinking of her, but I gave him as many facts as possible, in order that I might discover what he would think of her. When I had finished my account of the interview of the morning before, I could see that a very decided impression had been made upon him. His countenance twitched, he smiled, he looked upon the floor. For a moment I thought he was going to laugh.

"This amuses you," I remarked.

"Yes," he replied, his face having recovered its ordinary composure, "it is a little funny. Mother Anastasia seems to be a good deal of a manager."

"Yes," I said reflectively, "that is true. It is quite plain that, perceiving an opportunity of a private conference with me, she took advantage of the circumstances. We could have had an ordinary chat just as well in one place as another, but it was easy to see that she did not wish the boy who was unhitching the horse to hear even the first words of our conversation. As you say, she is a good manager, and I had my suspicions of that before you mentioned it." As I said this I could not help smiling, as I thought how surprised he would be if he knew in what direction my suspicions pointed. "Do you know," I continued, "if it is necessary that the head of a sisterhood should be a life member of it?"

"I have never heard," he answered, "but I have been informed that the organization of the House of Martha is a very independent one, and does not attempt to conform itself to that of any other sisterhood. The women who founded it had ideas of their own, and what rules and laws they made I do not know."

For a few moments I walked up and down the room; then I asked, "How did Mother Anastasia come to be the Mother Superior?"

"I have been told," said Walkirk, "that she gave most of the money for the founding of the institution, and it was natural enough that she should be placed at the head. I have an idea that she would not have been willing to enter the House except as its head."

"It is about four years since it was established, is it not?" I asked; and Walkirk assured me that I was correct.

All this information ranged itself on the side of conviction. She was just the woman to try a thing of this kind for a stated time; she was just the woman not to like it; and she was just the woman whose soul could not be prevented from whispering that the gates of the bright world were opening before her. But why should her soul whisper this to me? The whole matter troubled me very much.

I determined not to base any action upon what had thus forced itself upon my mind. I would wait. I would see what would happen next. I would persist in my determination never to give up Sylvia. And I will mention that there was a little point in connection with her which at this time greatly annoyed me: whenever I thought of her, she appeared before me in the gray dress of a sister, and not as I had seen her on the island. I wished very much that this were not the case.

XL

AN INSPIRATION

I now found myself in an embarrassing situation. All my plans and hopes of tidings from Sylvia, or of any possible connection with her, were based upon Mother Anastasia. But would it be wise for me to continue my very friendly relations with the Mother Superior? On my side these relations were extremely pleasant, though that did not matter, one way or another. But would it be kind and just to her to meet with her on the footing I had enjoyed? In every point of this affair I wished to be honorable and considerate. Acting on these principles, I went away for two weeks. It was very hard for me to absent myself for so long a period from Arden, but it was my duty. To take the chances of another meeting with Mother Anastasia, following close upon the recent one, which had made so forcible an impression upon me, would be imprudent. A moderate absence might be of great advantage.

On my return I took to strolling about the village, especially in the neighborhood of the House of Martha; and if, in these strolls, I had met the Mother Superior, I should not have hesitated to accost her and ask news of Sylvia. For more reasons than one, I felt it was highly desirable that I should impress it on the mind of Mother Anastasia that my interest in Sylvia had not in the least abated.

But several days passed, and I met no one clad in gray bonnet and gown. I was disappointed; there were a good many questions about Sylvia which I wished to ask, and a good many things in regard to her that I wished to say. I might go to the House of Martha and boldly ask to see the Mother Superior; but a step like that might produce an undesirable impression, and naturally the position in which I had placed myself regarding Sylvia would prevent my going to visit her.

As I could do nothing for myself in this matter, I must ask some one to help me, and there was no one so willing and able to do this as my grandmother. She could go to the House of Martha and ask what questions she pleased. I went to the dear old lady and made known my desires. She laid down her knitting and gave me her whole attention.

"Now tell me exactly what it is you want," she said. "You cannot expect to be asked to take tea with the sisters, you know, though I see no reason why you should not. Say what they will, they are not nuns."

"What I want," I replied, "is to know how Sylvia is, what she is doing, all about her. I do not even know that she is still there."

"My dear boy," said my grandmother, very tenderly, "I suppose that even if you are obliged to give up all hope of ever having Sylvia for your own, you will want to know every day for the rest of your life just how she is getting on."

"Yes," I answered, "that is true."

"Poor fellow," said the old lady, her eyes a little dimmed as she spoke, "the fates have not been using you well. Is there anything else you want me to inquire about?"

"Oh, yes," I answered. "I take a great interest in the institution."

"Which is natural enough, since Sylvia is there," interpolated my grandmother.

"And I should be glad," I continued, "to know anything of interest regarding the sisterhood, from the Mother Superior down."

"Mother Anastasia is a very fine woman," said my grandmother, "and I should think you would be likely to be greatly interested in her. I am going to make some inquiries about the rules of the House of Martha. I see no reason why the sisters should not occasionally accept invitations to tea."

This remark startled me, and I was prompted to make a cautionary observation. But I restrained myself; in cases like this interference would be likely to provoke comment, and by my grandmother's desire I went to order the carriage.

In less than an hour she returned. I was promptly at hand to receive her report.

"Well," said she, "I have visited the sisters, but I am sorry I did not see Mother Anastasia. She was away."

"Away!" I exclaimed. "Where has she gone?"

"She went to Washington more than a week ago," was the answer.

"For a long stay?" I asked quickly.

"The sisters did not know," continued my grandmother, "but their impression is that she will return in a few days."

I knitted my brows.

"You are disappointed, and so am I. I intended to ask her here to tea next Friday, and to urge her, if she did not too greatly object, to bring Sylvia with her. There is nothing like quiet intercourse of that kind to break down obstacles."

"Alas," I said, "I am afraid there are obstacles"—

"But do not let us talk about them," she interrupted. "Nobody knows what will happen, and let us be as happy as we can."

"Did you see Sylvia?" I asked.

"Oh, yes," she answered, "and I had some talk with her, but it did not amount to much. She is trying to make a regular nun of herself,—that is, if a Protestant can be a nun,—but I do not think she will ever succeed. She admitted that she greatly disliked the ordinary work of the sisters, and wished to employ herself in some way which would be just as lucrative to the institution, and yet not so repugnant to her. Now you can see for yourself that that will not do. If she intends to be a sister of the House of Martha, she must do as the other sisters do. She cannot always expect to be an exception. At present she is learning typewriting."

I gave a great start. "Typewriting!" I exclaimed.

"Yes," said my grandmother. "Is it not odd that she should have taken up that? She has a machine, and practices steadily on it. She showed me some of her printed sheets, and I must say, so far as I am concerned, that I should prefer plain handwriting, where the letters are not so likely to get on top of one another. She wanted to know if I could give her any advice about getting work, when she thought she could do it well enough; but of course I know nothing about such things. My hope is that she will get to dislike that as much as she does nursing and apothecary work, and to find out that her real duty is to live like an ordinary human being, and so make herself and other people truly happy."

I do not know that there is any inherent connection between a typewriting machine and the emotions and sentiments of love, but in this case such a connection instantly established itself in my mind. It seemed plain to me that Walkirk's suggestion to Sylvia had taken root; and why did she wish to typewrite, if she did not wish to typewrite for me? Was this an endeavor of her tender heart to keep up a thread of connection with me which should not be inconsistent with the duties, the vows, and the purposes of her life? Dear girl! If the thing could be managed, she should typewrite for me as much as she wished, even if she piled the letters on one another as high as the Great Pyramid.

With much enthusiasm, I communicated to Walkirk my intention to employ Sylvia in typewriting, and requested his assistance in regard to the details of the business. I could easily furnish her material enough. I had lots of things I should like to have copied, and I was ready to prepare a great deal more. My under-study made no allusion to my previous reception of his suggestion about typewriting, but brought his practical mind to bear upon the matter, and advised that preliminary arrangements should be made immediately. In a case like this it was well to be in time, and to secure the services of Miss Raynor at once. I agreed with Walkirk that it was very wise to take time by the forelock, but Mother Anastasia was the only person who could properly regulate this affair, which should be instantly laid before her; and as it was impossible to find out when she would return to Arden, I felt that it was my duty to go to her. When I mentioned this plan to Walkirk, he offered to go in my place, but I declined. This was a very delicate affair, to which no one could attend as well as I could myself.

"Walkirk," said I, "do you suppose that the Mother Superior will appear in Washington under her real name, or as Mother Anastasia? And, by the way, what is her real name?"

"Is it possible," exclaimed Walkirk, "that you do not know it? It is Raynor,—Miss Marcia Raynor. She is a cousin of the younger lady."

"Oh, yes, I know that," I replied; "but it never occurred to me to inquire what name Mother Anastasia bore before she entered the House of Martha. The first thing for me to do is to get her Washington address."

"And may I ask," continued Walkirk, "how you are going to do that?"

I was not prepared to give an immediate answer to this question.

"I suppose," I remarked presently, "that it would not do to ask for the address at the House of Martha, but I could go to Sylvia's mother. I should like to call there, any way, and I have no doubt she would know where Mother Anastasia would be likely to stop."

My under-study shook his head. "Pardon me," he said, "but I do not think it would be wise to go to Mrs. Raynor. She would be sure to connect her daughter with your urgent desire to see Mother Anastasia, and she would not hesitate to question you on the matter. I think I understand her disposition in regard to you and Miss Raynor, and I am very certain that when she heard of the typewriting scheme she would instantly put her foot on it; and if I am not mistaken," he continued, with a noticeable deference in his tone, "that is the only reason you can give for your wish to confer with Mother Anastasia."

I strode impatiently up and down the room. "Certainly it is," said I, "and although it is reason enough, I suppose you are right, and it would not do to offer it to Mrs. Raynor; and, for the matter of that, Mother Anastasia may think it a very little thing to take me down to Washington."

"I had thought of that," said Walkirk, "and that was one reason why I proposed to go in your stead."

I made no answer to this remark. My mind was filled with annoying reflections about the unreasonableness of people who insist upon knowing people's reasons for doing things, and my annoyance was increased by the conviction, now that I looked more closely into the matter, that the only reason I could give for hastening after Mother Anastasia in this way was indeed a very little one.

"Walkirk," I exclaimed, "can't you think of some other reason for my seeing the Mother Superior without delay?"

"Truly," he replied, smiling, "it is rather difficult. You might offer to build an annex to the House of Martha, but such a matter could surely wait until the return of the Mother Superior."

I sniffed, and continued to stride. I must see Mother Anastasia in Washington, because there I might have a chance of speaking to her freely, which I could not expect to have anywhere else; and yet how was I going to explain to her, or to any one else, my desire to speak with her at all? It might have been difficult to explain this to myself; at all events, I did not try to do it. Suddenly an idea struck me.

Frank R. Stockton

"Annex!" I cried,—"capital!"

"My dear sir," said Walkirk, rising in much agitation, "I hope you do not think that I seriously proposed your building an annex to"—

"Building!" I interrupted. "Nonsense! The annex I am thinking of is quite different; and yet not altogether so, either. Walkirk, don't you think that a man in my position could do a great deal to help those sisters in their good work? Don't you think that he could act as an outside collaborator? I am sure there are many things he could do which might not be suitable for them to do, or which they might not want to do. For instance, this business that has taken Mother Anastasia to Washington. Perhaps it is something that she hates to do, and I might have done as well as not. I have a mind to propose to her to go in and take all this sort of thing off the hands of the sisters. I think that is a good practical idea, and it is very natural that I should wish to propose it to her at the very time she is engaged in this outside business."

"In a word," remarked Walkirk, "you would make yourself a brother of the House of Martha."

I laughed. "That is not a bad notion," I said; "in fact, it is a very good one. I do not know that I shall put the matter exactly in that light, but a brother of the House of Martha is what I should like to be. Then I should be free to discuss all sorts of things, and to do all sorts of things. And I could be of a lot of service, I am sure. But I shall approach the matter cautiously. I shall begin with a simple offer of service, and, perhaps, for the present I may drop the typewriting plan. Now for Mother Anastasia's address. I must get that without delay."

Walkirk did not seem to have paid attention to this last

remark. His mind appeared occupied with amusing reflections.

"I beg your pardon," he said, in apologizing for his abstraction, "but I was thinking what a funny thing it would be to be a brother of the House of Martha. As to the address—let me see. Do you remember that lady who was staying with Mrs. Raynor, at her island, who called herself a Person,—Miss Laniston?"

"Of course I remember her," I answered, "and with the greatest disgust."

"I happen to know her address," said Walkirk, "and I think she is more likely to give you the information you want than Mrs. Raynor. If you do not care to confer with her, I can go to the city"—

"No, no, no!" I exclaimed. "She might object to giving you the address; I shall insist that she give it to me. I think I can manage the matter. She owes me something, and she knows it."

In fact, I did not care to trust Walkirk with this affair. It was plain that he did not thoroughly sympathize with me in the project. I was afraid he might make a blunder, or in some way fail me. Any way, this was a matter which I wished to attend to myself.

XLI

MISS LANISTON

At eight o'clock that evening I was at the house of Miss Laniston. The lady was at home, and received me. She advanced with both hands extended.

"Truly," she cried, "this is the most charming instance of masculine forgiveness I have ever witnessed."

I took one of her hands; this much for the sake of policy. "Madam," I said, "I am not thinking of forgiveness, or unforgiveness. I am here to ask a favor; and if you grant it, I am willing that it shall counterbalance everything between us which suggests forgiveness."

"Dear me!" she exclaimed, leading the way to a sofa. "Sit down, and let me know my opportunities."

I did not want to sit down, but, as I said before, I felt that I must be politic, and so took a seat on the other end of the sofa.

"My errand is a very simple one," I said. "I merely want to know the address of Mother Anastasia, in Washington."

The lady folded her hands in her lap, and looked at

me steadily.

"Very simple, indeed," she said. "Why do you come to me for this address? Would not the sisters give it to you?"

"For various reasons I did not care to ask them," I replied.

"One of them being, I suppose, that you knew you would not get it."

I did not reply to this remark.

"If you know the address," I inquired, "will you kindly give it to me? It is necessary that I should have it at once."

"To telegraph?" she asked.

"No, I am going to her."

"Oh!" ejaculated the lady, and there was a pause in the conversation. "It does not strike me," she said presently, "that I have any authority to tell gentlemen where to find Mother Anastasia, but I can telegraph and ask her if she is willing that I shall send you to her."

This proposition did not suit me at all. I was quite sure that the Mother Superior would not consider it advisable that I should come to her, and would ask me to postpone my communication until she should return to Arden. But Arden, as I had found, would be a very poor place for the long and earnest interview which I desired.

"That would not do," I answered; "she would not understand. I wish to see her on an important matter, which can be explained only in a personal interview."

"You excite my curiosity," said Miss Laniston. "Why don't

you make me your confidante? In that case, I might decide whether or not it would be proper to give you the address."

"Impossible," I said,—"that would be impossible."

Miss Laniston's eyes were of a blue gray, and very fine ones, and she fixed them upon me with a lively intentness.

"Do you still hope," she asked, "to marry Sylvia Raynor? Surely you must know that is impossible. She is now a member for life of the sisterhood."

"I know all that," I replied impatiently. "It is not about that matter that I wish to see the Mother Superior."

"Is it then about Mother Anastasia herself? Do you wish to marry her?"

I sprang to my feet in my excitement. "Why do you speak to me in that way," I exclaimed, "and about a woman who is at the head of a religious institution, and whose earthly existence is devoted to it?"

"Not at all," quietly answered the lady. "Mother Anastasia is not a life member of the sisterhood of the House of Martha."

At these words my blood began to boil within me in a manner which I could not comprehend. My eyeballs seemed to burn, as I stood and gazed speechlessly at my companion.

"You take such an interest in these sisters," she said, "that I supposed you knew that Mother Anastasia joined the sisterhood only for a term of years, now nearly expired. She was made Mother Superior because those who helped form the institution knew that no one else could so well fill the place, especially during its first years. I was one of those persons."

I do not remember a time when my mind was in such a state of ungovernable emotion. Not only was I unable to control my feelings, but I did not know what they were. One thing only could I comprehend: I must remove this impression from the mind of Miss Laniston, and I could think of no other way of doing it than to confide to her the business on which I wished to see Mother Anastasia. I reseated myself on the sofa, and without delay or preface I laid before her my plan of collaboration with the sisters of the House of Martha; explaining how much better a man could attend to certain outside business than the sisters could do it, and showing how, in a manner, I proposed to become a brother of the House of Martha. Thus only could I defend myself against her irrational and agitating suppositions.

She heard me to the end, and then she leaned back on the sofa and laughed,—laughed until I thought the people in the street must hear her. I was hurt, but said nothing.

"You must excuse me," she said, when she was able to speak, "but this is so sudden my mind is not prepared for it. And so you wish to become a brother of the House of Martha? I would be solemn about it if I could, but really I cannot," and again she laughed.

I was about to retire, but she checked me.

"Do not go," she said; "do not be angry. Forget that I laughed. Now perhaps I can help you. I will make you a promise. If you will agree faithfully to tell me how Mother Anastasia receives your proposition, I will give you her address."

"Promise," I said severely. "You may remember that this is

not the first time you have made me a promise."

"Don't bring up that old affair!" she exclaimed. "What I did then could not be helped. When we had our talk about the sister with whom you had fallen in love, I had no idea she was Sylvia Raynor, the daughter of my hostess. When I discovered the truth, I had to drop the whole affair. Any person of honor would have done that. I could not help its being funny, you know."

I had become calmer, and was able to be politic again.

"If Mother Anastasia will allow me," I said, "I am willing to promise to tell you what she thinks of my plan."

"Very good," she replied, "it is a bargain. She is stopping with a friend, Mrs. Gardley, at 906 Alaska Avenue. I address her as 'Miss Raynor,' because I always do that when I have a chance, but I think it will be well for you to ask for Mother Anastasia."

I arose, and she followed my example.

"Now, then," said she, "we are friends," and her sparkling eyes seemed to have communicated their merriment to the gems upon the white hand which she held out to me.

I took the hand, and as I did so a politic idea flashed up within me. If I must be friends with this woman, why not make use of her? This was a moment when she was well disposed to serve me.

"If you are willing to consider me a friend," I replied, still holding her hand, "you will not refuse to tell me something which I have long wanted to know, and which I ought to know."

"What is it?" she asked.

"What was the trouble, which caused Sylvia Raynor to enter the House of Martha?"

She withdrew her hand and reflected for a moment.

"Man is an inquisitive animal," she answered, "but we cannot alter his nature, and there is some excuse for your wanting to know all about Sylvia. She is out of your reach, of course, but you have certainly taken as much interest in her as a man can take in a woman. The matter is not a close secret, and I suppose I may as well tell you that the cause of her entering the sisterhood was nothing at all out of the common. It was simply a thwarted love affair. You don't like that, I can see by your face."

"No, I do not like it, and I am very sorry to hear it."

"My dear sir," said she, "you must be early on hand and prompt in action to be Number One with a girl like Sylvia; but then, you know, a Number One seldom counts. In this case, however, he did count, for he made a Number Two impossible."

"Not so," I cried hotly. "I am Number Two, and shall always continue so."

She laughed. "I am afraid," she said, "that it will be necessary for a brother of the House of Martha to get rid of that sort of feeling."

"How was she thwarted?" I asked quickly.

"The story is briefly this," replied Miss Laniston: "A certain gentleman courted Sylvia's cousin, and everybody supposed they would be married; but in some way or other he treated her badly, and the match was broken off; then, a few years later, this same person fell in love with Sylvia, who knew nothing of the previous affair. The young girl found him a most attractive lover, and he surely would have won her had not her mother stepped in and put an extinguisher upon the whole affair. She knew what had happened before, and would not have the man in her family. Then it was that Sylvia found the world a blank, and concluded to enter the sisterhood."

"Do you mean," I asked, "that the cousin with whom the man was first in love was Marcia Raynor, Mother Anastasia?"

"Yes," answered Miss Laniston, "it was she. You do not like that?"

Like it! A cold and tingling pain ran through my body, and there sprang up in me an emotion of the intensest hatred for a person whom I had never seen.

My feelings were such as I could not express; the situation was one which I could not discuss. I took leave of Miss Laniston without giving sufficient consideration to her expression of countenance and to her final words now to be able to say whether they indicated amusement or sympathy.

XLII

THE MOTHER SUPERIOR

Seldom, I think, has a berth in a sleeping-car held a more turbulent-minded man than I was during my journey from New York to Washington. The revelation that the same man had loved and been loved by Mother Anastasia and by Sylvia had disquieted me in a manner not easy to explain; but I knew that I was being torn by jealousy, and jealousy is a passion which it is sometimes impossible to explain.

An idea which came into my mind in the night increased the storm within me. I imagined that the wretch who had made suit to both Marcia and Sylvia was Walkirk. He knew a good deal about these women; sometimes I was surprised to discover how much he knew. Perhaps now, acting in a base disguise, he was endeavoring to make of me a stepping-stone to his ultimate success with one or the other. Hound! I would crush him!

My thoughts ran rapidly backward. I remembered how zealous he had been in following Miss Raynor's yacht. He had told me of his conversations with Sylvia, but what reason had I to believe he spoke the truth? That any man should have loved these two women filled me with rage. That that man should be Walkirk was an insupportable thought. I was not only jealous but I felt myself the victim of a treacherous insult.

It was seven o'clock when I reached Washington, but, although I had arrived at my destination, I could give no thought to the object of my journey until I had discovered the truth about Walkirk. That was all-important.

But of whom should I inquire? I could think of no one but Miss Laniston. I had been a fool not to ask her the name of the man when I was with her. But I would telegraph to her now, and ask for it. She might be asleep at that hour, but I believed she was a woman who would awake and answer my question and then go to sleep again.

I immediately went to the telegraph office, and sent this message: "What is the name of the man of whom we spoke last evening? It is necessary that I know it. Please answer at once." She would understand this. We had spoken of but one man.

For nearly an hour I walked the floor and tossed over the morning papers, and then came the answer to my message. It was this: "Brownson. He is dead."

There is a quality in the air of Washington which is always delightful to me, but I think it has never affected me as it did that morning. As I breathed it, it exhilarated me; it cheered and elated me; it rose-tinted my emotions; it gave me an appetite for my breakfast; it made me feel ready for any enterprise.

As soon as I thought it proper to make a morning call I went to number 906 Alaska Avenue. There I found a large and handsome house, of that independent and highly commendable style of architecture which characterizes many of the houses of Washington. I had not yet made up my mind whether I should inquire for Mother Anastasia or

"Miss Raynor." I did not know the custom of Mother Superiors when traveling or visiting, and I determined, as I ascended the steps, to be guided in this matter by the aspect of the person who opened the door.

It has always been interesting to me to study the character, as well as I can do so in the brief opportunity generally afforded, of the servants who open to me the doors of houses. To a certain degree, although of course it does not do to apply this rule too rigidly, these persons indicate the characters of the dwellers in the house. My friends have disputed this point with me, and have asserted that they do not wish to be so represented, but nevertheless I have frequently found my position correct.

I prefer to visit those houses whose door service is performed by a neat, good-looking, intelligent, bright-witted, kindly-tempered, conscientious, and sympathetic maidservant. A man is generally very unsatisfactory. He performs his duty in a perfunctory manner. His heart is not in it. He fears to say a word more than he thinks absolutely necessary, lest you should imagine him new in service, and had not lost his interest in answering questions.

But even if the person you ask for be not at home, it is sometimes a pleasure to be told so by an intelligent maid, such as I have mentioned above. One's subsequent action is frequently influenced by her counsel and information. Frequently she is able to indicate to you your true relation with the household; sometimes she assists in establishing it.

When the door before me opened, I saw a colored woman. I was utterly discomfited. None of my rules applied to a middle-aged colored woman, who gazed upon me as if she recognized me as one whom she carried in her arms when an infant. Actuated by impulse only, I inquired for "Miss Raynor."

"I reckon," said she, "you's got to de wrong house. Dat lady doan' live hyar."

"Well, then," I asked quickly, "is there a lady here named Mother Anastasia?"

The woman showed thirty-two perfectly developed teeth.

"Oh, dat's she? You means de sister. She's hyar, yes, sah. Want to see her?"

I stated that I certainly desired to see her.

"She's gone out now, sah, an' dere's no tellin' when dey'll git back. Dey ginerally all gits back 'bout dark. Commonly jist a little arter dark."

"Not return before dark!" I exclaimed. "That is bad. Can you give me any idea where I might find Mother Anastasia?"

"I 'spects you kin fin' her mighty easy. Mos' likely, she's at de Patent Office, or at de Army and Navy Buildin', or de White House, or de Treasury, or de Smifsonian, or de Navy Yard, or de new 'Servatory, or on de avenue shoppin', or gone to de Capitol to de Senate or de House, one; or perhaps she druv out to Arlin'ton, or else she's gone to de 'Gressional Libr'y. Mos' likely she's at one or de odder of dem places; an' about one o'clock, she an' Mis' Gardley is mighty sure to eat der luncheon somewhar, an' arter that I reckon they'll go to 'bout four arternoon teas. I doan' know 'xactly whare de teas 'll be dis arternoon, but ye kin tell de houses whar dar is a tea inside by de carriages a-waitin',— an' ef it aint a tea, it's a fun'ral,—and all yer's got to do is to go inside an' see if she's dar."

I could not refrain from smiling, but I was greatly discouraged. How could I wait until evening for the desired interview?

"If you is kin to de sister," said the woman,—"an' I reckon you is, for I see de likeness powerful strong,—she'll be mighty glad to see ye, sah. Want me ter tell her ye'll come back this evening, if you doan' fin' her before dat?"

I desired her to give such a message, and went away well pleased that the woman had not asked my name. It was desirable that Mother Anastasia should not know who was coming to call on her.

I am, as I have said before, much given to the consideration of motives and all that sort of thing, and, in the course of the day, I found myself wondering why I should have taken the trouble to walk through the Patent Office and half a dozen other public buildings, continually looking about me, not at the objects of interest therein, but at the visitors; that is, if they were ladies. Why this uneasy desire to find the Mother Superior, when, by quietly waiting until evening, I was almost certain to see her? But in the midst of my self-questionings I went on looking for Mother Anastasia.

I finished my long ramble by a visit to the gallery of the House of Representatives. A member was making a speech on a bill to establish a national medical college for women. The speech and the subject may have interested some people, but I did not care for either, and I am afraid I was a little drowsy. After a time I took a cab and went to my hotel. At all events, the long day of waiting was nearly over.

Early in the evening I called again at Mrs. Gardley's house, and to my delight I was informed that the lady I desired to see was at home.

When Mother Anastasia came into the drawing-room, where I awaited her, she wore the gray gown of her sisterhood, but no head covering. I had before discovered that a woman could be beautiful in a Martha gown, but at this moment the fact asserted itself with peculiar force. She greeted me with a smile and an extended hand.

"You do not seem surprised to see me," I said.

"Why should I be?" she answered. "I saw you in the House of Representatives, and wondered why you should doze when such an interesting matter was being discussed; and when I came home, and heard that a gentleman answering your description intended to call on me this evening, I declined to go out to the theatre, wishing to be here to receive you."

I was disgusted to think that she had caught me napping, and that she had been near me in the House and I had not known it, but I said nothing of this.

"You are very good," I remarked, "to give up the theatre"—

"Oh, don't thank me," she interrupted; "perhaps you will not think I am good. Before we say anything more, I want you to tell me whether or not you came here to talk about Sylvia Raynor."

Here was a blunt question, but from the bottom of my heart I believed that I answered truly when I said I had not come for that purpose.

"Very good," said Mother Anastasia, leaning back in her chair. "Now I can freely say that I am glad to see you. I was dreadfully afraid you had come to talk to me on that forbidden subject, and I must admit that this fear had a very powerful influence in keeping me at home this evening. If you had come to talk to me of her, I would have had something very important to say to you, but I am delighted that my fears were groundless. And now tell me how you could help being interested in that grand scheme for a woman's college."

"I have never given it any thought. Do you care for it?"

"Care for it!" she exclaimed. "I am enlisted in the cause, hand and heart. I came down here because the bill was to be brought before the House. If the college is established,—and I believe it will be,—I expect to be one of the faculty."

"You are not a physician?" said I.

"Oh, I have studied and practiced medicine," she answered, "and expect to do a great deal more of it before we begin operations. The physician's art is my true vocation."

"And you will leave the House of Martha?" I asked.

"Yes," she replied. "The period for which I entered it has nearly expired. I do not regret the time I have spent there, but I must admit I shall be glad to leave the sisterhood. That life is too narrow for me, and perhaps too shallow. I say nothing against it in a general way; I only speak of it as it relates to myself. The very manner in which I rejoice in the prospect of freedom proves to me that I ought to be free, and that I did a wise thing in limiting the term of my sisterhood."

As Mother Anastasia spoke there was a glow of earnest pleasure upon her face. She was truly very happy to be able to talk of her approaching freedom.

I am a prudent man and a cautious one. This frank enthusiasm alarmed me. How deftly she had put Sylvia out of sight! How skillfully she had brought herself into full view, free and untrammeled by vows and rules,—a woman as other women!

The more I saw of Mother Anastasia the better I liked her, but I perceived that she was a woman with whom it was very necessary to be cautious. She was apt, I thought, to make convictions of her presumptions. If she presumed that my love for Sylvia was an utterly hopeless affection, to be given up and forgotten, I did not like it. It might be that it was hopeless, but I did not care to have any one else settle the matter for me in that way,—not even Mother Anastasia.

"Of course," I remarked, "I am glad that you have concluded to withdraw from a vocation which I am sure is not suited to you, and yet I feel a little disappointed to hear that you will not continue at the head of the House of Martha, for I came to Washington on purpose to make you a proposition in regard to that institution."

"Came to Washington on purpose to see me, and to make a proposition! What can it possibly be?"

I now laid before her, with considerable attention to detail, my plan for working in cooeperation with the House of Martha. I showed her the advantages of the scheme as they had suggested themselves to me, and as an example of what could be done I mentioned Sylvia's fancy for typewriting, and demonstrated how easily I could undertake the outside management of this very lucrative and pleasant occupation. I warmed up as I talked, and spoke quite strongly about what I—and perhaps in time other men—might do for the benefit of the sisterhood, if my proposition were accepted.

She listened to me attentively, her face growing paler and harder as I proceeded. When I had finished she said:—

"It is not at all necessary for me to discuss this utterly preposterous scheme, nor even to refer to it, except to say that I plainly see its object. Whatever you have persuaded yourself to think of your plan, I know that its real object is to reestablish a connection with Sylvia. You would know, if you would allow yourself to think about it, that your absurd and even wicked scheme of typewriting, companionship in work, and all that stuff, could only result in making the girl miserable and perhaps breaking her heart. You know that she loves you, and that it has been a terrible trial to her to yield to her conscience and do what she has done; and you know, furthermore,—and this more than anything else darkens your intention,—that Sylvia's artless, ingenuous, and impulsive nature would give you advantages which would not be afforded to you by one who did not love you, and who better understood the world and you."

"Madam," I exclaimed, "you do me an injustice!"

She paid no attention to this remark, and proceeded: "And now let me tell you that what you have said to me to-night has changed my plans, my life. I shall not leave Sylvia exposed to your cruel attacks,—attacks which I believe will come in every practical form that your ingenuity can devise. It was my example that brought that girl into the House of Martha, and now that she has vowed to devote her life and her work to its service I shall not desert her. I will not have her pure purpose shaken and weakened, little by little, day by day, until it falls listless and deadened, with nothing to take its place. Therefore, until I know that you are no longer a source of danger to her, I shall remain Mother Superior of the House of Martha, and rest assured that while I am in that position Sylvia shall be safe from you." And with that she rose and walked out of the room.

XLIII

WAS HIS HEART TRUE TO POLL?

Never before had any one spoken to me as Mother Anastasia had just spoken. Never before had I felt as I felt in leaving the house where she had spoken to me. I did not admit all that she had said; and yet not even to myself could I gainsay her statements. I was not convinced that I had been wrong, but I could not help feeling that she was right. I was angry, I was mortified, I was grieved. The world seemed cold and dark, and the coldest and darkest thing in it was the figure of Mother Anastasia, as she rose to leave me.

When I reached New York, I bethought myself of my promise to Miss Laniston. It tortured my soul to think of what had happened; I knew it would torture it still more to talk of these things. But I am a man who keeps his promises; besides, I wanted to see Miss Laniston. I did not like her very much, but the people whom I did like seemed to be falling away from me, and she was a woman of vigorous spirit, to whom one in my plight would naturally turn. That she could give me any encouragement was not likely, but she might offer me an enheartening sympathy; and, more-over, she was well acquainted with Mother Anastasia, and there were a good many questions I wanted to ask about that lady.

I found Miss Laniston at home, but I was obliged to wait a good while before she made her appearance.

"If you were any other man in this world," she said, "I should have felt obliged to excuse myself from seeing you, for I am engaged on most important business with a modiste who is designing a gown for me; but I am perfectly wild to hear about your interview with Mother Anastasia, and I was afraid, if I sent you away, that you would not come back again; so tell me about it, I pray you. I know you have seen her, for you look so uncommonly glum. I am afraid that you have not yet become a brother of the House of Martha."

There was nothing inspiring about this badinage, but I braced myself to the work, and told her what had happened in Washington.

"This is truly dreadful," she declared. "Of course I had no idea that Mother Anastasia would consider your plan as anything more than the wild outreachings of a baffled lover, but I did not imagine that she would take it in this way. This is very bad."

"It is," I answered. "Everything is knocked from under me."

"Oh, bless you," said the lady, "I wasn't thinking of you, but of Mother Anastasia. It was the happiest news I can remember when I heard that she was soon to drop that name and all that belonged to it, and to begin a life in which she would be a woman among her peers, no matter with what sex they happen to be classed. But if she stops short and remains in that miserable House of Martha, the result is bound to be disastrous. If she believes it is necessary to spend her life in protecting Sylvia from your assaults, she is the woman to spend her life in that way."

"What her friends should do," said I, "is to convince her that it is not necessary."

Miss Laniston gazed upon me fixedly. "You think it would be a great pity for a beautiful woman—a remarkably fine woman like Mother Anastasia—to hide herself away in that make-believe convent?"

"Indeed I do," I answered, with animation.

"And since one fine woman is shut up for life in that prison, you think it a shame that another one should remain within its walls?"

I assented warmly.

"Now, then," remarked Miss Laniston, rising, "it is absolutely necessary for me to go to the Frenchwoman, who, I know, is fuming for me, and whose time is very precious. I shall be with you again in about twenty minutes, and during that time I wish you would make up your mind with whom you are in love,—Mother Anastasia or Sylvia Raynor. When that point is settled, we will see what can be done."

It was a man of a bewildered mind who was left alone in that drawing-room. I did not understand what had been said to me, but now that ideas of this kind had been put into words, there seemed to be a certain familiarity about them. How dared she speak to me in that way? What ground had she for such words?

And yet—Sylvia was shut up for life in the House of Martha. I could not gainsay that.

I could not put my thoughts into form, and with my mind in chaos I strode up and down the room until Miss Laniston returned.

"What an uneasy person you are!" she said. "Have you settled that little point?"

"Settled it! There is nothing to settle."

She laughed. "I am not so sure about that. I thought I saw a change in the wind when you were here last, and it is natural enough that it should change. What is the good of its blowing steadfastly from the north, when the north is nothing but ice?"

"You have no right to talk in that way!" I exclaimed angrily. "I utterly repudiate your supposition."

"Come, come," she said, "let us be practical. I really take an interest in you, you know, and besides that, I take an interest in my friends; and it is quite plain to me that you must not be allowed to wander about in a detached way, making all sorts of trouble. You have made a good deal already. So if we must consider Sylvia Raynor as really out of the race, on account of being tied up by her sisterhood obligations, we must turn our attention to Mother Anastasia, who probably has not yet done anything definite in regard to retaining her position in the House of Martha. If anything can be done in this direction, it will be entirely satisfactory, because, if you get the ex-Mother Superior, of course you will be content to leave the young sister alone."

"Madam, you insult me!" I cried, springing to my feet.

"By which, I suppose," she answered, "you wish me to understand that your heart is true to Poll,—by Poll meaning Sylvia Raynor."

"You know that as well as I do," I replied. "I have taken you into my confidence; I have told you that I loved her, that I should always love her; and it is unwomanly in you"—

"That will do," she interrupted,—"that will do; don't say hard words to one of your best friends. If you will continue to be true to Poll, not as the sailor was in the song, but constant and steadfast in all sorts of weather, and without any regard to that mere material point of eventually getting her for your own, why then I am your fast friend to the end, and will do everything that I can to soften your woes and lighten your pathway; and all the reward I desire for my labors is the pleasure of knowing that there is at least one man in the world who can love truly and unchangeably without seeing any chance ahead of him of winning the woman he loves. Do you think you can fill that position?"

I looked at her sternly, and answered: "I have said all upon that point that is necessary to say. When I love a woman, I love her forever."

"Very good," said Miss Laniston,—"very good; and I dare say your little side flights didn't mean anything at all. And now I shall talk with Mother Anastasia as soon as possible, and make her understand that she has no right to sacrifice herself to Sylvia or any one else. If I can get her started off on the right road, I will see what I can do with the new Mother Superior, whoever she may be. Perhaps you may yet be able to establish that delightful brotherhood of the House of Martha. Any way, I promise you you shall have something. It may not be much and it may not be often, but it shall be enough to keep your love alive, and that, you see, is my great object. I want to make of you a monument of masculine constancy."

As I took leave of her, Miss Laniston gave my hand a vigorous pressure, which seemed to me to indicate that her intentions were better than her words. As I went away my mind was quieter, though not cheered. There was in it a certain void and emptiness, but this was compensated for by a sense of self-approbation which was strengthening and comforting. I was even able to smile at the notion of the interview between Miss Laniston and Sister Sarah, when the former should propose my plan of the brotherhood.

XLIV

PRELIMINARY BROTHERHOOD

When I returned to Arden, I gave Walkirk an outline of what had occurred, but I did not go into details, having no desire that the preposterous idea which had gotten into the head of Miss Laniston should enter that of my under-study. Walkirk was not in good spirits.

"I had hoped something," he said, "from your interview with Mother Anastasia, though perhaps not exactly in the line of a brotherhood. I thought if she came to thoroughly understand your earnestness in the matter, she might use her influence with Miss Raynor, which at some time or other, or in some way or other, might result to your advantage, and that of the young lady. I had and still have great belief in the capabilities of Mother Anastasia, but now I am forced to believe, very much against my will, that there is no hope ahead. With Mother Anastasia decidedly against us, the fight is lost."

"Us," I repeated.

"My dear sir," said he, "I am with you, soul and body."

Without a word I took him by the hand, and pressed it warmly.

"What do you think of continuing your recitals of travel?" Walkirk said to me later in the day. "I should think they would interest you, and I know they were vastly interesting to me. You must have a great deal more to tell."

"I have," I answered, "but I shall not tell it now. Instead of talking about travels, I have determined to travel. At present it is awkward for me to remain here. It is impossible for me to feel independent, and able to do what I please, and know that there are persons in the village who do not wish to meet me, and with whom it would be embarrassing and perhaps unpleasant to meet. I know I must meet them some time or other, unless they shut themselves up, or I shut myself up. That sort of thing I cannot endure, and I shall go to Turkey and Egypt. Those countries I have not visited. If it suits you, I shall take you with me, and I shall also take a stenographer, to whom I shall dictate, on the spot, the materials for my book."

"Do you mean," asked Walkirk, "that you will dispense altogether with that preparatory narration to me of what you intend afterwards to put into your book? I consider that a capital plan, and I think you found it of advantage."

"That is true," I answered; "the plan worked admirably. I did not propose to work in that way again, but I will do it. Every night I will tell you what I have done, and what I think about things, and the next morning I'll dictate that material, revised and shapen, to the stenographer, who can then have the rest of the day to write it out properly."

"A capital plan," said Walkirk, "and I shall be charmed to go with you."

I was indeed very anxious to leave Arden. I could not believe that Mother Anastasia had ever imagined any of the stuff that Miss Laniston had talked about, but she certainly had

Frank R. Stockton

shown me that she was greatly offended with me, and nothing offends me so much as to have people offended with me. Such persons I do not wish to meet.

I did not immediately fix a date for my departure, for it was necessary for me to consider my grandmother's feelings and welfare, and arrange to make her as happy as possible while I should be gone. In the mean time, it was of course necessary that I should take air and exercise; and while doing this one morning in a pretty lane, just out of the village, a figure in the House of Martha gray came into sight a little distance ahead of me. Her back was toward me, and she was walking slower than I was. "Now, then," thought I, "here is a proof of the awkwardness of my position here. Even in a little walk like this, I must run up against one of those sisters. I must pass her, or turn around and go back, for I shall not slow up, and appear to be dogging her footsteps. But I shall not turn back,—that does not suit me." Consequently I walked on, and soon overtook the woman in gray. She did not turn her head as I approached, for the sisters are taught not to turn their heads to look at people. After all, it would be easy enough for me to adopt the same rule, and to pass her without turning my head, or paying the slightest attention to her. This was the manner indeed in which the general public was expected to act toward the inmates of the House of Martha when met outside their institution.

When I came up with her, I turned and looked into the bonnet. It was Sylvia. As my eyes fell upon the face of that startled angel, my impulse was to throw my arms around her, and rush away with her, gray bonnet, shawl and all, to some distant clime where there were no Houses of Martha, Mother Anastasias, or anything which could separate my dear love and me; but I crushed down this mad fancy, smothered, as well as I could, my wild emotions, and said, as calmly as possible,—

"Good morning, sister."

Over the quick flushes of her face there spread a smile of pleasure.

"I like that," she said; "I am glad to have you call me sister. I thought you would be prejudiced against it, and would not do it."

"Prejudiced!" I said; "not a bit of it. I am delighted to do so."

"That is really good of you," she said; "and how have you been? You look a little wan and tired. Have you been doing your own writing?"

"Oh, no," I said; "I have given up writing, at least for the present. I wish I could make you understand how glad I am to call you sister, and how it would joy my heart if you would call me brother."

"Oh, that would not do at all," she said, in a tone which indicated surprise at my ignorance; "that would be quite a different thing. I am a sister to everybody, but you are not a brother to anybody."

"When you hear what I have to say about this," I answered, "you will understand what I mean by wishing to be called brother. May I ask where you are going?"

"I am going to visit a sick person in that little house at the bottom of the hill. Sister Agatha came with me, but she had the toothache, and had to go back. I expect Sister Sarah will send some one of the others to join me, for she always wants us to go about in couples."

"She is entirely right," said I; "I did not know she had so

much sense, and I shall make one of the couple this time. You ought not to be walking about here by yourself."

"I suppose I ought to have gone back with Sister Agatha," said she, "but I didn't want to. I'm dreadfully tired of staying in the House of Martha, trying to learn typewriting. I can do it pretty well now, but nothing has come of it. Sister Sarah got me one piece of work, which was to copy a lot of bad manuscript about local option. I am sure, if I am to do that sort of thing I shall not like typewriting."

"You shall not do that sort of thing," said I; "and now let us walk on slowly, while I tell you what I meant by the term brother." I was in a whirl of delight. Now I would talk to one who I believed would sympathize with my every thought, who would be in harmony with my outreachings, if she could do no more, and from whom I need expect neither ridicule nor revilings. We walked on slowly, and I laid before her my scheme for the brotherhood of the House of Martha.

I was not mistaken in my anticipation of Sylvia's sympathy. She listened with sparkling eyes, and when I finished, clapped her hands with delight.

"That is one of the best plans that was ever heard of in this world," she said. "How different it would make our life at the institution! Of course the brothers wouldn't live there, but we should see each other, like ordinary people in society, and everything would not be so dreadfully blank, and there is no end to the things which you could do, which we cannot do, unless with a great deal of trouble. The usefulness of your plan seems to have no limits at all. How many brothers do you think we ought to have?"

"I have not considered that point," I said; "at present I know of but one person, besides myself, who would have the necessary qualifications for the position."

"I expect," she said, looking at me with a twinkle of fun in her eye, "that if you had the selection of the other brothers they would be a tame lot."

"Perhaps you are right," I said, and we both broke into a laugh.

"I wish I could tell you," said Sylvia, "how much I am charmed with your idea of the brotherhood. I haven't enjoyed myself so much for ever so long."

We were now nearing the little house at the bottom of the hill. An idea struck me.

"Who is it that you are going to visit?" I asked.

"It is an old man," she said, "who has the rheumatism so badly that he cannot move. He has to take his medicine every hour, and his wife is worn out sitting up and giving it to him, and Sister Agatha and I were sent to take care of him during the morning, and let the poor old woman get some sleep."

"Very good," said I, "here is a chance for me to make a beginning in my scheme of brotherhood, and that without asking leave or license of anybody. I will go in with you, and help you nurse the old man."

"I expect you can do it splendidly," said Sylvia, "and now we can see how a brotherhood would work."

We entered a little house, which apparently had once been a good enough home for humble dwellers, but which now showed signs of extreme poverty. A man with gray hair, and placid, pale face, was lying on a bed in one corner of the room into which the door opened, and in a chair near by sat an old woman, her head bobbing in an uneasy nap. She roused when we entered, and seemed glad to see us.

"He's about the same as he was," she said, "an' as he's loike to be width thim little draps of midicine; but if you're a docther, sir, it ain't for me to be meddlin', an' sayin' that one of thim Pepper Pod Plasters width howles in it would do more good to his poor back than thim draps inside of him."

"Rheumatism is not treated externally so much as it used to be," I said. "You will find that internal medication will be of much more service in the long run."

"That may be, sir," said she; "but it won't do to make the run too long, considtherin' he hasn't been able to do a sthroke of work for four weeks, an' if ye'd ever tried one of thim plasters, sir, ye'd know they's as warmin' as sandpaper an' salt; but if I kin git a little slape, it will be better for me than any midicine, inside or out."

"That's what we came to give you," said Sylvia; "go into the other room, and lie down, and you shall not be called until it is time for your dinner."

The woman gave a little shrug, which I imagine was intended to indicate that dinner and dinner-time had not much relation to each other in this house, and going into an adjoining room, was probably soon fast asleep.

"It would be better to begin by giving him his medicine. I know all about it, for I was here yesterday. I forgot to ask his wife when she gave it to him last," said Sylvia, "but we might as well begin fresh at the half-pasts."

She poured out a teaspoonful of the stuff, and administered

it to the old man, who opened his mouth, and took it placidly.

"He is very quiet and very patient," said Sylvia to me in an undertone,—and it is impossible for me to describe how delightful it was to have her speak to me in such a confidential undertone,—"he doesn't talk any," she continued, "and doesn't seem to care to have anybody read to him, for when Sister Agatha tried that yesterday, he went to sleep; but he likes his brow bathed, and I can sit on this side of his bed and do that, and you can find a chair and sit on the other side, and tell me more about your plan of brotherhood."

There was no other chair, but I found a box, on which I seated myself on the other side of the old man's cot, while Sylvia, taking a bottle from her pocket, proceeded to dampen the forehead of the patient with its pleasantly scented contents.

I did not much like to see her doing this, nor did I care to discuss our projects over the body of this rheumatic laborer.

"It strikes me," I said, "that it would be a good idea to put on that bay rum, or cologne, or whatever it is, with a clean paint-brush, or something of the kind. Don't you dislike using your fingers?"

Sylvia laughed. "You have lots to learn yet," she said, "before you can be a brother; and now tell me what particular kind of work you think the brothers would do. I hardly think nursing would suit them very well."

I did not immediately answer, and Sylvia's quick mind divined the reason of my reluctance.

"Let us talk *en francais*," she said; "that will not disturb this good man, and he can go to sleep if he likes."

"*Tres bien*," I said, "*parlons nous en francais.*"

"*Il serait charmant,*" said she; "*j'aime la belle langue.*"

The old man turned his head from one to the other of us; all his placidity vanished, and he exclaimed,—

"*Ciel! Voila les anges l'un et l'autre qui vient parler ma chere langue.*"

"Good gracious!" exclaimed Sylvia, "I thought he was Irish."

The patient now took the talking business into his own hands, and in his dear language told us his tale of woe. It was a very ordinary tale, and its dolefulness was relieved by the old man's delight at finding people who could talk to him like Christians. One of his woes was that he had not been long enough married to his wife to teach her much French.

"I wish," interpolated Sylvia to me, "that we had kept on in English. It would have been much more satisfactory. I expect one of the other sisters will be here before very long, and before she comes I wish you would tell me how you are getting on with your book. I have been thinking about it, ever and ever so much."

"I am not getting on at all," said I; "without you there will be no book."

At this Sylvia knit her brows a little, and looked disturbed.

"That is not a good way to talk about it," she said, "unless, indeed, the book could be made a part of the brotherhood work, in some way. The publisher might want a typewritten copy, and if I should make it, I should know the end of the story of Tomaso and Lucilla. You know I had almost given up ever knowing what finally happened to those two."

"You shall know it," said I; "we shall work together yet. I can think of a dozen ways in which we can do it, and I intend to prove that my brotherhood idea is thoroughly practicable."

"Of course it is," said Sylvia; "isn't this practical?" and she bedewed the patient's brow so liberally, that some of the perfume ran into his eyes, and made him wink vigorously.

"*Merci, mademoiselle*," said he, "*mais pas beaucoup, mais pas beaucoup*!"

"A capital practical idea has just occurred to me," I said; "do you think you shall be here to-morrow?"

"I expect to come here," she answered, "for I take a great deal of interest in this old man. Mother Anastasia is still away, and I expect that Sister Sarah will send me again, for this is the kind of work she believes in. She has a very poor opinion of typewriting; but, of course, a sister will come with me."

"There is one coming to join you now," I said; "I see her gray figure on the top of the hill. As she will not understand matters, and as I do not wish to talk any more about my plans, until I am better able to show how they will work, I think it will be well for me to retire; but I shall be here to-morrow morning, and it would suit my plans very well if another sister comes with you."

Sylvia looked around at the approaching gray figure.

"I think that is Sister Lydia," she said, "at least, I think I recognize her walk, and so it might be well for you to go. If it were Sister Agatha it wouldn't matter so much. Of course, when your plan is all explained and agreed to, it will not make any difference who comes or goes."

"Very true," said I, "and now I think I will bid you good-morning. Be sure and be here to-morrow."

She shook hands with me, across the prostrate form of the rheumatic Frenchman, who smiled, and murmured, "*Bien, bien, mes anges,*" and she assured me that I might expect her on the morrow.

XLV

I MAKE COFFEE AND GET INTO HOT WATER

I do not like to do anything which looks in the least underhanded, but I must admit that I left that wretched cottage by the back door, and taking a path through some woods, made a wide circuit before returning to the village.

As soon as I reached my house, I called Walkirk from his writing, and rapidly gave him instructions in regard to the execution of an idea which had come into my mind during my brotherhood labors of the morning.

I told him to hasten to the scene of my building operations, and to take away all the carpenters, painters, and plasterers he could crowd into a two-horse wagon, and to go with them to the house of the rheumatic Frenchman, from which I knew the sisters would have departed before he reached it. I promised to join him there, and at the same time that he set out on his errand, I hurried to a shop in the village, the owner of which combined the occupations of cabinet maker and undertaker, and who generally kept on hand a small stock of cheap furniture. From this I selected such articles as I thought would be suitable or useful in a small house, which at present contained nothing too good for a bonfire, and ordered them sent immediately to the Frenchman's cottage.

I reached this wretched little house a few minutes before the arrival of Walkirk and the wagon-load of mechanics. My under-study had entered heartily into my scheme, and by his directions the men had brought with them everything needed to carry out my plans, and in a very short time he and I had set every man to work.

There were carpenters, plasterers, painters, paper-hangers, and a tinner and glazier, and when they learned that I wanted that little house completely renovated in the course of the afternoon, they looked upon the business as a lark, and entered into it with great spirit. The astonished woman of the house did not understand what was about to happen, and even when I had explained it to her, her mind seemed to take in nothing except the fact that the house ought to be cleaned before the painting and paper-hanging began, but there was no time for delays of this sort, and the work went on merrily.

When the furniture arrived, the woman gave a gasp, for the last time the vehicle which brought them to her house had been there, it had taken away her previous husband. But a bureau and table and a roll of carpet assured her of its different purpose, and she turned in with a will to assist in arranging these articles.

Before dark the work was all done. The rheumatic Frenchman was lying on a shining new bedstead, a box of Pepper Pod Plasters had been placed in the hands of his delighted wife, a grocery wagon had deposited a load of goods in the kitchen, the mechanics in gay spirits had driven away, and Walkirk and I, tired, but triumphant, walked home, leaving behind us a magical transformation, a pervading smell of paint and damp wall-paper, and an aged couple as much dazed as delighted with what had happened.

Soon after breakfast the next day, I repaired to the bright

and tidy little cottage, and there I had my reward. Standing near the house a little in the shadow of a good sized evergreen-tree, which I had ordered transplanted bodily from the woods into the little yard, I beheld Sylvia approaching, and with her a sister with a bandaged face whom I rightly supposed to be the amiable Sister Agatha.

When the two came within a moderate distance of the cottage they stopped, they looked about them from side to side, and it was plain to see that they imagined they were on the wrong road. Then they walked forward a bit, stopped again, and finally came towards the house on a run.

I advanced to meet them.

"Good morning, sisters," said I. The two were so much astonished that they did not return my greeting, and for a few moments scarcely noticed me. Then Sylvia turned.

"How in the world," she exclaimed, "did all this happen? It must be the same house."

I smiled. "It is very simple," said I; "this"—and as I spoke I waved my hand towards the cottage—"is an instance of the way in which the brothers of the House of Martha intend to work."

"And you did this?" exclaimed Sylvia, with radiant eyes.

I explained to the eagerly listening sisters how the transformation had been accomplished, and with a sort of reverent curiosity they approached the house. Sister Agatha's astonishment was even greater than that of Sylvia, for she had long known the wretched place.

"It is a veritable miracle," she said, "see this beautiful white fence, and the gate; it opens on hinges!"

"Be careful," said I, as they entered the little yard, "some of the paint may yet be wet, although I told them to put as much drying stuff in as was possible."

"Actually," cried Sylvia, "a gravel walk up to the house!"

"And the outside a daffodil yellow, with fern green blinds!" said Sister Agatha.

"And the eaves tipped with geranium red!" cried Sylvia.

"And a real tree on each side of the front door, and new steps!" exclaimed Sister Agatha.

When they entered the house the amazement and delight of the two sisters was a joy to my soul. They cried out at the carpet on the floor, the paper on the walls, the tables, the chairs, the bureau, the looking-glass, the three framed lithographs on the wall, the clock, and the shining new bedstead on which their patient lay.

"If Mother Anastasia could but see this," cried Sylvia, "she would believe in the brotherhood."

"He sez yer angels," said the woman of the house, coming forward, "that's what he sez; an' he's roight too, for with thim Pepper Pod Plasters, an' the smell of paint in the house which he hates, he'll be out o' doors in two days, or I'm much mishtaken."

Sylvia and I now approached the old man to see what he thought about it. He was very grateful, and said nothing about the smell of paint, but we found him with a burning desire in his heart which had been fanned into flames by the arrival of the groceries on the day before. He eagerly asked us if we could make coffee; when he was well he could make it himself, but since he had been lying on that bed, he had not tasted a drop of the beloved liquid. His wife did not drink it, and could not make it, but as we could speak French, and had sent coffee, he felt sure that we could compound the beverage, so dear to the French heart.

"The angels make coffee," he said, in his best patois, "otherwise what would Heaven be?"

Both of the angels declared that the good man should have some coffee without delay, but Sylvia said to me, that although she had not the least idea how to make it, she was quite sure Sister Agatha could do it. But that sister, when asked, declared that she knew nothing about coffee, and did not approve of it for sick people, but if the man did not like the tea his wife made, she would try what she could do.

But this offer was declined. The old man must have his coffee, and as there was no one else to make it, I undertook to do it myself. I thought I remembered how coffee had been made, when I had been camping out, and I went promptly to work. Everybody helped. The old woman ground the berries, Sister Agatha stirred up the fire, and Sylvia broke two eggs, in order to get shells enough to clear the liquid.

It was a good while before the coffee was ready, but at last it was made, and Sylvia carried it to our patient in a great bowl. She sat down on one side of the bed to administer the smoking beverage with a spoon, while I sat on the other side and raised the old man's head that he might drink the better. After swallowing the first tablespoonful, the patient winked.

"I hope it did not scald his throat," said Sylvia, "Do you know what 'scald' is in French?"

"I cannot remember," said I, "you had better let the next

spoonful cool a little,"—but the patient opened his mouth for more.

"*C'est potage*," he said, "*mais il est bon.*"

"I am sorry I made soup of it," I said to Sylvia, "but I am sure it tastes like coffee."

We continued to feed the old man, who absorbed the new-fangled broth as fast as it was given to him, until a voice behind me made us both jump.

"Sister Hagar," said the voice, "what does this mean?"

"Goodness, Mother Anastasia," cried Sylvia, "you made me scald the outside of his throat."

At the foot of the bed stood Mother Anastasia clad in her severest gray, her brows knit and her lips close pressed.

"Sister Hagar," she repeated, "what is all this?"

I let down the old man's head, and Sylvia, placing the almost empty bowl upon the table, replied serenely:—

"Mr. Vanderley is making a beginning in brotherhood work—the brotherhood of the House of Martha, you know. I think it would work splendidly. Just look around and see what he has done. He has made this charming cottage out of an old rattle-trap house. Everything you see in one afternoon, and lots of provisions in the kitchen besides. Sisters alone could never have done this."

Mother Anastasia turned to me.

"I will speak with you, outside," she said, and I followed her into the little yard. As soon as we were far enough from the house to speak without being overheard, she stopped, and turning to me, said:—

"You are not content with driving me from the life on which I had set my heart, back into this mistaken vocation, but you are determined to make my lot miserable and unhappy. And not mine only, but that of that simple-hearted and unsuspecting girl. I do not see how you can be so selfishly cruel. You are resolved to break her heart, and to do it in the most torturing way. But you shall work her no more harm. I do not now appeal to your honor, to your sense of justice; I simply say that I shall henceforth stand between you and her. What misery may come to her and to me from what you have already done I do not know, but you do no more."

I stood and listened with the blood boiling within me.

"Marcia Raynor," I said—"for I shall not call you by that title which you put on and take off as you please—I here declare to you that I shall never give up Sylvia. If I never speak to her again or see her I shall not give her up. I make no answer to what you have charged me with, but I say to you that as Sylvia's life and my life cannot be one as I would have it, I shall live the life that she lives, even though our lives be ever apart. For the love I bear her, I shall always do the work that she does. But I believe that the time will come when people, wiser than you are, will see that what I proposed to do is a good thing to do, and the time will come when a man and a woman can labor side by side in good works, and both do better work because they work together. And to Sylvia and to my plan of brotherhood, I shall ever be constant. Remember that."

Without a word or change in her expression she left me, went into the house, and closed the door behind her. I did not wish to make a scene, which would give rise to injurious gossip, and therefore walked away, though as I did so I turned to look in at the open window, but I did not see Sylvia; I only saw the bandaged face of Sister Agatha looking out at me, more mournful than before.

As I rapidly walked homeward, I said to myself, "Now I declare myself a full brother of the House of Martha. I shall take up their cause, and steadfastly work for it whether they like it or not."

XLVI

GOING BACK FOR A FRIEND

When I reached home, I looked up my grandmother and told her everything that had happened. My excitement was so great that it was necessary I should talk to some one, and I felt a pang of regret when I remembered that latterly I had given no confidences to her.

My grandmother listened eagerly and without interrupting me, but as I spoke she shook her head again and again, and when I had finished, she said:—

"My dear boy, if you understood the world and the people in it as well as I do, you would know that that sort of thing could never, never work. Before long you and Sylvia would be madly in love with each other, and then what would happen nobody knows. It may be that Mother Anastasia has not fully done her duty in this case, or it may be that she has done too much, and other people may have acted improperly and without due thought and caution; but be this as it may, it is plain enough to see that your poor heart has been dreadfully wrung. I wish I had known before of this brotherhood notion, and of what you intended to do, and I would have told you, as I tell you now, that in this world we must accept situations. That is the only way in which we can get along at all. Sylvia Raynor has gone, soul

Frank R. Stockton

and body, into this Martha House, which is the same as a convent, and to all intents and purposes she is the same as a nun. Now there is no use fighting against that sort of thing. Even if she should consent to climb over the wall, and run away with you, I do not believe you would like a wife who would do that, after all she had vowed and given her solemn word to."

"My dear grandmother," I said, "all that you say may be true, but it makes no difference to me; I shall always be faithful to Sylvia."

"Perhaps so, perhaps so," said my grandmother, "but you must remember this: it may be all very well to be faithful, but you should be careful how you do it. In some respects Mother Anastasia is entirely right, and your faithfulness, if injudiciously shown, may make miserable the life of this young woman." I sighed but said nothing. My grandmother looked pityingly upon me.

"I think you can do nothing better than to go and travel as you have proposed. Stay away for a year. Dear knows, I do not want to keep you from me for all that time, but the absence will be for your good. It will influence your life. When you come back, then you will know yourself better than you can possibly know yourself now. Then you will be able to see what you truly ought to do, and I promise you that if I am alive I will help you do it."

I took the dear old lady in my arms, and her advice to my heart. I acknowledged to myself that at this conjuncture the wisest thing, the kindest thing was to go away. I might not stay away for a year, but I would go.

"Grandmother," I said, "I will do what you advise. But I have something to ask of you: I have vowed that I will be a brother of the House of Martha, and that I will do its work, with or without the consent of the sisters, and with or without their companionship. Now if I go, will you be my substitute? Will you, as far as you can, assist the sisters in their undertakings, and do what you think I would have done, had I been here?"

"I cannot change a dilapidated hut into a charming cottage in one afternoon," she said, placing both hands on my shoulders as she spoke, "but I will do all that I can, and all that you ought to do, if you were here. That much I promise."

"Then I will go," I said, "with a heavy heart, but with an easier conscience."

Walkirk entirely approved of an immediate start upon the journey which I had before proposed. I think he feared that if it was postponed any longer, I might get some other idea into my head which would work better than the brother-hood scheme, and that our travels might be postponed indefinitely.

But there was a great deal to be done before I could leave home for a lengthy absence, and a week was occupied in arranging my business affairs, and planning for the comfort and pleasure of my grandmother while I should be away. Walkirk engaged the stenographer, and was the greatest possible help to me in every way, but notwithstanding his efforts to relieve me of work that was a busier week for me than any week in my whole life. This was an advantage to me, for it kept me from thinking too much of the reason for my hurried journey.

At last the day arrived on which the steamer was to sail, and the generally cool Walkirk actually grew nervous in his efforts to get me ready to start by the early morning train for the city. In these efforts I did not assist him in the least. In fact had he not been with me I think that I should not have tried to leave home in time to catch the steamer. The more I thought of catching the steamer, the less I cared to do so; the more I thought of leaving home, the less I cared to do so. It was not that I was going away from Sylvia that made me thus reluctant to start. It was because I was going away without taking leave of her,—without a word or even a sign from her. I ground my teeth as I thought of how I had lost the only chance I had had of bidding her farewell, and of assuring her that, no matter what happened, I would be constant to her and to the principles in which we had both come to believe. I had been too much excited on the morning I had left her in the Frenchman's cottage to think that that would be my last chance of seeing her; that thereafter Mother Anastasia would never cease to guard her from my speech or sight. I should have rushed in, caring for nothing. People might have talked, but Sylvia would have known that prohibitions and separations would make no difference in my feeling for her.

And now I was going away without a word or a sign, or even the slightest trifle which I could cherish as a memento of her. There was a blankness about it all which deadened my soul.

But Walkirk was inexorable. He made every arrangement, and even superintended my farewell to my grandmother, and gently but firmly interrupted me, as I repeated my entreaties that she would speedily find out something about Sylvia, and write to me. At last we were in the carriage, with time enough to reach the station, and Walkirk wiped his brow, as would a man who had had a heavy load lifted from his mind.

We had not gone a quarter of the distance when the thought suddenly struck me, Why should I go away without a memento of Sylvia? Why had I not remembered my friend

Vespa, the wasp, whose flight around my secretary's room had made the first break in the restrictions which surrounded her; had first shown me a Sylvia in place of a gray-bonneted nun? That dead wasp, pinned to a card on the wall of my study, was the only thing I possessed in which Sylvia had a share. I must go back and get it; I must take it with me.

When I shouted to the coachman to turn, that I must go back to get something I had forgotten, Walkirk was thrown into a fever of anxiety. If we did not catch this train we would lose the steamer; the next train would be three hours later. But his protestations had no effect upon me. I must have Sylvia's wasp, no matter what happened.

Back to the house we dashed, and up-stairs I ran. I took down the card to which the wasp was affixed, I found a little box in which to put it, and while I was looking for a rubber band by which to secure the lid, a servant came hurriedly into the room with a telegram for me. I tore it open. It was from Miss Laniston and read thus:—

"Come to me as soon as you can. Important business."

"Important business!" I ejaculated. "She can have no business with me that does not concern Sylvia. I will go to her instantly." In a few seconds I was in the carriage, shouting to the man to drive as fast as he could.

"Yes, indeed," said Walkirk, "you cannot go too fast."

I handed my companion the telegram. He read it blankly.

"It is a pity," he said, "if the business is important. All that can be done now is to telegraph to her that she must write to you in London by the next steamer."

"I shall do nothing of the kind," said I, "I am going to her the instant we reach New York."

Walkirk clenched his hands together, and looked away. He had no words for this situation.

My temper was very different.

"What a wonderful piece of luck!" I exclaimed. "If we had kept on to the station, by this short cut, the telegraph boy, who of course came by the main road, would have missed me, and there would not have been time for him to get back to the station before the train started. How fortunate it was that I went back for that wasp."

"Wasp!" almost screamed Walkirk, and by the way he looked at me, I know he imagined that I was temporarily insane.

We caught the train, and on the way I explained my allusion to the wasp so far as to assure Walkirk that I was no more crazy than men badly crossed in love are apt to be.

"But are you really going to Miss Laniston?" he said.

"I shall be able to drive up there, give her fifteen minutes with five as a margin, and reach the steamer in time. You can go directly to the dock, and attend to the baggage and everything."

My under-study sighed, but he knew it was of no use to make any objections. He did not fail, however, to endeavor to impress upon me the importance of consulting my watch while listening to Miss Laniston's communication.

My plan was carried out; we separated as soon as we reached the city, and in a cab I rattled to Miss Laniston's house.

XLVII

I INTEREST MISS LANISTON

When I reached Miss Laniston's house that lady was at breakfast, but she did not keep me waiting long.

"Truly," she said, as she entered the drawing-room, "you are the most expeditious person I ever knew. I knew that you would come to me, but I did not suppose you would even start as soon as this."

"I had already started when I received your telegram," I said.

"To come here?"

"No, to sail for Europe."

"Well, well!" she exclaimed, "from this moment I shall respect my instincts, a thing I never did before. When I woke this morning my first thought was of the message I intended to send to you, and I intended to attend to it immediately after breakfast; but my hitherto unappreciated instincts hinted to me that no time should be lost, and I called my maid, and dispatched the telegram immediately. Moral: Do all the good you can before you get up in the morning. Why are you starting for Europe?"

Frank R. Stockton

"I haven't time to tell you," I said, "in fact, I can only remain a few minutes longer, or I shall lose the steamer. Please tell me your business."

"Is Sylvia the cause of your going away?" she asked.

"Yes," I said; "is she the reason of your wishing to see me?"

"Most certainly," she answered; "when does your steamer start?"

"By ten o'clock," I said.

"Oh, bless me," she remarked, glancing at the clock, "you have quite time enough to hear all I have to say, and then if you do not catch the steamer it is your own fault. Sit down, I pray you."

Very reluctantly I took a seat, for at last the spirit of Walkirk had infected me.

"Now," said she, "I will cut my story as short as possible, but you really ought to hear it before you start. I made a visit to Arden, on the day after you performed the grand transformation scene in your brotherhood extravaganza. I should have been greatly amused by what was told me of this prank, if I had not seen that it had caused so much trouble. Sylvia was in a wretched way, and in an extremely bad temper. Marcia was almost as miserable, for she was acting the part of an extinguisher not only to Sylvia's hopes and aspirations, but to her own. So far as I could see there was no way out of the doleful dumps in which you seemed to have plunged yourself and all parties concerned, but I set to work to try what I could do to straighten out matters; my principal object being, I candidly admit, to enable Marcia Raynor to feel free to give up her position of watch-dog, and go to her National College, on which her soul is set. But to accomplish this, I must first do something with Sylvia; but that girl has a conscience like a fence post, and a disposition like a squirrel that skips along the rails. I could do nothing with her. She had sworn to be a Sister of Martha for life, and yet she would not consent to act like an out and out sister, and give up all that stuff about typewriting for you, and the other nonsensical notions of co-Marthaism, with which you infected her. She stoutly stuck to it, in spite of all the arguments I could use, that there was no good reason why you and she, as well as the other sisters and some other gentlemen, could not work together in the noble cause of I don't remember what fol-de-rol. Pretty co-Marthas you and she would make!

"Then I tried to induce Marcia to give up her fancies of responsibilities and all that, and to leave the girl in the charge of the present Mother Inferior, an elderly woman called Sister Sarah, who in my opinion could be quite as much of a griffin as the case demanded. But she would not listen to me. She had been the cause of her cousin's joining the sisterhood, and now she would not desert her, and she said a lot about the case requiring not only vigilance, but kindness and counsel, and that sort of thing. Then I went back to the city, and tried my hand on Sylvia's mother, but with no success at all. She is like a stone gate-post, and always was, and declared that as Sylvia had entered the institution because Marcia was there, it was the latter's duty to give up everything else, and to throw herself between Sylvia and your mischievous machinations and to stay there until you were married to somebody, and the danger was past."

"Machinations!" I ejaculated,—"a most unreasonable person."

"Perhaps so," said Miss Laniston, "but not a bit more than the rest of you. You are the most unreasonable lot I ever met with. Having failed utterly with the three women, I had some idea of sending for you, and of trying to persuade you to marry some one who is not under the sisterhood's restrictions, and so smooth out this wretched tangle, but I knew that you were more obstinate and stiff-necked than any of them, and so concluded to save myself the trouble of reasoning with you."

"A wise decision," I remarked.

"But I could not give up," she continued; "I could not bear the thought that my friend Marcia Raynor should sacrifice herself in this way. I went back to Arden in the hope that something might suggest itself; that a gleam of sense might be shown by the one or the other of the lunatics in gray for whose good I was racking my brains. But I found things worse than I had left them. Sylvia had stirred herself into a spirit of combativeness of which no one would have supposed her capable, and had actually endeavored to brow-beat her Mother Superior into the belief that a Brotherhood Annex was not only necessary to the prosperity and success of the House of Martha, but that it was absolutely wicked not to have it. She had gone on in this strain until Marcia had become angry, and then there had been a scene and tears, and much subsequent misery.

"I talked first with one doleful sister, and then with the other, with the only result that I became nearly as doleful as they. In my despair I went to Marcia, and urged her to acknowledge herself vanquished, to give up this contest, which would be her ruin, to show herself a true woman, and to take up the true work of her life. 'Oh, I couldn't do it,' she said, and she looked as if she were going to cry, a most unusual thing with her; 'if I went away, to-morrow they would be together, making mud-pies for the children of the poor.' I sprang to my feet. 'Marcia Raynor,' I cried, 'you made this House of Martha. You are the head and the front, the top and the bottom of it. You are its founder and its autocrat, it lives on your money,—for everybody knows that what these sisters make wouldn't buy their pillboxes,—and now, having run it all these years, and having brought yourself and Sylvia to the greatest grief by it, it is your duty to put an end to it, to abolish it.'"

"'Abolish the House of Martha?' she cried, with her great eyes blazing at me."

"'Yes,' I said, 'abolish it, destroy it, annihilate it, declare it null, void, dead and gone, utterly extinguished, and out of existence. You can do this, and you ought to do this. It is your only way out of the dreadful situation in which you have got yourself and Sylvia. Let the other sisters go to some other institutions, or wherever they like. You and Sylvia will be free, that is the great point. Now do not hesitate. Stop supplies, dissolve the organization, break up the House of Martha, and do it instantly.'"

"She made one step towards me and seized me by the wrist. 'Janet,' she said, 'I will do it.' And she did it that day. At present there is no House of Martha."

I sat and gazed at Miss Laniston without comprehending what I had heard.

"No House of Martha!" I ejaculated.

"That is precisely the state of the case," she answered; "the establishment was dissolved at noon yesterday. As I had had all the trouble of bringing this thing about, I considered that I had a right to tell you of it myself. I thought it would interest me to see how you took it."

I rose to my feet; I stepped towards her.

"No House of Martha," I gasped,—"and Sylvia?"

"Sylvia will go home to her mother, so she told me yesterday. I was present at the dissolution. I think she will probably come to the city this afternoon."

I snatched up my hat. "I must go to her instantly," I said. "I must see her before she reaches her mother. I have lost time already."

"Upon my word!" exclaimed Miss Laniston, "your way of taking it is indeed interesting. Not a word of thanks, not a sign of recognition"—

I had nearly reached the door, but now rushed back and seized her by the hand. "Excuse me," I said, "but you can see for yourself"—and with one violent shake I dropped her hand, and hurried away.

"Oh, yes," she cried, "I can easily see for myself," and as I left the house I heard her hearty laugh.

I sprang into my cab, ordering the man to drive fast for the railroad station. It mattered not to me whether Walkirk went to Europe or not. All I cared for was to catch the next train which would take me to Arden.

XLVIII

IN A COLD, BARE ROOM

When I reached Arden I took one of the melancholy vehicles which stand at our station, and very much astonished the driver by ordering him to take me, not to my own home, but to the House of Martha.

"You know they're busted up, sir," said the man, turning to me, as his old horse hurried us along at the best of his speed.

"But the sisters have not left?" I eagerly asked.

"Not all," he said, "but two or three of them went down this morning."

"Drive on quicker," I replied, "I am in a hurry."

The man gave the horse a crack with his whip, which made no difference whatever in our rate of speed, and said:—

"If you've got a bill agin any of them, sir, you needn't worry. The Mother is still there, and she's all right, you know."

"Bill? Nonsense!" said I.

"I'm sorry they're busted," said the man; "they didn't do much hackin', but they give us a lot of haulin' from the station."

As I hurried up the broad path which led to the front of the House of Martha, I found the door of the main entrance open, something I had never noticed before, although I had often passed the house. I entered unceremoniously, and saw before me, in the hallway, a woman in gray, stooping over a trunk. She turned, at the sound of my footsteps on the bare floor, and I beheld Sister Sarah. Her eyes flashed as she saw me, and I know that her first impulse was to order me out of the house. This of course she now had no right to do, but there were private rights which she still maintained.

"I should think," she said, "that a man who has done all the mischief that you have done, who has worked and planned and plotted and contrived, until he has undermined and utterly ruined the sisterhood of pious women who ask nothing of this world but to be let alone to do their own work in their own way, would be ashamed to put his nose into this house; but I suppose a man who would do what you have done does not know what shame is. Have you come here to sneer and jibe and scorn and mock, and gloat over the misfortunes of the women whose home you have broken up, ruined, and devastated?"

"Madam," said I, "can you tell me where I can find Miss Sylvia Raynor?"

She looked as if she were about to spring and bite.

"Atrocious!" she exclaimed. "I will not stay under the same roof,"—and she marched out of the door.

I made my way into the reception room. I met no one, and the room was empty, although I heard on the floor above the sound of many footsteps, apparently those of the sisters preparing for departure.

I looked around for a bell, or some means of making my presence known. The room appeared harder, barer, emptier than when I had seen it before. In a moment it was filled with all the light and beauty of the world. A door opened, and Sylvia entered.

"I saw you come," she said, advancing with outstretched hands, "and hurried down as soon as I could."

She was in her gray dress, but without shawl or head covering. Her face was filled with the most charming welcome. I hastened towards her. I did not take her hands, but opening my arms I folded her in them, and kissed her over and over again. With flushed face she pushed herself a little from me.

"Isn't this taking a great deal for granted?" she said.

"Granted!" I exclaimed, "think of what has been denied. Think of the weeks, the months"—

"We would a great deal better think somebody may come in here and see us," said Sylvia, pushing herself still farther from me.

"But didn't you expect me to rush to you the instant I heard you were a free woman? Did you suppose there was anything to be taken for granted between us?"

"Oh no," she said, "I think we understood each other pretty well, but then, don't you see, I didn't suppose it would be like this. I am expecting a trunk from New York every minute, and I thought when it came I should be dressed like other people. Now that I am not a sister, I did not want you to see me in these dreary clothes. Then I would go to my mother's house, and I thought you would call on me there, and things would go on more regularly; but you are so impetuous."

"My dearest love," said I, "it fills me with rapture to take you in my arms in the same dress you wore when I fell in love with you. Often and often as I looked at you through that grating have I thought that it would be to me the greatest joy on earth if I could take you in my arms and tell you that I loved you."

"You thought that!" exclaimed Sylvia; "it was very wrong of you."

"Right or wrong, I did it," said I, "and now I have her, my dear little nun, here in my arms."

She ceased to push and looked up at me with a merry smile.

"Do you remember," she said, "the morning the wasp came near stinging me?"

"Indeed I do," I said vehemently.

"Well, before that wasp came," she continued, "I used to be a good deal afraid of you. I thought you were very learned and dignified, but after I was so frightened, and you saw me without my bonnet, and all that, I felt we were very much more like friends, and that was the very beginning of my liking you."

"My darling," I exclaimed, "that wasp was the best friend we ever had. Do you want to see it?" and releasing her, I took from my pocket the pasteboard box in which I had placed our friend Vespa. As she looked at the insect, her face was lighted with joyous surprise.

"And that is the same wasp?" she said, "and you kept it?"

"Yes, and shall always keep it," I said, "even now it has not ceased to be our friend." And then I told her how my desire to take with me this memento of her had held me back from the rolling Atlantic, and brought me to her. She raised her face to me with her beautiful eyes in a mist of tenderness, and this time her arms were extended.

"You are the dearest man," she said.

In less than a minute after she had spoken these words, Mother Anastasia entered the room. She stood for a moment amazed, and then she hastily shut the door.

"Really," she exclaimed, "you two are incomprehensible beings. Don't you know that people might come in here at any moment? It is fortunate that I was the person who came in at this moment."

"But you knew he was here?" said Sylvia.

"Yes. I knew that," the other replied, "but I expected you would both remember that at present this house might almost be considered a public place."

"My dear Marcia," said Sylvia, "if you knew him as well as I do, you would know that he would never remember any-thing about a place."

I turned to the ex-Mother Superior, who had already discarded the garb of the sisterhood, and was dressed in a dark walking suit.

"If you knew me as well as I know myself," I said, reaching to her both my hands, "you would know that my gratitude towards you is deeper than the deepest depths of the earth."

She took one of my hands.

"If you have anything to be grateful for," she said, "it is for the lectures I have given you, and which, I am afraid, I ought to continue to give you. As to what was done here yesterday I consider myself as much benefited as anybody, and I suppose Sylvia is of the same opinion regarding herself. But there is one person to whom you truly ought to be grateful—Miss Laniston."

"I know that," I said. "I have seen her; she told me what she did, and I treated her as I would treat a boy who had brushed my coat, but I shall make amends."

"Indeed you shall," said Sylvia, "and I will go with you when you do it."

"But you must not set yourself aside in this way," said I, addressing the older lady, "it was you who fanned my hopes of winning Sylvia when there seemed no reason why they should not fade away. It was you who promised to help me, and who did help me."

"Did you do that, Marcia?" asked Sylvia.

The beautiful woman who had been Mother Anastasia flushed a little, as she answered:—

"Yes, dear, but then you were only a sister on probation."

"And you wanted me to marry him?"

The other smiled and nodded, and in the next moment Sylvia's arms were about her neck, and Sylvia's lips were on her cheek.

I was very much affected, and there is no knowing how my

feelings and gratitude might have been evinced, had not the clumping of a trunk upon the stairs and the voices of sisters at the door called me to order.

Frank R. Stockton

XLIX

MY OWN WAY

When I went home to my grandmother, she was greatly surprised to see me, and I lost no time in explaining my unexpected appearance.

"Really, really," she exclaimed, "I was just writing you a letter, which I intended to send after you, so that you would get it when you arrived in London; and in it I was going to tell you all about the breaking up of the House of Martha, of which I first heard half an hour after you left me. I was glad you had not known of it before you started, for I thought it would be so much better for all the changes to be made while you were away, and for Sylvia to be in her mother's house, where she could get rid of her nunnish habits, and have some proper clothes made up. Of course I knew you would come back soon, but I thought your own mind would be in much better order for a little absence."

"My dear grandmother," I cried, "in mind and body I am in perfect order, and it is presence, not absence, which made me so."

"Somehow or other," said she, smiling, "the fates seem to help you to have your own way, and I am sure I am delighted that you will stay at home. And what has become of Mr. Walkirk?"

"Upon my word!" I exclaimed—"I do not know."

Towards evening Walkirk returned, looking tired and out of spirits. I truly regretted the carelessness and neglect with which I had treated him, and explained and apologized to the best of my ability. He was a good-natured fellow, and behaved magnanimously.

"Things have turned out wonderfully well," he said, as he took a seat, "but I shall be more delighted with the state of affairs when I am a little less fatigued. Minor annoyances ought not to be considered, but I assure you I have had a pretty rough time of it. As the hour for sailing drew near, and you did not make your appearance, I became more and more nervous and anxious. I would not allow our baggage to be put on board, for I knew a conference with a lady was likely to be of indefinite duration, and when at last the steamer sailed, I went immediately to Miss Laniston's house to inform you of the fact, and to find out what you proposed to do; but Miss Laniston was not at home, and the servant told me that a gentleman—undoubtedly you—had left the house nearly an hour before, and his great haste made her think that he was trying to catch a steamer.

"'People would not hurry like that,' she said, 'to catch a train, for there's always another one in an hour or two.'"

"Then I began to fear that in your haste you had gone on board the wrong steamer—two others sailed to-day, a little later than ours, and I went to their piers and made all sorts of inquiries, but I could find out nothing. Then I went to your club, to your lawyer's office, and several other places where I supposed you might go, but no one had seen or heard of you. Then a fear began to creep over me that you had had some greatly depressing news from Miss Laniston, and that you had made away with yourself."

"Walkirk!" I exclaimed, "how dared you think that?"

"Men in the nervous condition I was," he answered, "think all sorts of things, and that is one of the things I thought. Finally I went to Miss Laniston's house again, and this time I found her, and learned what had happened. Then I went to the pier, ordered the trunk sent back here, for I knew there was no question now of the trip to Europe, and here I am."

It was easy to see that whatever pleasure the turn in my affairs may have given Walkirk, he was disappointed at losing his trip to Europe; but I thought it well not to reopen his wounds by any allusion to this fact, and contented myself by saying the most earnest and cordial things about what he had done and suffered for me that day, and inwardly determining that I would make full amends to him for his lost journey.

In about ten days I received a message by cable from Liverpool, which was sent by my stenographer, informing me that he had gone aboard the steamer, as per agreement, and being busy writing letters to send back by the pilot, had not discovered that Walkirk and I were not on board until it was too late. The message was a long one, and its cost, as well as that of the one by which I informed the stenographer that he might come home, and the price of the man's passage to Liverpool and back, besides the sum I was obliged to pay him for his lost time, might all have been saved to me, had the fellow been thoughtful enough to make himself sure that we were on board before he allowed himself to be carried off. But little rubs of this kind were of slight moment to me at that time.

On the day after things had been taken for granted between

Sylvia and myself, I saw her at her mother's house, and I must admit that although it had given me such exquisite pleasure to feel that she was mine in the coarse gray gown of a "sister," it delighted me more to feel she was mine in the ordinary costume of society. She was as gay as a butterfly ought to be which had just cast off its gray wrappings and spread its wings to the coloring light.

I found Mrs. Raynor in a somewhat perturbed state of mind.

"I cannot accommodate myself," she said, "to these sudden and violent mutations. I like to sit on the sands and stay there as long as I please, and to feel that I know how high each breaker will be, and how far the tide will come in, but these tidal waves which make beach of sea and sea of beach sweep me away utterly; I cannot comprehend where I am. A week ago I considered you as an enemy with active designs on the peace of my daughter. I was about to write you a letter to demand that you should cease from troubling her. But I heard you were going to Europe, and then I felt that henceforth our paths would be smoother, for I believed that absence would cure you of your absurd and objectless infatuation; but suddenly, down goes the House of Martha, and up comes the enemy, transformed into a suitor, who is loved by Sylvia, and against whom I can have no possible objection. Now can not you see for yourself how this sort of thing must affect a mind accustomed to a certain uniformity of emotion?"

"Madam," said I, "it will be the object of my life to make you so happy in our happiness that you shall remember this recent tumult of events as something more gratifying to look back upon than your most cherished memories of tranquil delight."

"You seem to have a high opinion of your abilities," she

said, smiling, "and of the value of what you offer me. I am perfectly willing that you try what you can do; nevertheless I wish you had gone to Europe. Everything would have turned out just the same, and the affair would have been more seemly."

"Oh, we can easily make that all right," said I. "Sylvia and I will go to Europe on our bridal trip."

As I finished these words Sylvia came into the room, accompanied by Miss Laniston.

"Here is a gentleman," said my dear girl to her companion, "who has declared his desire to thank you for something you have done for him, and he has spoken so strongly about the way in which he intended to pour out his gratitude, that I want to see how he does it."

"Mr. Vanderley," said Miss Laniston, "I forbid you to utter one word of that outpouring, which you would have poured out yesterday morning, had it not been so urgently necessary to catch a train. When I am ready for the effusion referred to, I will fix a time for it and let you know the day before, and I will take care that no one shall be present at it but ourselves."

"Any way," said Sylvia, "he will tell me all about it."

"If he does," said Miss Laniston, "you will re-enter a convent."

L

MY BOOK OF TRAVEL

When the House of Martha had been formally abolished, the members of the sisterhood made various dispositions of themselves. Some determined to enter institutions of a similar character, while others who had homes planned to retire to them, with the intention of endeavoring to do what good they could without separating themselves from the world in which they were to do it. Sister Sarah was greatly incensed at the dissolution of the House, and much more so because, had it continued, she expected to be at the head of it. She declared her intention of throwing herself into the arms of the Mother Church, where a sisterhood meant something, and where such nonsense and treachery as this would be impossible.

I did not enjoy the autumn of that year to the extent that I should have enjoyed it had I been able to arrange matters according to my own ideas of what was appropriate to the case.

Sylvia lived in the city, and I lived in the country, and although I went to her whenever I could, and she and her mother dined several times with my grandmother, there were often long stretches, sometimes extending over the greater part of the day, when I did not see her at all.

Thus it was that I had sometimes to think of other things, and one morning I said to my under-study, "Walkirk, there is something I regret very much, and that is the non-completion of my book. I shall never finish it, I am sure, because every thing that has ever happened to me is going to be made uninteresting and tedious by what is to happen. Travel and life itself will be quite another thing to me, and I am sure that I will be satisfied with enjoying it, and shall not want to write about it. And so, good-by to the book."

"In regard to your book," said Walkirk, "I feel it my duty to say to you that there is no occasion for you to bid good-by to it."

"You are wrong there!" I exclaimed. "I shall never write it. I do not want to write it."

"Nevertheless," said Walkirk, "the book will be written. I shall write it. In fact I have written a great part of it already."

"What in the name of common sense do you mean?" I cried, staring at him in astonishment.

"What I am going to say to you," replied Walkirk, "may displease you, but I earnestly hope that you may eventually agree with me, that what I have done is for the general good. You may remember that when you first talked to me of your travels, you also handed me some of the manuscript you had prepared for the opening chapters of your book and gave me an outline of the projected plan of the work. Now as I have often told you, I considered the material for a book of travels contained in your experiences, as recited to me, as extremely fresh, novel and entertaining, and would be bound to make what publishers call a 'hit' if properly presented, but at the same time I am compelled to say that I soon became convinced that there was no probability that you would properly present your admirable subject matter to the reading world."

"Upon my word," said I, "this is cool."

"It is hard to speak to you in this way," he answered, "and the only way in which I can do it is to be perfectly straightforward and honest about it. I am at heart a literary man, and have, so far as I have the power, cultivated the art of putting things effectively; and I assure you, sir, that it gave me actual pain when I found how you were going to present some of the incidents of your journey, such as, for instance, your diving experiences in the maelstrom, or at least in the place where it was supposed to be, and where, judging from your discoveries, it may under certain conditions and to a certain extent really exist.

"There were a good many other points which I believe could be made of startling interest and value, not only to ordinary readers, but to scientific people, if they were properly brought out. I saw no reason that you would so bring them out, and I felt not only that I could do it, but that it would delight me to do it.

"My feeling on the subject was so strong that, as you may remember, I declined to act as your secretary. I am perhaps over-sensitive, but I could not have written your book as you would have dictated it to me, and as you did indeed dictate it to your various secretaries."

"Go on," I said, "I am perfectly charmed with my power of repressing resentment."

"Therefore it was," he continued, "that I set to work to write the book myself, founding it entirely upon your daily recitals. My plan was to write as long as I found you were in the humor to talk, and, in fact, if you lost interest in me as a listener I determined that I would then declare what I had done, show you my work, and implore you, if you felt like it, to give me enough subject matter to finish it.

"I have now stated my case, and I place it entirely in your hands. I will give you what I have written, and if you choose to read it and do not like it, you can throw it into the fire. The subject matter is yours, and I have no rights over it. But if you think that the work which you have decided to discontinue can be successfully carried on by me, I shall be delighted to go ahead and finish it."

"Walkirk," said I, "you have the effrontery of a stone sphinx; but let me see your manuscript."

He handed it to me, and during the rest of the morning, and for a great part of the night, after I had returned in a late train from the city, I read it. The next day I handed it to him.

"Walkirk," said I, "as my under-study go ahead and finish this book. You never came nearer the truth than when you said that that material is vastly interesting."

Walkirk was delighted and took up the work with enthusiasm. Whenever I had a chance I talked to him, and whenever he had a chance he wrote. However, at that time, I gave so much of my business to my under-study that he was not able to devote himself to his literary work as assiduously as he and I would have desired. In fact, the book is not yet finished, but when it appears I think it will be a success.

LI

A LOOSE END

I was now a very happy man, but I was not an entirely satisfied one. Looking back upon what had happened, I could see that there were certain loose ends, which ought to be gathered up before they were broken off and lost, or tangled up with something to which they did not belong.

It has always been my disposition to gather up the loose ends, to draw together the floating strands of circumstance, tendency, intention, and all that sort of thing, so that I may see what they are and where they come from. I like to know how I stand in relation to them, and how they may affect me.

One of the present loose ends was brought to my mind by a conversation with Sylvia. I had been speaking of her cousin Marcia Raynor, and expressing my pleasure that she was about to enter a new life, to which seemed so well adapted.

"Marcia is a fine woman," she said, "and I love her ever so much, but you know she has caused me a great deal of pain; that she has actually made me cry when I was in bed at night."

I assured her that I had never imagined such a thing possible.

"Of course," Sylvia continued, "I do not refer to the way she acted just before the House of Martha was broken up. Then she opposed everything I wanted to do, and would listen to no reason, but I wouldn't listen to her reasons either, and I was entirely too angry with her to think of crying on her account. It was before that, that she made my very heart sick, and all on your account."

"She was severe upon me, I suppose."

"Not a bit of it," said Sylvia, "if she had been severe, I should not have minded it so much, but it was quite the other way. Now just put yourself in my place and try to think how you would have felt about it. Here was I, fixed and settled for life in the House of Martha, and here were you, perfectly convinced—at least I was afraid you were convinced—that there was nothing for you to do but to give me up, and here was Marcia, just about to step out into the world a free woman, and at the same time taking a most wonderful interest in you, and trying to make you understand that you ought to let me alone, and all that sort of thing."

"In which she did not succeed at all," I said.

"So it appears," said Sylvia, "but I couldn't be sure about that at the time, you know, and if she had succeeded there was no earthly reason why you should not have become as much interested in her as she was in you, and then—but it's too dreadful to talk about; it used to make me fairly boil."

"You mean to say," said I, "that you were jealous of your Cousin Marcia."

"Yes," she answered, "there is no use in calling it by any other name; I was jealous, savagely so, sometimes."

Now this was a very high compliment, and I did not fail to express my satisfaction at having been the subject of such emotions. But one of the results of Sylvia's communication was to remind me of the existence of a loose end. I had never understood Mother Anastasia's feelings towards me. It had been very interesting to me to make conjectures about those feelings, and now that I could safely do more than conjecture I wished to do more, and to find out, if possible, if there had been any reasons for the construction I had placed upon the actions of the beautiful Mother Superior. Of course this was of no real importance now, but one cannot be brought into relations with such a woman as Marcia Raynor without wanting to know exactly what those relations were.

I had far too much prudence, however, to talk on this subject with Sylvia; if I talked with any one I must do it very cautiously. One morning I called upon Miss Laniston. That lady was informed on a great many points, and, moreover, was exceedingly free-spoken. I did not expect any direct information from her, but she might say something from which I might make inferences.

She thought I had come to thank her for what she had done for me, but I assured her that this ceremony must be postponed for the present, for Sylvia had instructed me to write my gratitude in a letter, which she thought would be a much preferable method than for me to pour it out in a private interview.

"Your Sylvia seems to be a jealous little body," she remarked.

"Oh, no," said I, "although, of course, it is natural enough

Frank R. Stockton

for persons in our state of mind to have tendencies that way. By the way, one of these tendencies on her part was rather odd. Do you know that at one time she was almost jealous of her cousin Marcia, at that time a gray-bonneted sister? As you know so much of our affairs I do not think I am going too far in telling that."

Miss Laniston seemed to be considering the subject.

"It is the commonest thing," she said presently, "to make mistakes about matters of this sort. Now, for instance, I once put some questions to you which seemed to indicate that there might be some reason for Sylvia's uneasiness. Didn't you think they pointed that way?"

"Yes, I did," I replied.

"And have you ever thought of it since?" she asked.

"Occasionally. Of course the matter is of no vital interest now. But at the time you spoke of it, I could not help wondering if I had said or done anything during my rather intimate acquaintance with Mother Anastasia which would give you good cause to put the questions to which you just now alluded."

"Well," said Miss Laniston, "you seemed to me, at the time, to be in a decidedly unbalanced state of mind, but I think I acted most unwarrantably in speaking of Marcia as I did. In fact, I often act unwarrantably. It is one of my habits. And to prove it to you, I am going to act unwarrantably again. Having brought the elder Miss Raynor before you in a way that might have led you to have undefined ideas about her, I am going to bring her before you again in order that those ideas may be exactly defined. It is all wrong, I know, but I like to set things straight, whether I do it in the right way or wrong way."

"That is exactly my disposition," I replied; "I always want to set things straight."

She left the room, and soon returned with a letter.

"When I decide positively to do a thing," she said, sitting down and opening the letter, "I think it just as well to drop apologies and excuses. You and I have decided that matters ought to be set straight, and so, here goes. Marcia has just written me a long letter in which she says a good deal about you and Sylvia, and I am going to read you a part of it which I think will straighten out some things which I may have made crooked, in my efforts to do good to all parties concerned—a dangerous business, I may say.

"'It is delightful to think,' thus Marcia writes,—'that Sylvia's life is at last settled for her, and that, too, in the right way. Of course, neither you nor I would be satisfied with a match like that; but Sylvia is not only satisfied with Mr. Vanderley, but I have no doubt that she will be perfectly happy with him. More than that, I believe she will supply his shortcomings, and strengthen his weaknesses, and as he has a naturally good disposition, and an ample fortune, I think Sylvia is to be sincerely congratulated. When we first spoke of this matter a good while ago I thought that if the Sylvia-Vanderley affair could ever be arranged, it would be a good thing, and I have not changed my opinion.' The rest of the letter," said Miss Laniston, folding it as she spoke, "chiefly concerns the new college, and I do not suppose it would interest you."

I agreed with her, and took my leave. The loose end had been gathered up.

LII

I FINISH THE SICILIAN LOVE-STORY

It might have been supposed that my little experience in gathering up loose ends would have deterred me from further efforts in this direction, but it did not.

I had left Miss Laniston without asking some questions I had intended to put to her. I wished very much to know—I thought it was my right to know—something definite about the Mr. Brownson who had formerly been connected, so to speak, with the Misses Raynor. I hated this subject as I hated the vilest medicine, but I felt that I must get the matter straightened in my mind, yet I could not say anything to Sylvia about it. And after what Miss Laniston had read to me I could not ask her anything, even if my mind had been sufficiently composed to formulate questions. She was a very plain-spoken person. Too much so, perhaps.

Walkirk was very different; in fact, I think he erred on the other side. I am sure that he would have liked to conceal from me anything that would give me pain. In the course of his life he had met a great many people; he might know something about Brownson. Any way, I would throw out some feelers in that direction.

"Yes," I remarked to him, in the course of a conversation about the late Mother Superior, "what she is going to do is a very fine thing,—a noble enterprise, and she is just the sort of person to go into it, but after all I would rather see her married to the right sort of man. A woman like that owes it to society to be married."

"I fancy," said Walkirk, "that she has permanently left the marrying class. When she broke with Brownson, I think she broke with marriage."

"What were the points of that?" I asked. "Did you ever happen to hear anything about him?"

"I knew him very well," answered Walkirk. "Those were his prints I was cataloguing just before I entered your service. He had then been dead a year or more, and I was working for the estate."

I arose and went to the window. I wiped my forehead, which had become moist. If this man had known Brownson, why should he not know all? Was he familiar with both engagements? It made me sick to think of it. There was no sense or reason in such emotion, for it was not likely that Sylvia's engagement had been a secret one; but I had a proud soul and could not bear to think that people about me, especially Walkirk, should be aware of Sylvia's attachment, slight as it may have been, to another than myself. I heartily wished that I had not spoken of the subject.

Still, as I had spoken of it, I might as well learn all that I could.

"What sort of a man was this Brownson?" I asked. "What reason was there that Miss Marcia Raynor should have cared for him?"

"He was a fine man," said Walkirk. "He was educated, good-looking, rich. He was young enough, but had been a bachelor too long, perhaps, and had very independent ways. It was on account of his independence of thought, especially on religious matters, that he and Miss Marcia Raynor had their difficulties, which ended in the breaking of the engagement. I am quite sure that she was a good deal cut up. As I said before, I do not think that she will consider marriage again."

I took in a full breath of relief. Here Walkirk had told the little story of Brownson, and had said nothing of any subsequent engagement. Perhaps he knew of none. This thought was truly encouraging.

"Perhaps you are right," I said, "she may know better than any of us what will suit her. Any way I ought to be satisfied; and that reminds me, Walkirk, that I have never expressed to you, as strongly as I wished to do it, my appreciation of the interest you have taken in my varied relations with Miss Sylvia Raynor, and for the valuable advice and assistance you have given me from time to time. For instance, I believe that your reluctance to have me go away from Tangent Island was due to your discovery that the island belonged to Sylvia's mother, and, therefore, there was some probability that she might come there."

Walkirk smiled. "You have hit the truth," he said.

"I have sometimes wondered," I continued, "why a man should take so much interest in the love affairs of another. When one engages an under-study, he does not generally expect that sort of thing."

"Well," said Walkirk, "when a man engages as an under-study, or in a similar capacity, he often performs services, without regard to his duty and salary, simply because they interest and please him. Now it struck me that it would be a curious bit of romantic realism if two beautiful women, who on account of one man had become nuns in a convent, or what was practically the same thing, should both be taken out of that convent and brought back to their true life in the world by another man."

"Two women"—I gasped.

Walkirk smiled, and his voice assumed a comforting tone.

"Of course that sort of thing has its rough points for the second man, but in this case I do not think they amount to much. Brownson's affair with the younger lady would have come to an end as soon as she had discovered the rocks in his character, but her mother broke it off before it came to that. But I do not think she would have gone into the sisterhood, if it had not been for the man's death very soon after the breaking of the engagement. This affected her very much, but there was no reason why it should, for he was killed in a railway accident, and I am positively certain that he would have married some one else if he had lived long enough."

I had nothing to say to all this. I walked slowly into my study and shut the door. Surely I had had enough of picking up loose ends. If there were any more of them I would let them flap, dangle, float in the air, do what they please; I would not touch them.

*   *   *   *   *

That evening I spent with Sylvia. In the course of our conversation she suddenly remarked:—

"Do you know we have had so much to do and so much to talk about, and so much to think about and plan, that I

Frank R. Stockton

have had no chance to ask you some questions that I have been thinking about. In the first place I want you to tell me all about Mr. Walkirk. How long has he been with you? Are you always going to keep him? What does he do? What was his business before he came to you? Was he always an under-study for people? It has struck me that that would be such an odd occupation for a man to have. And then there is another thing,—a mere supposition of mine, but still something that I have had a sort of curiosity about: supposing that the House of Martha had not been broken up, and it were all fixed and settled that I should stay there always, and supposing cousin Marcia had left us, and had gone into her college work, just as she is doing now—do you think that you would have had any desire to study medicine?

"And then there is another thing that is not a question, but something which I think I ought to tell you,—something which you have a right to know before we are married."

"Sylvia," said I, interrupting her, "let me give you a little piece of wisdom from my own experience: The gnawings of ungratified curiosity are often very irritating, but we should remember that the gnawings of gratified curiosity are frequently mangling."

"Indeed!" she exclaimed, "is that the way you look at it? Well, I can assure you that what I have to tell is of no importance at all, but if you have anything to say that is mangling, I want to hear it this very minute."

"My dear Sylvia," said I, "we have had so much to do and so much to talk about, and so much to think about and plan, that I have had no chance to finish the story of Tomaso and Lucilla."

"That is true," she cried, with sparkling eyes; "and above all things I want to hear the end of that story."

I sat by her on the sofa and finished the story of the Sicilian lovers.

"In some ways," she said, "it is very much like our story, isn't it?"

"Except," I answered, "that the best part of ours is just beginning."

ABOUT THE AUTHOR

**Frank R. Stockton** (April 5, 1834 - April 20, 1902), was an American writer and humorist, best known today for a series of innovative children's fairy tales that were widely popular during the last decades of the 19th century. Stockton avoided the didactic moralizing common to children's stories of the time, instead using clever humor to poke at greed, violence, abuse of power and other human foibles, describing his fantastic characters' adventures in a charming, matter-of-fact way in stories like "The Griffin and the Minor Canon" (1885) and "The Bee-Man of Orn" (1887), which was republished in 1964 in an edition illustrated by Maurice Sendak.

Born in Philadelphia, Stockton was the son of a prominent Methodist minister who discouraged him from a writing career. He supported himself as a wood engraver until his father's death in 1860; in 1867, he moved back to Philadelphia to write for a newspaper founded by his brother. His first fairy tale, "Ting-a-ling," was published that year in The Riverside Magazine; his first book collection appeared in 1870.

He died of a cerebral hemorrhage in 1902. His collected works, 23 volumes of stories for adults and children, were published between 1899 and 1904.

Choose from Thousands of 1stWorldLibrary Classics By

A. M. Barnard
Ada Leverson
Adolphus William Ward
Aesop
Agatha Christie
Alexander Aaronsohn
Alexander Kielland
Alexandre Dumas
Alfred Gatty
Alfred Ollivant
Alice Duer Miller
Alice Turner Curtis
Alice Dunbar
Allen Chapman
Alleyne Ireland
Ambrose Bierce
Amelia E. Barr
Amory H. Bradford
Andrew Lang
Andrew McFarland Davis
Andy Adams
Angela Brazil
Anna Alice Chapin
Anna Sewell
Annie Besant
Annie Hamilton Donnell
Annie Payson Call
Annie Roe Carr
Annonaymous
Anton Chekhov
Archibald Lee Fletcher
Arnold Bennett
Arthur C. Benson
Arthur Conan Doyle
Arthur M. Winfield
Arthur Ransome
Arthur Schnitzler
Arthur Train
Atticus
B.H. Baden-Powell
B. M. Bower
B. C. Chatterjee
Baroness Emmuska Orczy
Baroness Orczy
Basil King
Bayard Taylor
Ben Macomber
Bertha Muzzy Bower
Bjornstjerne Bjornson

Booth Tarkington
Boyd Cable
Bram Stoker
C. Collodi
C. E. Orr
C. M. Ingleby
Carolyn Wells
Catherine Parr Traill
Charles A. Eastman
Charles Amory Beach
Charles Dickens
Charles Dudley Warner
Charles Farrar Browne
Charles Ives
Charles Kingsley
Charles Klein
Charles Hanson Towne
Charles Lathrop Pack
Charles Romyn Dake
Charles Whibley
Charles Willing Beale
Charlotte M. Braeme
Charlotte M. Yonge
Charlotte Perkins Stetson
Clair W. Hayes
Clarence Day Jr.
Clarence E. Mulford
Clemence Housman
Confucius
Coningsby Dawson
Cornelis DeWitt Wilcox
Cyril Burleigh
D. H. Lawrence
Daniel Defoe
David Garnett
Dinah Craik
Don Carlos Janes
Donald Keyhoe
Dorothy Kilner
Dougan Clark
Douglas Fairbanks
E. Nesbit
E. P. Roe
E. Phillips Oppenheim
E. S. Brooks
Earl Barnes
Edgar Rice Burroughs
Edith Van Dyne
Edith Wharton

Edward Everett Hale
Edward J. O'Biren
Edward S. Ellis
Edwin L. Arnold
Eleanor Atkins
Eleanor Hallowell Abbott
Eliot Gregory
Elizabeth Gaskell
Elizabeth McCracken
Elizabeth Von Arnim
Ellem Key
Emerson Hough
Emilie F. Carlen
Emily Bronte
Emily Dickinson
Enid Bagnold
Enilor Macartney Lane
Erasmus W. Jones
Ernie Howard Pie
Ethel May Dell
Ethel Turner
Ethel Watts Mumford
Eugene Sue
Eugenie Foa
Eugene Wood
Eustace Hale Ball
Evelyn Everett-green
Everard Cotes
F. H. Cheley
F. J. Cross
F. Marion Crawford
Fannie E. Newberry
Federick Austin Ogg
Ferdinand Ossendowski
Fergus Hume
Florence A. Kilpatrick
Fremont B. Deering
Francis Bacon
Francis Darwin
Frances Hodgson Burnett
Frances Parkinson Keyes
Frank Gee Patchin
Frank Harris
Frank Jewett Mather
Frank L. Packard
Frank V. Webster
Frederic Stewart Isham
Frederick Trevor Hill
Frederick Winslow Taylor

Friedrich Kerst
Friedrich Nietzsche
Fyodor Dostoyevsky
G.A. Henty
G.K. Chesterton
Gabrielle E. Jackson
Garrett P. Serviss
Gaston Leroux
George A. Warren
George Ade
Geroge Bernard Shaw
George Cary Eggleston
George Durston
George Ebers
George Eliot
George Gissing
George MacDonald
George Meredith
George Orwell
George Sylvester Viereck
George Tucker
George W. Cable
George Wharton James
Gertrude Atherton
Gordon Casserly
Grace E. King
Grace Gallatin
Grace Greenwood
Grant Allen
Guillermo A. Sherwell
Gulielma Zollinger
Gustav Flaubert
H. A. Cody
H. B. Irving
H.C. Bailey
H. G. Wells
H. H. Munro
H. Irving Hancock
H. R. Naylor
H. Rider Haggard
H. W. C. Davis
Haldeman Julius
Hall Caine
Hamilton Wright Mabie
Hans Christian Andersen
Harold Avery
Harold McGrath
Harriet Beecher Stowe
Harry Castlemon
Harry Coghill
Harry Houidini

Hayden Carruth
Helent Hunt Jackson
Helen Nicolay
Hendrik Conscience
Hendy David Thoreau
Henri Barbusse
Henrik Ibsen
Henry Adams
Henry Ford
Henry Frost
Henry James
Henry Jones Ford
Henry Seton Merriman
Henry W Longfellow
Herbert A. Giles
Herbert Carter
Herbert N. Casson
Herman Hesse
Hildegard G. Frey
Homer
Honore De Balzac
Horace B. Day
Horace Walpole
Horatio Alger Jr.
Howard Pyle
Howard R. Garis
Hugh Lofting
Hugh Walpole
Humphry Ward
Ian Maclaren
Inez Haynes Gillmore
Irving Bacheller
Isabel Cecilia Williams
Isabel Hornibrook
Israel Abrahams
Ivan Turgenev
J.G.Austin
J. Henri Fabre
J. M. Barrie
J. M. Walsh
J. Macdonald Oxley
J. R. Miller
J. S. Fletcher
J. S. Knowles
J. Storer Clouston
J. W. Duffield
Jack London
Jacob Abbott
James Allen
James Andrews
James Baldwin

James Branch Cabell
James DeMille
James Joyce
James Lane Allen
James Lane Allen
James Oliver Curwood
James Oppenheim
James Otis
James R. Driscoll
Jane Abbott
Jane Austen
Jane L. Stewart
Janet Aldridge
Jens Peter Jacobsen
Jerome K. Jerome
Jessie Graham Flower
John Buchan
John Burroughs
John Cournos
John F. Kennedy
John Gay
John Glasworthy
John Habberton
John Joy Bell
John Kendrick Bangs
John Milton
John Philip Sousa
John Taintor Foote
Jonas Lauritz Idemil Lie
Jonathan Swift
Joseph A. Altsheler
Joseph Carey
Joseph Conrad
Joseph E. Badger Jr
Joseph Hergesheimer
Joseph Jacobs
Jules Vernes
Julian Hawthrone
Julie A Lippmann
Justin Huntly McCarthy
Kakuzo Okakura
Karle Wilson Baker
Kate Chopin
Kenneth Grahame
Kenneth McGaffey
Kate Langley Bosher
Kate Langley Bosher
Katherine Cecil Thurston
Katherine Stokes
L. A. Abbot
L. T. Meade

L. Frank Baum
Latta Griswold
Laura Dent Crane
Laura Lee Hope
Laurence Housman
Lawrence Beasley
Leo Tolstoy
Leonid Andreyev
Lewis Carroll
Lewis Sperry Chafer
Lilian Bell
Lloyd Osbourne
Louis Hughes
Louis Joseph Vance
Louis Tracy
Louisa May Alcott
Lucy Fitch Perkins
Lucy Maud Montgomery
Luther Benson
Lydia Miller Middleton
Lyndon Orr
M. Corvus
M. H. Adams
Margaret E. Sangster
Margret Howth
Margaret Vandercook
Margaret W. Hungerford
Margret Penrose
Maria Edgeworth
Maria Thompson Daviess
Mariano Azuela
Marion Polk Angellotti
Mark Overton
Mark Twain
Mary Austin
Mary Catherine Crowley
Mary Cole
Mary Hastings Bradley
Mary Roberts Rinehart
Mary Rowlandson
M. Wollstonecraft Shelley
Maud Lindsay
Max Beerbohm
Myra Kelly
Nathaniel Hawthrone
Nicolo Machiavelli
O. F. Walton
Oscar Wilde

Owen Johnson
P.G. Wodehouse
Paul and Mabel Thorne
Paul G. Tomlinson
Paul Severing
Percy Brebner
Percy Keese Fitzhugh
Peter B. Kyne
Plato
Quincy Allen
R. Derby Holmes
R. L. Stevenson
R. S. Ball
Rabindranath Tagore
Rahul Alvares
Ralph Bonehill
Ralph Henry Barbour
Ralph Victor
Ralph Waldo Emmerson
Rene Descartes
Ray Cummings
Rex Beach
Rex E. Beach
Richard Harding Davis
Richard Jefferies
Richard Le Gallienne
Robert Barr
Robert Frost
Robert Gordon Anderson
Robert L. Drake
Robert Lansing
Robert Lynd
Robert Michael Ballantyne
Robert W. Chambers
Rosa Nouchette Carey
Rudyard Kipling
Saint Augustine
Samuel B. Allison
Samuel Hopkins Adams
Sarah Bernhardt
Sarah C. Hallowell
Selma Lagerlof
Sherwood Anderson
Sigmund Freud
Standish O'Grady
Stanley Weyman
Stella Benson
Stella M. Francis

Stephen Crane
Stewart Edward White
Stijn Streuvels
Swami Abhedananda
Swami Parmananda
T. S. Ackland
T. S. Arthur
The Princess Der Ling
Thomas A. Janvier
Thomas A Kempis
Thomas Anderton
Thomas Bailey Aldrich
Thomas Bulfinch
Thomas De Quincey
Thomas Dixon
Thomas H. Huxley
Thomas Hardy
Thomas More
Thornton W. Burgess
U. S. Grant
Upton Sinclair
Valentine Williams
Various Authors
Vaughan Kester
Victor Appleton
Victor G. Durham
Victoria Cross
Virginia Woolf
Wadsworth Camp
Walter Camp
Walter Scott
Washington Irving
Wilbur Lawton
Wilkie Collins
Willa Cather
Willard F. Baker
William Dean Howells
William le Queux
W. Makepeace Thackeray
William W. Walter
William Shakespeare
Winston Churchill
Yei Theodora Ozaki
Yogi Ramacharaka
Young E. Allison
Zane Grey

www.ingramcontent.com/pod-product-compliance
Lightning Source LLC
Chambersburg PA
CBHW031057260626
47172CB00001B/113